GLITTERING PROMISE

From the devastation of war-torn Europe to America's golden shores, they struggled to create a bold, new future out of the ruins of a shattered past . . .

Jana Horvath—Scarred by a childhood filled with wartime violence and terror, she yearned to build a new life . . . and learn to love . . . in America!

Rachel von Weitzman—Stronger than she'd ever dreamed she could be, she saved herself and Jana from certain death, braving unspeakable horrors for a chance to live without fear . . .

Merek Cetkovic—When the Nazis slaughtered his family, he vowed to dedicate himself to saving others . . . and to never leave himself open to the pain of needing anyone again . . .

Oberleutnant Fritz Walther — Driven mad by his lust for power and an obsessive desire for vengeance, he swore his hatred for Jana, Rachel and Marek would haunt them long after the war had ended . . .

PRISM

BY
ANNA
LAIN

ZEBRA BOOKS
KENSINGTON PUBLISHING CORP.

ZEBRA BOOKS

are published by

Kensington Publishing Corp.
475 Park Avenue South
New York, NY 10016

First printing: June, 1988

Printed in the United States of America

With love to Ben and Noah, for what they have been and what they will be.

PART ONE
(1944-1945)

Chapter 1

Jana Horvath reached out and touched the cream-colored satin. Just one day shy of her seventh birthday, she was the perfect age to be awed by the splendor of the gown. Entirely handstitched in the immaculate tradition of the old world, it was designed with perfect simplicity. Picking up the eight-foot-long veil of delicate Brussels lace, she held it up to the light that shone brightly through the dormer windows.

"It's so beautiful, Buba," said the child to her grandmother. "May I wear it when I get married?"

"Of course you may," replied Rachel von Weitzman, as she leaned over to kiss her. "And I shall pin the same brooch on the gown that I wore on my wedding day. You will be the loveliest bride in all of Budapest."

"Thank you, Buba." Jana spoke with the naive enthusiasm that belongs so naturally to the young.

Rachel's pure green eyes took on the cast of remembrance. Her voice was low and resonant, but it still harbored a lilt of youth that hinted at the girl she had once been. "It was a grand day, when your grandfather and I were married. After the ceremony, we celebrated in this very house. Champagne and laughter. That's what I remember. And we had a string quartet from the conservatory. So elegant, Jana. So loving, this house filled with family, with friends. Extraordinary," she said, her voice drifting as she explored the happy reaches of memory.

"What else is in the trunk?" asked Jana.

"We'll save that for another day," her grandmother answered firmly. "I'm certain that the family has already begun tea without us, we've been here in this attic for so long."

"But —" the child protested. Before she could further her cause, she was interrupted by a loud pounding that reached up to them ominously from three floors below. Eva, the maid who had been with them for thirty years, must have been standing near the door, for it was opened immediately.

A moment later, Jana and Rachel heard her shocked cry. The sound was stopped with a thud. The hard, insistent voices of the Hungarian police took over. Then, Jana heard her mother scream.

Immobilized with terror, Rachel stood next to the trunk, still holding her wedding gown.

"What is it, Buba?" whispered the child in a choked voice.

Rachel could hear her husband, Josef, his voice raised in anger and indignation. Her daughter's wail formed an obscene lietmotif to his words.

Then there was silence.

10

Shaking her head, Rachel's eyes glazed with the realization of what was happening. Instantly, she made a hideous decision. "Come, Jana," she whispered to the child. "We must go to the hiding place, just as we practiced."

"But—"

"No objections now," Rachel replied with an unnatural calm as she folded the wedding gown and veil carefully and replaced it in the trunk. Then she closed the lid softly. "Come with me."

They walked to the far side of the attic. As immaculate as a parlor, it had become the repository for three generations of family history.

Inserting her fingers carefully between two bricks next to the large chimney that ran up the north side of the early nineteenth century house, Rachel pushed a concealed button, then pulled with the strength of her entire body. A door, concealed artfully in the bricks, slowly opened.

"Inside now," she said to the whimpering child.

They moved into the tiny room and Rachel pulled the heavy door closed behind them.

Even through the bricks, the voices of the three remaining members of the family could be heard once again above the ugly din of the Hungarian police. Jana could hear her grandfather's mighty cry, her mother's scream, her father's strong voice. This was followed shortly by the sound of a truck engine starting. The sound faded into the afternoon. Then there was nothing.

Jumping from her grandmother's lap, Jana

groped for the latch on the door.

"No!" hissed Rachel, as she grabbed the child. The sound of a thousand chimes rang through the air. It must be the crystal, she thought, imagining the exquisite prisms from the chandelier falling to the ground and shattering.

Jana struggled. But when she heard the strong male voices grow louder, she stopped. Rachel covered Jana's mouth as she listened to the men enter the attic. Silent, the woman and child heard the sounds of trunks being opened, crates being overturned, as they huddled only inches away in the hiding place that had been constructed five months previously as an extension to the chimney.

"No one here," pronounced a disembodied voice. In the hiding place, they listened as the footsteps receded down into the main part of the house.

Still Rachel did not move. They dared not risk a noise that would reveal their existence. Silence surrounded them like a shroud as they crouched mute and stunned in the dark.

Just when Rachel began to believe that they might be safe at last, she heard new noises drifting up from the parlor two floors below. At first, she could not distinguish what the sounds were. Just a low, rumbling sort of buzz, periodically interrupted by the slam of a door or an unidentified crash.

Ever so slowly, the noises moved closer.

"Look in the drawer over there." It was a man's voice, harsh and urgent.

"The desk . . . see what's inside!"

"The trunk!" said another, this voice a woman's. Rachel heard the lid of the ornate, barrel-topped truck being opened, the soft rustling of silk and lace. She felt violated as she imagined coarse, dirty hands running over her wedding gown. She felt soiled, as if she were still wearing the dress.

There were many of them now, buzzing, exploring, urgent in their greed. They were strangers who recognized the wealth that the house represented. When they saw the family and the elderly servant being dragged away and placed in the dun-colored German trunk, they knew there would be treasures inside the house. They waited patiently until another truckload of soldiers had pilfered the house for the most obvious valuables. And then they took their turn.

But not all the voices belonged to strangers. For Rachel heard one voice say, "Look for the jewels. Von Weitzman is a rich Jew. His father's father was a jeweler. There are jewels hidden someplace."

This remark propelled the people into a new frenzy of activity. Like locusts gone mad over the sight of a ripe and succulent crop, they tore open everything, stealing with indiscriminate greed anything that appeared to have value.

Little escaped their voracious appetite for the oppulent luxury that spilled from every corner of the house: Sevrès china and English silver; leather-bound books in five languages, although most of the pillagers could not even read; French porcelain and Persian carpets; Renaissance paintings, Chinese silk and damask. All of it they pawed and plundered in the wake of the vulturous raid of the Hungarian police who carried out the orders of the SS command with extreme efficiency and enthusiasm.

Once the Jews had been detained, the police stole the most valuable property in order to enhance the glory of the Reich. The remainder—often a fortune in itself—was left to be picked over and plundered by rapacious, anonymous hoardes.

The strangers ravaged the attic, buzzing like the mindless insects they had become. They tore open everything in sight, destroying the carefully-packed history of four generations.

In the hiding place, the light that seeped through the cracks around the eaves began to grow dim. And in the attic, with the waning of the light, the people began to drift reluctantly away.

The silence of night came gently, and with it came fear. Abandoned and helpless, Rachel and Jana huddled together, surrounded by the silence that followed in the wake of this sudden storm. Only the memories of the anguished cries of their family were left behind in testament that they had ever even existed.

Unwilling to risk even the light of a candle which Josef had thoughtfully placed with the supplies in the tiny room, Rachel whispered to her grandchild. "Let's try to get comfortable now. We will spend the night here."

Jana's eyes opened wide. "But, Buba! It's so dark in here. Please . . . light a candle."

"We mustn't," Rachel said, her voice gentle but firm. She lay down beside Jana on a thick down quilt and gathered the child into her arms. "See? We can be comfortable. And I'll take care of you," she added with more determination than she felt.

"Oh, Buba," wailed Jana softly. "It's so black in here. So very black. Maybe there are ghosts or . . . spiders . . . " she whispered, shuddering in the arms of her grandmother as she imagined hairy, creepy creatures crawling over her as she slept.

Never before had darkness been so threatening, so filled with visions of unspeakable images and loathesome dreams. She longed for the comfort of her own bed with its silk coverlet and the touch of lace that bordered her thick, down pillow. She longed for the arms of her father and mother and grandfather, all of whom knew how to comfort her when fear overcame her courage. Alone with her grandmother now, Jana lay stiff and silent with her eyes wide open, trying to make out shapes that might assault her in the darkness. Finally, exhausted and tormented, she slept.

As the light of false dawn crept through the cracks, Rachel stirred. For a moment she believed that she was sleeping beside her beloved Josef in their canopied bed, covered happily with silk and the quiet contentment of loving. For a moment she was blessed with forgetfulness. For a moment she was free of pain. Then reality assaulted her.

The house had been silent for hours now. Still, Rachel did not trust this new silence that carried such malevolence and forboding in its arms.

Lying quietly as she held Jana, Rachel thought of her husband, Josef. She was grateful to him for building this tiny room and stocking it with food and clothing. But her gratitude was mixed with a terrible regret that she had been the one to be left behind. This room, hidden and secret, was Josef's last gift to her. She remembered then how the rest of the family had teased him for his silly precautions.

"Oh Papa," their daughter, Olga, had said to Josef when he announced his intentions to build the hiding place. "We aren't in danger. Our family has been titled for three generations. We occupy a prominent place in the city. And Stefan," she said as she looked fondly at her husband, "is a professor of history at the University. Besides, he's a Christian."

"But we are Jews," Josef had replied stoically as he carried more bricks up the steep stairs to the attic. "We are Jews who refused to convert. And until we can find safe passage out of Budapest, this room will be our refuge."

"She's right," Stefan agreed, siding with his wife. "The Weitzman's are a prominent family in Budapest. You belong to the best clubs. There is no need to take such extreme precautions."

"Don't strain yourself, Josef," cautioned Rachel. She, too, wanted desperately to believe that no harm could come to them. She pushed the ugly rumors she had heard into that safe corner of her memory

16

that could be locked. And now they must be opened, Rachel thought; they must be examined. I must use everything I know to insure our safety.

Just three weeks before, Adolph Eichman, himself, had come to Budapest in order to begin the implementation of the final solution for the citizens of Hungary. Starting with the provinces, he divided the country into six zones, each of which would be methodically cleansed of the scourge of the Jews. Budapest would be last. But he must have made an exception in the case of the wealthy and recalcitrate jeweler who had voiced so many objections at the first meeting of the Judenrat.

Just a few days before, Josef had come home and informed his family that the yellow star had at last come to the Jews of Budapest.

Two years earlier, Prime Minister Kallay had rejected the German demands to introduce the wearing of the ugly yellow badges. But now they were a new and harsh reality, along with the impending "resettlement" of the Jews.

All this Josef had learned at the meeting of the Judenrat, the group of prominent Jewish leaders established by Eichman for the express purpose of carrying out his orders. And all this had hardened Josef's conviction that the family must flee the city it had known for five generations.

The irony was that Josef had finally succeeded in arranging passage out of Budapest for the entire family. Tomorrow morning, before the first light of day, Miklos would be waiting for them on the quay.

17

Rachel was grateful that they lived so near to the Danube. Their elegant house on Batthyány Square, near Margaret Bridge, was only a block from the river. From the cobbled street by the house, one could stand and see the Parliament Building across the water where it stood in majestic splendor between Margaret Island and the Chain Bridge.

Josef had spent many hours down by the river, the Danube he loved so passionately. That was why he had chosen the river as their means of escape. He felt safe with it, as if he were entrusting the lives of his family to an old friend.

It had not been easy, this arrangement that Josef had made. And he had tried other avenues before this one. Rachel remembered the day that Josef had gone to his friend, Lázló Dénes, a man to whom Josef gave all his engraving business. Her husband had sought out this man in order to ask him to forge some false papers for him and his family. But his request had been turned down.

"Lázló?" Rachel uttered in disbelieve when Josef told her. "Lázló turned you down?" Rachel said. "But you started him in his business . . . you sent people, customers to him, you loaned him money. He even engraved my brooch . . . The 'always Rachel' on my brooch. He . . . he turned you down?"

Josef could only nod. "Lázló is afraid," he said sadly. That was all, that was the only excuse he offered for the deadly betrayal of a man he had known for thirty years. "Lázló is afraid." That night Josef wept. Because he was afraid, too.

And he continued to be afraid, right up until the time when he heard the Swedish Legation in Budapest. For several months, it had been working quietly to save the endangered citizens of the city.

Josef von Weitzman was lucky. He was the beginning of many people whose rescue would be arranged through this mission. It was April, and efforts had begun to be implemented to save the Jews. Later, the Swedish government would bring in an aristocratic Swede with the unlikely name of Raoul Wallenberg to form a special committee to aid the Jews and other victims of the Reich. He was a man unique to his times, a man destined to be called a saint. Wallenberg spent the war years in Budapest devoted to the singleminded pursuit of saving lives. There was nothing he would not risk, no person he would not confront. He issued special passports that declared the carrier to be under the protection of the government of Sweden; he placed those in danger in special apartment buildings, over which flew the protective flag of his country. When the round-ups began, he would go to the railway station where the boxcars were waiting and march off two hundred victims to safe apartments, as he brazenly waved official papers in the faces of the stunned Hungarian police.

A hero in his own time, he was a man who nurtured the seeds of salvation that had been planted earlier when Josef approached the legation on a rainy morning in early April of 1944.

Josef had sat nervously across the desk from a

harried-looking diplomat.

"You are a wealthy man?" the diplomat inquired gently.

"Yes," Josef answered.

"Do you think you can get your family as far as Belgrade?"

"I believe it can be arranged," Josef said.

"I know it is dangerous," continued the diplomat. "Belgrade is no place to be. But we have friends there, Partisans who will take you on to the coast. It's been done before. It's risky, I know." He paused, trying to assess the character of this stranger who was placing his life and the lives of his family in another man's hands. "But it is a greater risk to remain in Budapest. I hear stories . . . terrible stories . . . as I'm sure you do. We both know, Herr von Weitzman, that the time is coming soon when it will no longer be safe in this city. Already it has begun in the provinces. It is only a matter of time . . ." he said, his voice drifting into the horrors that the future would surely bring.

And thus it had been arranged. Three weeks before, when Miklos' barge had pulled into the quay filled with scrawny chickens that he would sell to hungry customers up and down the Danube, Josef had asked his friend to take them to Belgrade. Reluctantly, this hearty man of the river had agreed. Everything had been set, had been worked out with meticulous logic and planning.

Except the SS had arrived first. Now, only two members of the family remained. And they were

20

alone. A forty-seven-year-old woman and her seven-year-old granddaughter, alone and virtually helpless in a tiny brick room.

As she surveyed the cramped space around her with the aid of the increasing light of morning, Rachel von Weitzman appreciated the thoroughness of her husband's preparations. Josef had planned their escape with the same precision he employed when he repaired a fine old pocket watch. He had thought of everything: food, clothing, utensils and most important of all, money in the form of jewels.

She looked at the leather satchels that had been filled with supplies for five people. But now there would only be two, Rachel thought, as she reached over and touched Jana gently.

The child awakened slowly at first, easing her body out of its cramped position before jerking suddenly with the realization that the true nightmare was just beginning.

Rubbing her eyes, Jana asked in a tiny, frightened voice, "Has daylight come?"

"Yes, darling," her grandmother whispered. "Remember now to whisper. We must not be heard."

Jana started to cry then. Always before when she was sad, her grandmother would take her in her arms and hold her close until the tears disappeared. This time it was different.

Rachel took Jana's face between her hands and held it tight. Speaking in a whisper that carried the weight of a command, she said, "Hush now. No tears. We must save them for another time. Now we must think. And we must prepare. The two of us, Jana, we are all that is left. Just you and I. And, if we are to get out of here . . . to survive . . . then we must behave accordingly. Do you understand?"

Jana nodded. "I think so, Buba."

"Listen carefully to me, my love. We must spend the day here. We will have some light from the cracks there," she explained, pointing to the eaves. "And while there is light, we will prepare for our journey."

"But where will we go?" Jana asked. She could not possibly imagine living anywhere except in this lovely and comfortable house. This was all she had known, all she had ever wanted. It was here that she had learned to talk, to take her first step, to read. It was here that she was loved and coddled and cared for. It was the place that defined her past and safeguarded her future. It was home.

"First we shall travel down the river," Rachel explained. "Then a friend will take us to the coast. It will be a long and difficult journey. And, in the mean time, we must prepare."

"But what about Papa and Momma and Grandpa?" Jana asked. "Will we go fetch them before we leave?"

"We cannot do that. They will follow later," Rachel said, begging God's forgiveness for telling this lie.

"But how will they find us?" Jana asked. "How will they know where to go?"

"Jana, my love," Rachel said, her voice cracking

22

with the effort of speaking, knowing she could carry the lie no further. "They have been taken from us. But we must have faith. . . . We must have faith in the fact that, if it is possible, they will find us."

"And we must go now without them?"

"Yes."

Jana cried even harder then. The thought of a journey without the comfort of her father and mother left her limp with fear.

"No!" hissed Rachel. "You must not cry. Listen carefully to me, my child." She paused, wondering how to explain this madness to such a small child. "All your life, Jana, you have lived well. Lived like a child. But I must now ask you now to behave like an adult. It is a terrible thing to ask of one so young. I know that. But there is no choice. From now on, you must put childish things behind you. We are the last of the von Weitzmans. We must survive. . . . We shall. It is a difficult lesson to learn. But tears are no longer a luxury we can afford. The weeping must wait until the day comes that we are safe in America with your father's relatives. Then, every tear that you have saved can be shed. And I promise you that I will hold on to you until the last one has fallen."

Rachel stopped then, searching the innocent purity of her granddaughter's face. Even in the dim light, she was beautiful. Jana had the green eyes of her grandmother and the fine sculptured bones of her mother, all of which promised beauty. Her face, delicate and slightly angular, was surrounded by a mass of golden curls. She was a lovely child whose inward sensitivity matched the loveliness of her outward appearance.

If it is the last thing I do—and it may well be—Rachel vowed to herself, I will save this child. Then she spoke. "Do you understand what I am telling you, Jana? Do you understand how important it is?"

"I think so, Buba."

"Promise me you will be a good girl, that you will be strong and do as I say. Promise . . . for me and . . . all of us."

"I promise, Buba. I promise."

Leaning over to kiss the tears from Jana's eyes, Rachel smiled encouragingly. "Now. We must get to work. There is much to be done before nightfall."

Taking the three satchels that had been packed with supplies, Rachel explained how they would have to put all their belongings into one bag. "And perhaps that small one there for you to carry," she added in a effort to make Jana feel useful.

Laying everything out before them, they chose carefully. Extra clothes were placed in the bottom of the bag. Then, three long, hard sausages and some cheese, the silver and mother-of-pearl folding knife, additional woolen mittens, socks and scarves and an extra pair of shoes for each. There was also sulfa powder wrapped in small packets and some precious tablets of aspirin.

Rachel picked up the large and cumbersome family Bible. Tucked inside were precious family photographs. This was the book which held the history of the von Weitzman's for five generations. Rachel weighed the book in her hands. Slowly, sadly, she shook her head. "It is too heavy."

"But, of course we will take it anyway. How could you leave that behind?" Jana asked.

"We must," Rachel answered. "We cannot afford to carry anything this heavy."

"No. . . ." Jana wailed softly, remembering how important this book had been to her grandfather. She recalled how he would sit at night, quiet and content in his rocking chair, as he read the Old Testament by the light of the lamp.

"This is only the first of many difficult decisions," Rachel said firmly. "The first of many. We must learn to make wise decisions, not sentimental ones."

"But what will Grandpa do when he finds us and discovers that we don't have his Bible?"

"He will understand."

"How do you know?" Jana persisted.

"Because that is the kind of man he is," Rachel replied, knowing that she spoke the truth. Then she busied herself with packing two bars of soap, gauze for bandages, chocolate for energy, extra underwear and a change of clothing. And, finally, the jewels.

Josef had sewn them into the elaborate heavy, round leather straps of the satchel. Stitched separately inside the handle were a dozen loose diamonds, the largest on the sides of the handle and the smallest in the middle. There was also one four carat emerald and a sapphire of the same size.

Rachel's husband had worked the stones skillfully into the ornate design of the straps. But Rachel could feel them all, hard and lumpy, as she lifted the bag to test its weight.

Josef had also wrapped a filigreed platinum and diamond ring into the extra pair of Jana's socks, an article of clothing so small that it would be of little use to some stranger tempted to steal it.

"Is that everything?" Jana asked as she watched her grandmother buckle the satchel.

"Almost."

"Isn't there room for the Bible?" Jana asked plaintively, still hoping that her grandmother would change her mind.

"No," Rachel answered, her patience wearing thin.

"What will we do with it?"

Rachel thought a moment. "We will put it in this satchel and leave it here. Perhaps we will return one day to claim it."

Jana nodded, resigned to the decision. "Is there anything else?" she asked.

"Just the brooch," Rachel answered as she lifted it out of the tiny glove leather pouch that had been made especially for it. Taking it carefully in her hand, Rachel brought out the gift that her husband had given her on their wedding day; the gift that she had worn pinned proudly to the satin of her elegant gown that now rested in the soiled hands of some greedy stranger.

26

Even in the dim light, the diamond in the middle of the brooch radiated fire, as if it had a brilliant life of its own. The perfectly round center stone weighed almost seven carats. Expertly faceted to insure that its full beauty would be exposed, in daylight it was the color of a pale blue sky, a rarity in the esoteric world of diamonds. Josef had bought the brooch from Charles Lewis Tiffany, himself, on his only trip to America. Set in eighteen carat gold, the diamond was surrounded with rare American fresh water pearls, rose-white and perfectly matched.

"Please, Buba, may I hold it?" Jana asked eagerly, forgetting for a moment where she was.

Rachel handed the brooch to her. "Josef used to tell me," she said, "That the diamond is known for its hardness and durability. But that the pearl, although it appears to be soft and fragile, is a tough and lusterous gem. That is how we must be, Jana — like the pearl."

Turning it over carefully, Jana knew that if she caught the light just right, she would see the famous Tiffany signature on the back of the brooch. Underneath it, engraved in beautiful script by Josef's friend Lásló, were two simple words, "Always Rachel."

"Where will we hide it?" Jana asked suddenly.

"I don't know," answered her grandmother. "Josef did not know, either. It will take some thought because this cannot be hidden so easily."

Looking at Jana's long, thick hair, Rachel said,

"Turn around. Let me try something."

Rachel separated the longer strands of hair that covered the back of Jana's head. Then she lifted up the top mass of hair for Jana to hold. She took some of the strands underneath and divided them into five small cords, twisting each one before tying a knot in it. She took a needle and thread from the basket on the floor. Working very carefully, she stitched the small pouch to the knots of Jana's hair, working meticulously to make certain that it was firmly secured. When she was finished, she brushed the top hair over the brooch. But she could still see the lump it formed.

Experimenting, she took all of Jana's hair and twisted it into a knot on the back of her head, using tortoise shell pins to secure it.

"There," Rachel said, satisfied with her work. "It cannot be seen."

Jana raised her hand to the back of her head where she could feel the pull of the extra weight.

"Touch it one time now," Rachel said carefully. "Feel it, get used to the idea of its being there. Then you must never reach up there again to give anyone the idea that there is something hidden in your hair. You must behave as if you have always worn your hair in such a grown-up fashion, Jana. You must never tell anyone about the brooch that you carry."

Jana nodded, understanding the words, but not the solemn importance of them. She could not understand that her life might depend on it. For in her child's world, people went away, just like her parents

28

might go for a week in the country. But they did not die. Dying was forever, and therefore it was unthinkable, least of all for a little girl who would be seven years old in the morning.

"Now," said Rachel, "we are ready. We will leave before the first light of day. And, until then, we must try to get some sleep."

But sleep did not come easily for Jana that night. It was worse than the night before. The darkness was more threatening. It was peopled with monsters, with malignant creatures of the dark. Tormented with visions too terrible to tell, with thoughts too frightening to express, Jana tossed and turned in Rachel's arms, moaning softly in her troubled sleep.

In the middle of the night, she dreamed of being ripped from the arms of her mother, of being condemned to live alone in filth and squalor. She tried to run, but her tormentors were faster and stronger. She tried to scream, but no sound emerged. They closed in on her, these horrible men, pulling at her arms, her clothes. "Aahh . . ." she said. And then she screamed. It was loud and piercing, heavy with hopelessness and terror.

Before she could open her eyes, she felt a hand clamp harshly over her mouth.

"Shhh," Rachel whispered as she put her arms around the trembling child, terrified that the scream would reveal their presence in this supposedly empty house. "Hush now . . . I'm with you," she soothed, rocking Jana back and forth.

Struggling, Jana tried to escape the hold of her

grandmother. She was unable to separate the reality of her present situation from her night terror. The dream had stripped her, had bared her worst fears. She could not stop shaking, could not stop thinking of the possibility of an endless night in which she would be trapped forever in the dark dread of her own worst dreams.

In the morning, Jana had forgotten almost everything that had happened during the last twenty four hours. It was simply too terrible to remember. Later, she would only remember the dark, the loathesome, terrifying dark.

Rachel lay next to Jana, alert to the sounds of the house, to any indication that there might be people searching for them. Perhaps, she thought, a scream in the middle of the night is no longer so unusual; now, in these terrible times, it is ignored.

Rachel had not slept for more than two or three hours. It was still dark, but she risked striking a match to look at her watch, extinguishing it quickly so that the light would not filter through the cracks above.

It is time, she thought, as she touched Jana gently. Time to go.

They prepared in silence, occasionally striking a match in order to find something lost in the darkness. They dressed carefully in the costumes of rather shabby peasants. Rachel tied a colorful kerchief around Jana's head, thankful it would provide additional covering for the brooch. It was the brooch that would buy them a new life in America, she thought. Freedom.

"These pants are itchy, Buba," Jana complained.

"Then they are itchy," replied Rachel in a matter-of-fact tone of voice.

Jana did not understand this new attitude of her grandmother's. Before, if she had complained of something itchy, Rachel would have said, "Then take them off, my love, do not wear them." Jana had counted on that. She had always known where she stood, where the boundries of acceptable behavior were set. Now, in this new game, there seemed to be no rules. She could not understand that there was simply no more room in their lives for perfunctory sympathy. That had been stolen from her two days earlier, along with her china tea set and her porcelain dolls.

"But I hate the way the pants scratch," Jana persisted. "I won't wear them."

Rachel turned to her. "Those pants were made from your grandfather's overcoat. They are warm and they will keep you from freezing. Even though it is April, there will be many cold nights ahead. You will be grateful for their warmth long after you have forgotten how they feel."

"I won't," Jana said sulkily.

Rachel took a deep breath. "Times have changed now, Jana," she said as she caressed Jana's face. "Everything has changed. And if we are to live, we must change with them. You are a Horvath and a von Weitzman. You must be as strong as your history. It won't always be this way. I promise."

Jana nodded, temporarily resigned to this new way of thinking.

Taking one more look around the room, feeling in the dark corners for things that might have been overlooked, Rachel reached over and touched Jana. The room had grown insufferably tiny and Rachel was grateful that they would be leaving it, no mater what risk awaited them.

"Remember, my love," Rachel said. "You are a grown-up now. It is your seventh birthday today and you are setting out on a great adventure. You have become an adult and you must now behave like one."

"Yes, Buba," Jana replied with subdued obedience, wondering what it would be like, this being a grown-up. The only thing she knew for certain was that she must try not to cry or complain. That belonged to her past.

Rachel pushed hard on the door with the heavy false brick front. It opened slowly as she put her full weight against it. Then they stepped out of the hiding place. The attic was a terrible sight, even in the dim light of dawn. For a moment, she was stunned by the chaos.

"Buba!" Jana cried. "Look what they've done!" In her alarm, she forgot the terror of the attic. Turning from the shocking sight, Jana stepped back toward the hiding place. Then she froze. Never! she thought. I'll never go back in that dreadful place again. I'll never be trapped in the dark again. Never! Gasping for air, suddenly overcome with relief that she was free, Jana tugged Rachel's hand. "Let's get out of here, Buba!" she whimpered softly. "Let's get out now!"

Still stunned from the dismay of seeing the attic, Rachel nodded. It took all her strength to pull herself together. She listened carefully for voices, for signs of other people. The house was silent.

Together, they walked through the ravaged attic, then moved down the steep steps to the main part of the house.

"Oh look!" cried Jana, pointing to her china doll that lay smashed at the bottom of the stairs.

"Hush!" whispered Rachel. "You must not talk unless it is absolutely necessary. Pretend this is the house of a stranger," she said sadly. "Pretend that it never belonged to us."

Everywhere, piles of discarded household items lay in messy heaps on the floor. Every drawer and shelf had been ransacked, every nook and cranny had been pillaged, every item of furniture that could possibly be moved had been stolen.

As they passed the pantry on the ground floor, Jana saw something gleaming in the corner, a dull reflection from the waning moon. Letting go of her grandmother's hand, she walked to the corner and picked it up. It was her very own baby cup, the one made of heavy silver that had belonged first to her mother. "Olga von Weitzman, born 7 November 1917" had been engraved in Gothic script on the front of the cup. And underneath, "Jana Horvath, born 10 April 1937" had been etched deeply into the hand-hammered silver. Touching it for a moment, Jana looked at her grandmother for silent permission. Then she placed it gently in the small leather bag she carried.

Without a backward glance, they walked stiffly out the door of their home. They went out through the gate in the high brick wall surrounding the lovely back garden, then headed towards the quay where Miklos would be waiting. "But only until sunrise," Rachel remembered Josef saying. "Miklos will not wait past the first light of day."

Before they reached the corner, they could smell the pungent fishy odor rising from the river. They could also hear German voices riding ominously on the soft cloud of darkness that was their only protection.

Pulling Jana into the shadow of the last house before the river, Rachel stopped. For a moment, she thought she would vomit. Swallowing hard, she stood still, willing herself to remain calm as she waited for her heart to stop its wild and erratic pounding.

Rachel had heard stories. Not just about families stolen away in the middle of the night; but of soldiers taking their way with women, especially ones who had an edge of attractiveness about them.

Standing in the gossamer shelter of the shadows, Rachel leaned over and whispered to Jana. "Look . . . humble. But do not look frightened. That has always been enticing to men who carry guns."

Jana grabbed Rachel's skirt. Taking her hand away, Rachel whispered urgently to Jana. "Now remember, you must behave like a grown-up. Don't cling to my skirt, child. That shows you're frightened. It takes only one man's hand patting your head in kindness to encourage others to touch you also. And their touch could be different," she added ominously.

Jana nodded, forcing her tears back into their source. She did not quite understand what her grandmother meant about men touching her, but she sensed its threat. Besides, she was so relieved to be gone from the terrifying darkness that the hiding place had wrapped around her, Jana promised herself that she would behave exactly as her grandmother demanded. Anything was better than being placed in such a horrifying, suffocating place, she thought, knowing she would do anything to avoid it in the future. She would never forget that place. Nor would she forget her grandmother's dark warning about the strange ways that men touch.

Rachel looked up at the sky. It would not be long before the sun peeked over the horizon, she speculated. There is no time now for a detour around the soldiers. This is our last chance and we must take it. Miklos cannot leave without us.

She calculated coldly for a moment, then made up her mind. Reaching silently into her satchel, she moved her fingers into the side pocket where she touched the mother-of-pearl handle of the knife she carried. She pulled it out and opened it. A glint of light reflected off its razor-sharp blade, and she quickly hid it from Jana's sight.

"What are you doing?" Jana asked, knowing that something was happening she did not understand.

"Shhh," whispered Rachel. "Turn your head away. Do not watch me."

Obeying without further question, Jana turned her head away. She did not see her grandmother lift her skirt, nor the way her hand trembled. She did not see the blood drain from Rachel's face, nor the expression of repulsion and dread that replaced the color.

"We will be ready to go in a minute, Jana. In just a minute."

Chapter 2

Jana waited silently, trying to remember the times she had walked past this very spot as she held her grandfather's hand. They would often walk down to the river together, and he would tell her stories to amuse her along the way. Those were lovely times, happy times, and Jana tried with all her might to recreate them in her imagination. That way, she would not have to think about what her grandmother was doing.

Rachel held the knife in her hand, then eased it gently up her leg. High up against her thigh, she thought, under the edge of my boomers where the cut won't show.

Afraid of the act itself, she hesitated. This might make the difference, she told herself. I must. Now.

Pushing the blade of the knife through the pale, smooth skin of her thigh, she drew it across her leg in a shallow slice almost two inches long. For an instant, there was only an obscene pink line of spreading flesh before the blood began to flow scarlet down the inside of her leg.

Totally unaware of the pain, Rachel wiped the blade of the knife on her skirt and replaced it in her satchel. Then she took her hand and covered it with blood. Leaning over, she smeared it between her thighs and down the inside of her legs, past her knees onto the long, grey woolen stockings. In the dark, the blood appeared black.

Trembling, Rachel stood up straight and collected her composure as she held her skirt up until she felt the blood begin to dry. Then she dropped the skirt before turning to Jana. "Now . . . courage, child. Courage," she whispered.

They walked quietly side-by-side around the corner. The German soldiers were there, smoking cigarettes and laughing among themselves. There were three of them, three conquerers, three men who regarded the Hungarian people with disdain. Rachel shuddered with fear at the very sight of their uniforms. The single menacing word of Auschwitz fluttered into her consciousness. Auschwitz.

She hoped that they could walk past the soldiers with a nod of indifference. That was her intention. But it was not possible.

"Whoa . . . not so fast. What have we here?" said the oldest of the soldiers as he noticed the lone woman and child. He shined a light first on Rachel's face, then Jana's. Moving the torch back to Rachel, she looked dumbly at him, as if she did not understand his language. Of course, she had spoken German fluently — along with French, Russian, English and Yiddish — since the age of fifteen. And she could, to her disgust, understand everything the man said.

"A woman . . . that's what we have here," said the soldier with a smile, answering his own malevolently innocent question. "And not so bad, either. A peasant . . . but not so bad." He spoke to his comrades as if he were giving them a lecture on the female of the species.

Even in the murky light, Rachel's attractiveness could be seen. The kerchief covered her luxurient auburn hair. But, even at the age of forty-seven, there was a distictive beauty about her. No amount of disguise could conceal the fine lines of her face, the smoothness of her skin. Her nose was long, but it was aristocratic instead of sharp. And her lips, drained as they were of color, still had that quality of generosity that one sees in a woman who has laughed often and loved well.

Hanging her head in what she hoped was a humble pose, Rachel stood before the soldiers as if she were their servant.

"She's a little old for my taste," the older man continued. "But as I was just saying, when there's a war on, a cunt is a cunt."

Rachel blanched inwardly, but smiled at the three men as if she had not understood a word. The mere thought of a strange man's hands running over her body made her want to run screaming into the night. No one had ever touched her except Josef and they had enjoyed — from the beginning — a loving and special relationship in the privacy of their bedroom. It took every ounce of strength that Rachel had to stand her ground without revealing her

39

fear.

As the light from the soldier's long flashlight moved from her face down over her full, voluptuous body, Rachel stood humbly before the men smiling dumbly during their arrogant inspection.

"Not so bad at all," said the second man, moving closer.

Jana started to step back, away from the possibility of being touched by this man. But remembering her grandmother's words, she held her ground.

"Not so bad," the man repeated. Drawing courage from his older comrade's initial advance, the soldier stood directly in front of Rachel. With a startling gesture, he reached out and grabbed her hair and kerchief, yanking her head backwards in order to see her face more clearly. The copper of her hair glinted in the light. Taking his rifle with the bayonet attached, the young man moved the blade downward to the ground.

"Are you frightened, old woman?" he asked with a leering smile. "Don't worry. I wouldn't do anything that you haven't already known before."

Still, Rachel kept her eyes cast downward, as if she were slightly simple and could not understand what he was expressing so very succinctly.

Hooking the blade of his bayonet under the edge of her long skirt, he raised it slowly, shining the light of his torch on her as he did it.

He stepped back. She could sense his admiration at the shape of her body. A slow grin spread over his lips. But as the light focused on her legs, then moved up, the grin changed to disgust as he caught sight of the blood.

Turning with open disdain to his comrades, he said, "Do you see it? Look! She's got her monthly curse and does not even have the sense to wear rags. Disgusting, these ignorant peasants!" He turned away. Rachel's skirt fell back down. Then the man spat on the ground. "Disgusting!"

"Go away, pig," said the third soldier with a dismissing wave of his hand. "Go away!"

Rachel nodded benignly, as if she barely comprehended the man's gesture of dismissal. She wanted to cry with relief, to weep with the passion and gratitude of a person whose death sentence has been commuted. At the same time, if she had possessed a weapon, she would gladly have killed all three soldiers.

But she restrained her impulses to do anything except take Jana by the hand and walk away with her head lowered. They made their way carefully to the edge of the steps and down to the quay where, in better times, lovers met in the romance of the river's darkness. But there were no lovers here. There were not boats here, either. The quay was empty.

Rachel's heart lurched at the thought that they had come this far only to be abandoned. There was no barge waiting for them. She looked up at the sky and saw the pale crimson light of dawn.

Our luck's run out, she thought desperately. We can't go back. We can't go forward. There's no time left. And no place to go.

Then she saw the boat. About a hundred yards down the river, it stood moored to a post, just north of the propeller boat jetties. Clearly, he had moved away from the possibility of inquisitive soldiers. She could barely make out Miklos moving about on the front deck of the barge as he folded a fishing net.

Restraining her impulse to run, Rachel took Jana's hand and walked slowly down the quay. When they reached the boat, they crossed the plank that connected it to land.

"I thought you weren't coming," Miklos said as he glanced at the sky. "Where are the others?"

"There are no others," Rachel replied, "They were taken away two days ago and we are the only ones left."

A stricken look crossed Miklos' face. "Ohhh . . . I'm sorry," he said sadly, shaking his head. "So sorry. Josef . . . he was a good man . . . a very good man."

"Yes," Rachel agreed stoically. She looked down at her granddaughter whose face was tight with her effort not to cry.

"Then you will still be going?" Miklos asked.

"Yes. It is too dangerous for us to stay."

Miklos paused a moment, then nodded. "Then we'll be off soon," he said in a voice that cracked with anxiety and pity. "Go below, both of you. You will find hot soup I made just this morning."

"Thank you, Miklos. Thank you," whispered Rachel with tears in her eyes. She understood the risk

42

this man was taking. He could be shot if it were discovered he was helping two Jews escape.

"Thank you," Jana squeaked, her voice barely audible.

"Ah . . . is that Jana?" Miklos said, bending over to the child's level.

She nodded.

"Well, it's nice to have you on board," Miklos said as he reached out to touch her head. But when she saw his hand coming towards her, Jana stepped back.

"What is this?" Miklos asked with a mixture of hurt and surprise. "You are afraid of me? Miklos? Your friend? Your grandfather's friend?"

Jana nodded, struggling to maintain her composure. "Buba says that men must'nt touch me," she said.

A quick glance was exchanged between Miklos and Rachel.

"You must do as your grandmother says," Miklos told Jana. "But you must also know that I would never harm you."

Jana looked at him, then nodded uncertainly.

"Come," Rachel said softly. "Let's go below and have some soup."

It was still early spring and the chill of winter had not yet left Budapest. Rachel ate her soup, grateful for its warmth. She looked up through the hatch, hugging her coat tighter around her as she bid her city good-bye. Gazing at the elegant domes and spires of the great Parliament building outlined against the dark silver and rose-colored sky, she nodded once in farewell, then turned away.

The unbearable thought that she was leaving this city forever washed over her consciousness, and somewhere deep inside something snapped. It was a sorrow and a severing, an ending and a beginning. Most of all it was a loss, a loss of home and love and security. It was almost more than she could bear. There was nothing left now except her own life and the life of her grandchild. That was all. And, at that moment, it would have to suffice.

It had been a rich life in Budapest, a full one. The city was a good home even for a Jew, especially a Jew who carried the title of Baron, as did Josef von Wietzman. It was a sophisticated city, one with a history of years of intermarriage and acculturation. The House of Lords even had a seat for the Chief Rabbi. But in the mid-thirties, under the malignant influence of the Nazis, anti-Semitism had markedly increased, and the atmosphere of the city turned ugly and ominous. Still, the Jewish population remained. For Jews were safer there than in almost any other city under German rule.

Despite all the evidence to the contrary, no one wanted to believe that anything horrendous would happen in Budapest. Rachel had heard that the deportations would come soon. The horrors that had been whispered about for years in other cities of Europe were now actually happening to her own family. And the ugly word entered her consciousness once more: Auschwitz. And she wondered if that was where her family would be sent.

Knowing she could not allow herself to dwell on the fate of her family Rachel turned her attention to Jana, making certain she ate her soup, fussing with her hair to assure that it still covered the precious brooch. By mid-morning, the barge had passed out of the city into the deceptively tranquil countryside. In ancient times, Celts had dwelt along the river's edge, but signs of their passing had been obliterated by the thick expanse of beech and willow trees that lined the banks. They were just now turning green, the tiny buds ready to burst into an ironic celebration of spring.

During lunch, Miklos informed Rachel that it would take five days to reach Belgrade. Rachel implored him to travel more quickly, but Miklos maintained that he could not change his routine; that the guards along the route knew him too well.

As it was, he stood out from the other barges, Miklos said. He was a rebel of sorts, a man who had refused to convert his barge from coke fuel to a barge that travelled in tandem with other boats, all pulled by a tug.

"I do not wish to depend on other men," he explained to Rachel.

This need to be independent had gained him the distinction of being one of the last of the individualists, a man who travelled the river unencumbered and alone. And it also made him stand out from the other barges. If he deviated from his normal course, he would risk arrousing the suspicion of the guards. Thus, he could not hurry past a town where he usually stopped for an entire afternoon.

The journey was agonizingly slow for Rachel, her days filled with anxiety and her nights with dread. Yet somehow she felt safe aboard the barge, separated by water from the constant threat of discovery.

Every afternoon, as they travelled lazily down the Danube, Miklos took out his nets and dropped them over the side of the barge. He fished for sturgeon and catfish that abounded in the river, one of which they would usually eat a short time later. The rest of the fish were dropped into a tank in the hold. By the third day, the air around the barge was filled with the pungent odor of fish.

Jana only complained once about the smell of the fish. Rachel's response was immediate and hard: "Be grateful you have food on your table."

With this curt reminder of the new rules of behavior, Jana nodded. Still, it was difficult for her to comprehend that her days of coddling were over and that in their place was a distinct lack of sympathy. Too young to believe she would ever die or that real harm could come to her, Jana had trouble understanding what had happened. But somewhere in Rachel's demeanor and the firm, impassive strength of her voice, Jana understood the importance of accepting these new rules, whether or not she liked or understood them.

Every day on the journey, Rachel hung a bucket

over the side of the barge and filled it with water. Then she and Jana bathed, using the treasured soap they had packed for their journey. This daily bath was as important to Rachel as her daily meals, and it never occurred to her to change her routine. It was as if this ritual, this ceremony of civilization, was a way of clinging to her sanity. And she refused to give it up for fear of what might take its place.

Sometimes she would imagine herself soaking in the large claw-footed Victorian tub in the marbled oppulence of her home.

She would soak in the scented water for half an hour, loving the warmth and relaxation it offered.

Then, after her morning bath, she would dress carefully and go downstairs for breakfast. There, Eva would serve the morning meal from silver platters and covered porcelain dishes.

There were moments during the river journey when Rachel could smell the freshly baked rolls, the strong, pungent aroma of the dark-roasted coffee. She could feel the sensation of the thin china cup as it touched her lips, the heavy weight of the silver fork, the sensual, soft comfort of a thick, luxurious carpet as she walked barefoot across it. She could see the prismatic reflection of light through hand-cut crystal and hear the delicate chime of the grandfather clock that stood gracefully in the marbled entry hall. This was what her life had been, what gave meaning to daily ritual, what lent beauty to the mundane. It had substance, significance. She thought of this frequently as she ran a cloth soaked with cold river water over her body, as she sipped coffee from a tin cup, as she lay at night on her hard mattress made of a thin layer of straw. Sometimes they would comfort her, these thoughts from another time, and sometimes the memories were more than she could bear. But always, she knew they belonged to her, even if she could no longer incorporate them into her newly impoverished life.

Midway through the trip, the barge crossed the border into Yugoslavia. Before reaching the final bend of the river, Miklos said curtly, "Go down into the hold. Do not make a sound and do not appear again until I come to get you."

Rachel sensed fear in the man's voice, his dread of being caught. With a nod, Rachel led Jana down into the smelly darkness where they took their places behind burlap bags of grain that Miklos used sparingly to feed his chickens en route.

As soon as Jana saw this awful, dark place to which she was suddenly condemned after almost three days of floating peacefully down the river, she stopped.

"No!" she said. "I won't go in there."

"You must," Rachel countered impassively, even as she wept inwardly for Jana's terror.

"I can't, Buba. I can't go in there. Please don't make me go in there." she begged. "It's dark and awful inside. I can't do it, don't make me do it."

"You must go in there with me, Jana. We have no choice." Rachel could feel the barge slowing down. She knew that soon they would be moored to enemy territory.

"No!" Jana cried. Tears of terror streamed down her face.

Rachel controlled her impulse to grab Jana's arm and drag her into the dark. If she gave in, Rachel knew beyond a doubt that Jana would scream, alerting the guards to their presence. And so she bent down and took Jana's face in her hands. Then she spoke to her, softly, confidently. "Jana, darling. Listen to me. You must do this for your mother and father. For Josef. I promise I won't leave you alone for one second. But we must hide. For if we are discovered here, we could die."

"Die?" Jana repeated, puzzled at the finality of the alien word that was suddenly being applied to her.

"Die," Rachel confirmed. "I want us to live. I want *you* to live, Jana. And in order to save ourselves, we must hide in the dark. You *must* do it. We have no choice."

Jana pressed her lips together in an effort to control herself. Rachel felt the barge stop.

"Will you do it for us?" Rachel whispered urgently. "For our family?"

Agonized, Jana nodded. Resigned, she tip-toed with her grandmother to their hiding place.

As soon as she was crouched in the darkness, held firmly in Rachel's arms, Jana began to whimper. "No Buba . . . not the dark again. Not the dark . . . please."

Rachel rocked her gently back and forth, moving

her hand closer to Jana's mouth so that she could clamp it shut if she sensed that the child might lose control. "Hush now," she whispered into Jana's ear. "Hush now. It's only for a little while. Stay here with me. I'll take care of you."

Rachel heard footsteps and voices on the deck above their heads. The border guards had boarded the barge.

"Same cargo, Miklos?" asked as strange voice.

"Very much the same," Miklos replied pleasantly. "And I have saved another plump hen for you."

"Ahh . . ." said the officer in appreciation, imagining the dinner he would enjoy that night.

Below, Rachel felt Jana tremble as she held the child tighter. She listened as the heavy boots walked across the deck to inspect the cage of chickens. She was alert to every passing step, able to ascertain exactly where they were on the deck above.

It seemed an eternity passed before Rachel heard the footsteps move to the side of the barge and then disappear. With a deep sigh of relief, she held Jana close and waited for the rocking motion of the barge to indicate they were floating in deep water.

Rachel and Jana crouched patiently in the hold, surrounded by a shroud of darkness. It seemed that hours passed, but Miklos did not come to fetch them. Rachel had begun to think that he would never come, that they would have to spend the remainder of the trip in this hellish place. But finally, Miklos appeared, trembling with the aftermath of fear that he had successfully repressed while he conversed so casually with the guards.

When he entered the hold, Jana did not move. Even when Miklos approached and spoke to her, she was immobile. It was as if she had ceased to function. Miklos leaned over and picked her up, speaking softly to her as he lifted her from Rachel's arms. Jana did not object to his touching her then. She could not even talk.

Rachel followed as Miklos took Jana into his living quarters and sat her in a chair. She watched as the child started to gulp in the air as she blinked against the sudden brightness of the light that filtered down the open hatch.

"I never knew," Miklos mumbled as he turned to the cupboard to pour himself a small drink of slivowitz. "I never knew how frightened a man could be."

"You did a fine job," Rachel said softly.

"A coward. I'm a coward," he replied, hearing only the voice of his own fear. "Never again."

"You were wonderful." Rachel countered. "Wonderful."

Having regained a semblance of life, Jana reached out then and touched Miklos softly on his arm. "Then why do you do it?" she asked innocently.

"For a friend," Miklos answered curtly. "I did it for a friend, your grandfather. And I'll never do anything like that again."

"I did it for him, too," Jana replied shyly. "And I think that you were very, very brave." An expression

51

of undisguised admiration shone from her face.

Miklos looked at her, at her simple trust in his strength, in his ability to save her life. "It was pretty easy when I look back on it," he said with wonder and a slow smile of pride.

They could hear the music of the csardas as the barge pulled into the Belgrade quay in the afternoon of the fifth day of their journey. It came from a cafe near the river, inviting the listener to dance, to sway to the beat of its insistent rhythm.

When she heard the music, Rachel was seized by the simple longing to leave the barge and walk into the cafe for a hot steaming cup of coffee and a pastry. She remembered the happy times then, the hours she had spent in Budapest at the Expressos talking with friends, laughing, participating in a ritual that was as natural as breathing to the citizens of that city. Much of the city's smart and chic social life revolved around these coffee houses. Listening to the music drove home to Rachel how cut off she was from everything that was kind and familiar. She wondered how long it would be before she could participate once again in this simple, human ritual.

During the afternoon, Rachel and Jana stayed below as Miklos sold his wares to the hungry citizens of Belgrade. If there was no money to purchase the goods, they would barter, a practice at which Miklos was a master. Rachel listened to him, admired his style, the manner in which he would cajole just one more yard of material or another apple from a customer whose desire for a chicken stew clouded his judgement. Miklos rarely finished second in these transactions.

Finally, with the sunset, Miklos came into the cabin where Rachel and Jana had been hiding.

"We made it," he said with growing pride, as he reached into the cabinet and pulled out a bottle of wine. Turning to Rachel, he smiled. "Your husband gave me this bottle months ago. All this time I have saved it. And now I think we should drink to him."

"No," said Rachel firmly, silently begging forgiveness for this heresy. "We will drink to your courage and your generosity." Better to celebrate the living than to mourn the missing, she thought pragmatically. I will have years for mourning.

Miklos filled her glass carefully, even poured a sip into a glass for Jana. Then the two refugees raised their glasses in a gesture of gratitude that they had come this far on their reckless and perilous journey.

After a dinner of spicy chicken stew that Rachel prepared with onions and paprika, Miklos stood up and rubbed his protruding belly.

"I thank you for that. It was a beautiful meal," he said with a courtly bow to Rachel. Hesitating guiltily for a moment, he continued. "Now I am going to go to the cafe. The sound of the zimbalon is too much with me tonight. I cannot hear that music without running to it."

Rachel listened to the pulsating gypsy rhythms floating over the river to the barge. It called to her, also. But she could not go.

"How is it you plan to leave the barge?" Miklos asked, uncomfortable with his question. He was clearly compromised by their presence and anxious for them to leave.

"Josef told me that we would be met," Rachel said with quiet dread. She did not know what was supposed to happen next. "I don't know how or who is to meet us. I did not have a chance to discuss it with him."

"Nor did I discuss it," Miklos said, his voice taking on a barely perceptible note of hardness. "I only know that I must leave here in the morning, whether anyone has come for you or not."

Rachel started to reply, but Miklos held up his hand.

"I cannot alter my route," he said. "You know that. From the first day, I told you. I cannot do it. To alter my route would be too suspicious."

"Then we will be gone by morning," Rachel replied, a note of resigned desperation in her quivering voice. She knew very well what it meant to be abandoned in Belgrade.

Although the city had been considered liberal in its policies towards the Jews before the war, the advent of the Nazis had stirred up the malignant stew of anti-Semitism. The German command had done an excellent job in Serbia. There were few Jews left now in Belgrade, where once there had been eight thousand. And those Jews who did remain were in constant jeopardy of being trapped by Serbian collaborators and turned over to the Germans.

Rachel knew this was no place to be caught. She and Jana would be shot or deported with no questions asked. There would be no mercy in Belgrade for a woman and a child with no papers; papers, in this case, that were far more valuable than diamonds.

Once Rachel agreed to leave, she could see the relief on Miklos' face. She understood that they were a dangerous burden to him, that he had done all he could. But now he wanted to be free of them.

Fumbling, Miklos finally repeated that he was going to the cafe. And, with an awkward gesture of farewell, he left Rachel and Jana to themselves.

Rachel waited all evening for some sign, some indication that their rescue would actually occur. But nothing happened. No one came, no message was delivered. She tried to keep Jana's spirits up, to give the child some measure of confidence that help would arrive. But, finally, around ten o'clock, she tucked Jana into bed. She rocked her in her arms, held her close and sang familiar lullabies, wondering if this would be the last time she would ever sing these simple songs. She wondered, too, if they would be alive by this time tomorrow.

Lying down beside the sleeping child, Rachel made the decision that she would wait until early morning before she and Jana left the barge. She would give it that much time. Perhaps it would be possible to escape under the cloak of dawn into the countryside. Perhaps it would be possible to create a miracle, she thought bitterly.

Awake in the single bunk, Rachel tried to formulate an alternate plan, anything besides being abandoned in this hostile city. She considered the possibility of paying Miklos with diamonds to take them downriver a little further, even as far as the Black Sea. She had heard of people there getting a boat to Israel. They could try their luck, she thought, though she doubted seriously that their lives would be in any less danger in Bulgaria. A Jew was no longer safe on the continent of Europe.

She must have drifted into a restless sleep, for the next thing Rachel knew, she heard the sound of footsteps on the deck above her. It was the blackest hour of night. She thought it must be Miklos returning from the cafe—and from his women—she added ruefully to herself. She lay quietly in the bunk and waited for him.

She watched the door. Then a man appeared in the doorway, his outlined figure clear against the night sky. Recognizing the faint silhouette of a German officer's uniform, Rachel's throat constricted with terror.

Frantically, she thought of Miklos, hoped for his return. Then it dawned on her how guiltily he had behaved about going to the cafe. He knew, of course, that Josef was a jeweler. A wealthy jeweler. And he could have made the natural assumption that Rachel would be carrying jewels with her, whether Josef was with her or not.

Miklos himself had said that he was a coward. Was he too much of a coward to face Rachel with his terrible betrayal? Was it easier to turn the woman and child into a German officer and collect a reward?

Rachel did not know whether to scream or to fight. She knew nothing except that death was close at hand.

A light from the torch swept the room and rested on Rachel's face. She closed her eyes, pretending to sleep. As the officer walked down the steps, Rachel hoped Jana would not awaken. It would be better, she thought, if the child were shot in her sleep.

Walking over to the side of the bed, the officer shielded the light with his hand. He stood directly over her. Then he spoke in perfect, cultured German. "Is this barge the 'Danube Mermaid?'"

Rachel opened her eyes. "Yes," she choked.

"von Weitzman?" asked the man in a voice so low that she could not hear him.

"Pardon me?"

"von Weitzman?" he repeated.

"Yes. That is my name," she answered.

"My name is Marek. I have come to take you to the coast."

Rachel gasped for air, taking in great gulps as her entire body started to shake. Her trembling woke up Jana.

"What is it?" asked the child, still half asleep.

"Hush now," Rachel whispered. "Lie quietly for a

moment until you are awake."

"Where are the others?" Marek asked.

"There are no others."

"But I was told that there would be an entire family," he replied, not bothering to hide his annoyance.

"The rest were taken away the day before we left Budapest. We are all that is left."

"There should be more," he protested. "I came to help a family."

"I'm sorry . . ." Rachel replied evenly, her voice drifting off inconclusively, wondering if he would abandon them.

"Families. That's why I work. What I do best."

"There's nothing I can do."

"Nor I," he said with thinly disguised resignation, as if his trip there had been for nothing. "So get up now and move. We must be on the other side of the city before daylight."

Since they were already dressed, it took only a few minutes for Rachel and Jana to prepare. Before they left, Rachel took her knife from the satchel and slit open one of the small compartments on the handle of the bag. Feeling the diamond drop into her hand, she took a piece of newspaper used for wrapping fish and folded the stone carefully inside. Laying it in the middle of Miklos' table, she wrote in pencil on the package: "Thank you forever." When that was done, she took one look around. Then, holding Jana's hand, they left the barge.

Marek had instructed them that they should walk directly in front of him in an orderly fashion, as if they were captives of the officer. Doing exactly as they were told, the three began their journey across the city.

As they walked through Belgrade, Rachel was overwhelmed at the condition of this once-lovely city. She knew, of course, about Hitler's rage against the country. The citizens of Yugoslavia had refused to acknowledge the Tripartate Pact that its leaders had signed with Germany. They had rebelled, overthrowing the government that had signed the pact, leaving Hitler in a frenzied rage.

Determined to wreak revenge on this rebellious country, Hitler postponed Operation Barbarossa — the invasion of Russia — for four weeks. It was a tactical error that would cost him dearly. But revenge and the destruction of Belgrade were more important to him at that moment.

In April, 1941, German armies poured over Yugoslavia's borders from Hungary, Bulgaria and Germany. Following Hitler's orders, Goering's Luftwafe raided Belgrade for three successive days and nights in a military exercise that Hitler dubbed Operation Punishment. And, indeed, it was just that. Bombing at rooftop level, Belgrade was defenseless, for the city had no anti-aircraft guns.

The result was the rubble through which they walked now: block after block of destruction, mile after mile of unbelievable ruin.

As it grew closer to dawn, the trio passed an increasing number of soldiers, both German and Hungarian. Marek would give a nod or a smart salute when he encountered them, then continue as if he were on official business. It was plain to the most casual observer that the German officer was disgusted by the two dirty peasants that it was his distasteful duty to deal with.

Finally reaching the edge of the city where buildings were mostly still intact, the bare light of dawn could just be made out. Glancing back, Rachel realized for the first time how very young their savior was.

He's a child, she thought as she looked at his unlined face, still not totally free of the soft edges of youth. No wonder he did not want to be seen too clearly in the light of day.

Veering off the road now, they had moved to within touching distance of some trees when they heard the one German word that they dreaded most: "Halt."

They turned to find themselves looking into the menacing barrel of a Luger.

Oberleutnant Fritz Walther stood before them, his hand steady as he held his pistol. In his late twenties, he prided himself on his instinct for recognizing suspicious behavior. A child of the streets, it was second nature to him. And so when he first saw the threesome walking on the road, he thought little of it. But it did occur to him that they walked a bit too purposefully, as if they knew more than he did.

Following them at a distance, he watched them move off the road and head towards the trees, and swung around ahead of them. Meeting them at the intersection where the field met the trees, he was their last obstacle before reaching the safe shelter of the woods.

The man standing in front of him was too young to be an officer, Walther thought. Even in this war, he's too young.

Marek tried to overcome his obvious disadvantage by speaking first, trying to take command of the confrontation. "How dare you stop me like this," he said arrogantly. "I am an officer of the Reich—"

"I shall tell you how I dare stop you, just as soon as you show me your papers," Oberleutnant Walther returned in a cool, hard voice.

Fearing the worst, Rachel pushed Jana behind her, covering the child with her body.

"The woman and child . . ." Walther said. "Who are they?"

"Prisoners."

"Who are they?" Walther persisted.

"The woman . . ." Marek began, thinking furiously about what to do, "the woman told me that I could . . . have her, if I would let them go free."

"Who are they?"

"Just peasants."

"She does not look like a peasant to me," Walther replied in a defiantly subdued voice, surveying Rachel as he spoke. He recognized the fine lines of an aristocrat in her face, the deep green eyes of a woman who has known beauty, the smooth skin of a woman who has not worked in the fields. Glancing at Jana, he considered her . . . no she is too young. I'll have the older one. It's been a long time, he thought, his penis hardening at the idea. Since he had been in Yugoslavia, he had seen few women he desired. The best ones hated the Germans. And Walther did not want just any woman. Oberleutnant Fritz Walther was particular, as any loyal officer of the Reich should be. Especially one who has never known riches, never known the feel of silk on his bed, nor an elegant woman lying next to him.

He motioned to Rachel with a jerk of his head. "Come," he said.

Leaving Jana next to Marek, Rachel walked over to the officer and stood directly in front of the pistol. She knew that Marek would take care of Jana if anything happened to her. And that knowledge made it easier for her to stand there.

Shoving her roughly to the side so that he could keep his primary opponent in the sight of his pistol, Walther grabbed Rachel's arm.

"I . . . I have a diamond," she managed to utter in German, fumbling for some way to bribe the man.

Not taking his eyes off Marek, the officer replied, "So do I, my dear lady. In case you did not know it, diamonds have become trifling commodities these days. Not so hard to come by as before, when the rich hoarded them all."

"This diamond is not trifling," replied Rachel,

making a decision that scoured her heart, leaving it raw and bleeding.

"Oh?" the man said cautiously. "Show it to me."

Walther was not above the appreciation of beauty. He had worked hard to get where he was. The son of a common laborer, he had grown up in a squalid apartment in the grand city of Dresden. He knew finer things. He was simply never allowed to touch them.

Oberleutnent Fritz Walther valued the army immensely. It had given him his first opportunity to raise himself up in the world, to become someone whose destiny embraced more than poverty and humiliation. He had vowed on his first day in the army that, if he survived the war, he would become a man of power and wealth, a man who could purchase the finest things life had to offer. Almost everything he did was directed towards that goal. And the means by which he was getting there were legitimate when it was convenient, and ruthlessly illegal when it was not. Therefore, taking a diamond from a helpless woman before he raped and then killed her was not at all unthinkable. As a matter of fact, he took a rather perverse pleasure in the thought.

"Please show me this extraordinary jewel," he said. His even, mock-pleasant voice did little to disguise the fact that this was a harsh and insolent command.

Rachel knew this was her last chance. They had touched the cover of the woods and their odds for survival would increase with every step they took. It was important to do anything to buy time until a means of escape could be devised. She had no choice. Now was not the time to make a pitiful offering of a small loose stone and risk enraging the German. She could not afford to be sentimental. The brooch would not buy their freedom in America; instead, it would purchase their lives in Yugoslavia.

Rachel spoke quietly to Jana and the child moved to her grandmother's side without a sound.

Rachel removed Jana's kerchief and pulled the pins from her hair. Jana stood still, as if she had been turned to stone. Even a seven year old could understand the threat this man represented.

As the thick, blond hair fell over her shoulders, the small leather pouch came readily into view. But it was still stitched to her hair. Rachel began to untangle it carefully, trying not to pull Jana's hair or hurt her in any way. As she worked, she caressed her granddaughter, attempting to soothe her fears.

Oberleutnant Walther watched impatiently as Rachel worked. Then he drew his knife from the sheath on his belt.

"Hold out her hair," he ordered.

Jana did not utter a word. She stood still before this monster and willed herself not to move, not to cry, trying her best to be the grown-up that her grandmother had asked her to be.

As Rachel held out Jana's hair, Walther took the knife and sawed at it roughly. The knife was razor sharp and the pouch came free quickly, leaving an ugly crop of short hair on the back of Jana's head. Still, Jana did nothing. She concentrated on how her mother used to brush her hair in the mornings, braiding it lovingly as she sang to her. Then she would tie a satin ribbon at the ends of the braids. Jana loved those moments with her mother. She wondered what her mother would think now if she could see the ugly shock of hair on the back of her head.

Holding the Luger, Walther opened the leather pouch and took out the brooch. "Ahh . . ." he exclaimed quietly, unable to look at the diamond without reacting to its unsurpassed beauty. "You were right," he said to Rachel indifferently.

Rachel straightened her body. Fear had passed from her consciousness. In its place was a desperate determination to get away from this man, to survive. "I have given you the brooch," she said with quiet dignity. "Now. Please let us go."

Walther looked at her, once again feeling the pleasurable stirring in his loins. "Yes," he replied. "I will let you go. But first there is a little favor I must ask of you." He smiled. "Come with me. You, too," he said to Marek and Jana. "Come into the woods."

The three of them walked into the trees with a pistol pointed at their backs.

Suddenly Marek stumbled over a branch in the path. He fell to the ground and grabbed his ankle.

"Get up," ordered the Oberleutnant, pointing the gun directly at Marek's head.

Marek rose slowly, taking the knife he had pulled from his boot and slipping it up his sleeve. Then he walked with the others to a dense grove of trees.

"Now," Walther said to Rachel as he grabbed her by the arm and pulled her away from Jana and Marek. "Lie down."

Rachel's worst fears were confirmed. This inhuman pig of a man intended to rape her, and she could do nothing about it. It was clear that if she objected in any way, she would be shot. Hoping for a miracle, Rachel glanced at Marek. His eyes were glazed with disgust at his own helplessness.

"Do not look to him for help," Walther said to Rachel. "Look to me. And do as I say."

Rachel stood still.

"Lie down!" the Oberleutnant barked. "Now!"

She could not seem to make herself move.

He reached out and shoved her roughly to the ground. The earth was cold, ungiving. Propelled into a heightened state of sensitivity, Rachel was aware of everything. The mark on her body where the German had touched her felt like a burn. She was acutely aware of the pine needles beneath her hand as it rested on the ground. She sensed Jana's terror and Marek's rage; she understood the Oberleutnant's lust. Each moment stood out as if it were separate from all the others. Each breath hung silently in the air as if it were charged with life. Each change in the light, each sound of the forest came to her as if it were brand new. Life was suspended. Time stopped.

"I told you to lie down," the German said.

Slowly, as an automoton would move, Rachel lay back.

"No," he said. "This way." He motioned that she should point her legs away from Jana and Marek.

Silently she moved her body around to accommodate his demand.

The German looked at Marek and Jana. "Step closer," he commanded.

Touching Jana on her shoulder, Marek moved her forward.

"No . . . please . . ." Rachel begged. "Not in front of the child. Please. Send them away."

"Pull up your skirt."

"Please send them away," she pleaded. "I promise I will cooperate. Just let him take her away so that she does not see this. Please."

"Pull up your skirt!" he barked.

"Please. I beg of you . . ."

"Do as I say!" the Oberleutnant hissed, a murderous rage flashing in his eyes.

Silently, Rachel raised her buttocks and slipped her skirt up to her waist, exposing the fine, firm lines of her legs.

"That is better."

"Close your eyes, Jana," Rachel said without turning her head. "Close your eyes, my love. Do not watch this."

The German knelt over her and landed a blow across Rachel's mouth. It jarred her head to the side. And, in that moment, she could see Jana's stricken expression as she opened her mouth in a silent scream. Rachel's face stung with the blow. She tasted the blood that trickled from her mouth down the side of her face. She dared not say another word.

The German officer straddled her roughly. Still holding his pistol, he trained it directly on Marek who stood no more than three feet away from Rachel's head. "Put your arms in the air," he said. Marek did as he was told.

Without looking at her, the Oberleutnant felt Rachel's body with his free hand. He groped up her leg until he touched her hand-embroidered silk bloomers. Glancing down quickly, a malevolent grin on his face, he exclaimed, "Ah . . . a lady in peasant's clothing."

Rachel looked at her captor and thought what a pleasure it would be to reach up and put her hand around his neck and squeeze the life from him.

Excited now, filled with the new sensation of exerting his full power and dominion over such a beautiful woman, Walther smiled to himself. This is the way it should always be, he told himself smugly. He enjoyed the hardness of the pistol he held in his hand. Power creates potency. See how hard it is, How it grows. I needn't worry ever again about being humiliated by a woman. This is what I need. Complete control.

He unbuttoned his pants and pulled out his penis. He was pleased with the rigid manifestation of his power and virtility. "You have probably never seen one like this before," he commented calmly to Rachel with a strange mixture of malice and pride. "It is not circumsized. It will be a new experience for a Jewess like you." He assumed correctly that she was fleeing because the long arm of anit-Semitism had reached out to her and the child.

No man had ever touched her besides Josef. Rachel tried desperately to recreate the passion she had felt for her husband, the happy and lusty times she had spent with him in their grand canopied bed. It suddenly seemed very important to her that she remember this before this monster on top of her spoiled her memory forever. She wanted her remembrance to be pure, to be whole, a treasure to be guarded inside her own head where this grotesque being could never reach. But memory could not obliterate present reality. Instead of closing her eyes to it in an attempt to avoid the brutality of what was happening to her, Rachel decided to confront him. She would not look away, she vowed to herself. She would not avert her eyes in shame. She would now allow him to perpetrate an anonymous act of rape.

I will not be cowed by this monster, she told herself. Nor will I forget what is happening. I will not allow him to make me non-human, closing my eyes to this abomination so it makes it easier for him to forget. This is a part of my life now. As it will be a part of Jana's. Poor child . . . poor, poor child. My darling baby.

Without warning, the Oberleutnant shoved himself roughly into her. It was difficult, because there was no moisture; nothing except dry, parched revulsion to receive his perverted virility.

Against her will, she winced. She did not want to give him the satisfaction of knowing that he was affecting her in any way. But she could not prevent that flash of reaction to the pain he caused her. In spite of this, she did not close her eyes. The pain was minimal now. It was outweighed by her sorrow for her granddaughter, for the confusion and horror that Jana must now be feeling.

With every second that passed, Rachel's rage grew. She felt it taking shape in her like a crazed animal ready to explode in its full measure of fury. She felt it boiling, churning inside, as if it were a living pulsating thing.

Walther stopped moving for a moment, reveling in the sensation of so completely dominating a woman . . . a woman of class, a lady. Even if she were a Jewess, she still had the mark of the upper class. And even if he did have to take her by force, it still felt good.

All the time he was moving inside Rachel, the German kept his pistol trained on Marek and the child who stood before him, both paralyzed with fear. Grinning wildly, he began to move faster. Jana was rigid with terror, unable to comprehend what was happening, yet knowing it was something deeply and irrevocably hideous. She understood clearly that an unspeakably savage act was being committed.

Jana was mesmerized by the expression on the

70

German's face, by the obvious pleasure he was deriving from this madness. She could not understand his pleasure. She longed to squeeze her eyes closed. But she could not. She watched everything as if she were trapped in a nightmare from which she could not awaken.

She watched as the man moved faster and faster. She looked down at her grandmother's face that was now contorted with an agony she had never seen. Rachel's eyes were open, but they were wild. There was a glazed quality about her expression, as if the vision she beheld was too unspeakable to acknowledge.

Jana wanted to cry out, to run to her grandmother and cover her with kisses, to tell her she would make it all right, that she would kiss away the pain.

The man moved faster now. And as Jana watched, she could see a kind of ecstasy spread over his face as he reveled in the fullness of his power.

Jana did not see Marek move his fingers downward to his sleeve, nor did she see the knife fly through the air with one swift flick of his wrist. But she did see the German's face contort with an alien pleasure; a pleasure that died instantly when the knife spread open the side of his cheek before glancing off the bone and moving down, entering his body between his shoulder and his heart.

Jana screamed. Stunned, Rachel felt warm blood spurt on her, felt the Oberleutnant's body slump over hers as he cried out in agony.

Moving with the grace and swiftness of a panther, Marek stepped over to Rachel and pulled the German's inert body from on top of her. Then, with no wasted motion, he removed the knife from the man, wiped it on the German's uniform and reached over to pick up the Luger.

Rachel opened her mouth in a kind of animal protest. But not a sound came out. It was a scream of silence, a scream that reflected an unremitting vision of hell. She lay on the ground, immobile, mute, the blood of her conquerer spread in destestable blotches over her face.

Looking down at her, Marek said, "Get up. Now."

But Rachel did not move.

Marek leaned over and grabbed Rachel by the arm. "Get up!" he ordered desperately. She struggled to rise, managing finally to pull herself to a sitting position.

In full control of his senses, Marek squatted down and took Rachel's face in his hands. "There is no time for that," he said clearly. "You must move. If you want to save your granddaughter, you must get up and come with me now. There is no time left."

Dazed, Rachel looked at Marek, his young face grim from witnessing many lifetimes of horror. And she looked at Jana, frail and stunned, her eyes dead, her body stiff.

"You must come with me now," Marek repeated slowly. "Jana must come with me. Time has run out."

In an automatic gesture born of another time, Rachel reached out and gripped the handle of her satchel. Then she stood and turned to Jana.

"Get your bag," she said, her voice like a robot. She was aware of Marek picking up the little bag and putting it in Jana's hand.

"We must go now," Marek said, urgently. Then he took each of them by a hand and began to run.

They stumbled at first, clumsy in their shocked state. But he held onto them, pulling them deeper and deeper into the sanctuary of the trees. Gradually, even though their brains were frozen in shock, their limbs began to function automatically. And they were able to move faster, hurling their bodies forward in desperate flight from the enemy.

They had travelled a half a mile when Rachel remembered.

"The brooch!" she cried out, coming to a halt. "I must go back and get it."

"Never!" Marek replied.

Rachel begged. "Please. Please let me go."

Marek's answer was to drag her forward, to continue running.

Chapter 3

It is a matter of conjecture whether Fritz Walther was an inherently wicked man, or whether he was just another person entangled in the snare of war.

It is possible that, had Marek's knife missed its mark, the Oberleutnant would have lived out his postwar days in a nondescript blur, working, marrying, having children and eventually becoming a responsible citizen of the republic. With a bitter and shabby whimper, he would have taken his menial place in society.

However, for the bloodied man who emerged from unconsciousness that bright April morning, that was no longer the case.

For a short while, Oberleutnant Fritz Walther lay still, the blood from his awful wounds flowing freely into the dark, moist earth. His head spinning, feeling like he was trapped in a childhood nightmare - unable to run, unable to call for help—he lay suspended in helplessness.

Sluggishly, his eyelids fluttered and then were still once more. Finally, he opened his eyes, struggling to focus on the dark shadows of the trees that hovered over his inert body. He did not know where he was, what he was doing there.

It took him several minutes to remember what had happened, to sort out the sequence of events that had taken place before he fell unconscious to the ground. With an effort born of greed, he moved his hand to his pocket. Feeling the hard lump formed by the brooch still resting within, he smiled.

With that smile came a pain that rose from hell. It tore through the side of his face, searing his severed nerve endings. Clumsily, he moved his hand up, his fingers delicately exploring the divided flesh. His smooth, unblemished skin gaped open in an unspeakable hole, the two sliced edges of his cheek curling outward, as if forming another mouth on his contorted face. At first, he did not understand. Then he realized with a moan that the slippery hardness he felt was his cheekbone, exposed completely by the cut of Marek's knife.

He cried out, horrified and bitter, attempting to rise from the ground. It was then that he realized he had sustained a wound just above his heart.

Finally understanding that there would be no help for him if he remained hidden in the trees, he began to move, to uncurl his wounded body from the center of its own agony.

Holding onto the trunk of a tree, he pulled himself to his feet. The cold air brushed his limp penis, hanging impotently from his rumpled pants. In his pride, he struggled to tuck it back inside before

75

staggering crazily from the cover of the low branches.

Taking a handkerchief from his tunic, he pressed the sides of his cheek together as best he could, then set out across the wide field that separated the woods from the road.

Had the canvas-covered truck filled with German soldiers not driven along the road at the particular moment, there is no doubt that the Oberleutnant would have died from shock and blood loss. But fortune also follows the unworthy, and when he sighted the dun-colored vehicle through a blur of tears and blood, he staggered towards it, waving his hand in a silent plea for help.

Deep into the forest by now, Marek was still running, pulling Jana and Rachel along with him. Stumbling madly away from the city, it was Marek who first heard the relentless wail of the siren that turned them officially into prey.

"Faster!" he implored them. "Time has run out!"

Marek knew beyond doubt that slow torture would not be good enough for a Partisan caught wearing the uniform of the Reich. Nor for Jews fleeing the tyranny of its long, savage arm.

Chapter 4

"Buba!" Jana gasped, barely able to speak. "No more. Please, Buba. No more. I have to rest."

Without stopping, Rachel answered. "Like the tears, Jana, rest must be delayed until another time. You are young and healthy and accustomed to exercise. You can keep up with us if you try harder. You must. Because you are a Horvath and a von Weitzman. And your mother and father would want you to do it."

Having regained enough of her senses to understand the dire threat of their situation, Rachel was as desperate as Marek now to find refuge. She had placed all her trust, her life, in the hands of this young man because she recognized plainly that his judgement, his actions, were the only hope they had.

Finally, panting heavily, he stopped. Deeply frightened now, he took stock of the ugly dilemma in which he found himself. For a moment, he was tempted to leave the woman and child, to abandon them to the mercy of the fates. He knew that he, alone, could escape. He had done it many times before. But he also knew that he would betray everything in which he believed if he saved himself at the expense of their lives.

He assumed that the enemy would begin its search along the banks of the Sava River on the route leading to the coast. It would be reasonable for the Germans to follow this course. They knew it was the route chosen by many enemies of the Reich to escape occupied territory.

Because of this, Marek could not follow his original plans for spiriting these people out of the country.

"You may rest for a moment," he said to them, his voice hard with anxiety and dread. He knew he must make a decision now, that he could not waste time wondering what to do.

Jana stood silent before him, looking at his face as if he were invincible. She could understand the German that Marek spoke. She had been speaking it with her family for two years and had become surprisingly proficient in the language of fairy tales and the enemy.

"We must change our plans," Marek said at last. "I can no longer take you to the coast. It would be too dangerous. They will look there for us first."

"But where will we go?" Rachel asked, mentally confronting her worst fear that this stranger would abandon them in the midst of the enemy.

"I will take you to the Partisans," Marek said. "To my uncle's division. That is where I stay when I am not running this . . . human ferry."

"But how will we get out of the country?" Rachel asked, alarmed at this sudden change in plans.

Marek looked directly at her. "I do not know."

"How long will we be there?"

"I do not know."

Jana, unable to understand the full impact of this decision, asked, "How far away is your uncle?"

"Very far," Marek answered, reaching out and touching her gently. He felt Jana flinch and withdrew his hand, instinctively understanding her fear. "My uncle's division is very far away," he began again, trying to gentle her anxiety with the calm tone of his voice. "It is southwest of here, deep into the mountains. It will take five days, maybe six, to get there." He paused, knowing that if he were travelling alone, the journey could be made in half that time. "Five days of constant movement and little sleep. For the first part of the journey, we cannot use the roads. Word travels fast about enemies of the Reich," he added. "So we must walk where there are no paths. It will be difficult, Jana. But I know you can do it."

He turned to Rachel, speaking plainly. "We must hurry, drive ourselves without mercy. Or we shall all die."

"We shall not die," Rachel replied, more to convince herself than the others.

Smiling at Jana, his expression hiding his fear, Marek asked, "Will you do it for me, Little One? Even though you are exhausted and hungry? I'll look after you. I'll take care of you so that you will not be afraid. Remember to do as I say, and you will be safe."

"I can do it," she answered with the simple naivete of a child.

"I'm sure you can," Marek said, wishing his faith were as simple and uncomplicated as the child's. "Now. We'll be off."

It was late afternoon when Marek heard the ominous buzz.

"Quick!" he said, grabbing Jana's hand and indicating to Rachel that she should follow. "Stuka!"

They divided into the shadow of some scrub oak, the only cover available to them. Then the three refugees watched as the lone plane came into sight over the ridge, making lazy circles overhead.

"Don't move," Marek instructed. "I did not think they would be looking in this direction so soon."

With every muscle in their bodies pulled into knots of perfect stillness, they waited while the predator searched meticulously for its prey. Rachel understood for the first time the nature of the hunt, and wondered if this were anything more than an amusing game for the pilot flying the plane.

After the plane disappeared over the far ridge, Marek made them wait for another ten minutes before venturing from their meagre cover.

"Now we must move even faster," Marek said, pointing up the steep mountain that they had just begun to climb. "We must be well into the forest up there before nightfall."

"I've never climbed a mountain before," Jana said.

"You'll be doing many new things now, Jana," Marek said.

Climbing as quickly as they could up the rocky slope, Marek hesitated then he saw the pink glow ahead, shining with an other-worldly incandescence.

"Snow," he said grimly. "We haven't time to search for clear ground where our tracks won't be seen."

The setting sun had turned the ground pale scarlet, now soft with purple shadows from the trees that crept over it, gracing it with irregular patterns of dark and light. It appeared beautifully benign to Rachel and she found it difficult to reconcile this with its inherent threat.

Staying in the shadows whenever possible, the trio made its laborious way to the snowline. Then they stopped, Marek scanning the ground for a possible route.

"There," he said, indicating some brown patches where rocks jutted through the snow. "We'll go that way."

Instructing Rachel to follow in his exact footsteps, he leaned over and swooped Jana into his arms. "Just for a few minutes, mind you, you get a free ride. Hold tight to your bag," he cautioned.

Stepping carefully on exposed rocks and clusters of pebbles, they made a zig-zag path to the shelter of the trees that lay ahead. Only three footsteps in the snow, when they were forced into it for lack of a connecting rock, revealed their presence. Without turning around, he told Rachel to take a stick and to brush over the footsteps once she was past. With luck, they would be hidden from searching eyes.

When they reached the edge of the trees, Marek set Jana down gently. "It will be dark soon," he explained, "but we cannot stop for the night so close to the open ground. We shall have to travel in the dark, Little One. You won't be frightened, because I will take care of you. And in a little while, we will make a shelter for the night."

Jana nodded, trusting him completely.

The shrouded silence of the forest surrounded the trio with both a sense of security and foreboding. The first time Rachel heard a limb, laden with the weight of snow, crack from a tree, she jumped in fear.

"No," whispered Marek. "It is not a gun. Just a falling branch."

Pausing for a moment by a tree near a tiny stream, Marek reached up to a branch, expertly stripping the bark from it after he had snapped it from the tree.

"You must get into the habit of eating the bark from these trees," he said quietly, beginning the first of many lessons of how to survive in this alien wilderness. "Later in the spring, when the tree is in bloom, the leaves will be tastier than this bark."

"But why should we eat the bark from a tree,"

Jana asked wide-eyed. "It must taste awful."

"We have no fruit in the mountains," Marek answered matter-of-factly. "Eating the leaves and bark of the beech tree prevents us from getting scurvy."

"What's scurvy?" Jana asked, putting a piece of bark into her mouth. Then she made an ugly face and spit it out. "Yech!" she exclaimed. "I don't care about scurvy! I won't ever eat that again."

"Scurvy is a disease that causes you to hurt all over," Marek explained. "Even your gums hurt. And, it if gets bad enough, your teeth will fall out. And then you won't be able to eat anything at all."

Jana nodded, thinking carefully about what Marek had just said. Then she took another piece of the bark and put it in her mouth. She chewed it quickly, then swallowed it.

"That's a good girl," Marek said. "Now come along."

They walked for two hours after dark had descended on the forest. They were silent, steady, bound by their common desire to reach the safety of shelter.

As they passed a clearing where the snow had fallen into deep drifts, Jana reached down and grabbed a handful of snow, shoving it greedily into her mouth.

"Don't swallow," Marek said suddenly when he saw what she had done. But he was too late.

Jana looked up at him inquiringly, her mouth frosted on the inside.

"Always warm the snow in your mouth first before you swallow. Icy snow in your stomach can make you sick."

"I'll remember next time," Jana said obediently. "It's just that I'm so tired and thirsty."

"I understand," Marek said. "It won't be long now."

They travelled for another quarter of a mile before Marek finally announced they could stop. "Here," he said simply, as he scanned the area for a proper resting place.

He stepped over to the trunk of a large tree that had fallen to the ground. It seemed dark and ominous in the weak light that filtered through the trees from the half moon.

Cutting pine bows from a nearby tree, Marek laid them across two poles he had leaned against the fallen trunk. It formed a crude shelter for them.

"We cannot afford to build a fire tonight," Marek said. "It you have extra clothing in your satchel, get it out so we can cover ourselves. We will need all the warmth we can gather."

He looked at Jana then. He could barely make out her face, her eyes wide and white from an exhaustion she had never known. Mud and dirt were streaked across her face. She was so exhausted, she could not even speak.

Marek leaned over and felt her shoes. "Take off your shoes. Both of you," he directed. "If your shoes are wet, soon you feet will be too tender to walk. In the morning, we'll pack our shoes with moss to insulate our feet from the wet and cold."

He paused, his heart going out to the child who had behaved so valiantly throughout the first day's journey. "I know you are hungry, Little One. It is too dark for me to find something for you to eat. I'm sorry we have no food."

Josef, thought Rachel. Thank you, Josef. Then she spoke, attempting, for Jana's sake, to inject a note of lightness into her hoarse, exhausted voice. "Ah, but we do have food," she said, reaching into her satchel and pulling out a sausage. She even managed a weak smile to accompany her words.

They ate slowly and silently, too tired to speak. Then, packing the extra clothing around them, they lay down, huddling together for warmth. Weary beyond anything she had ever known, Rachel held Jana close to her. They fell asleep instantly.

Sometime during the night, Rachel had a lovely and satisfying dream. Lying next to Josef, both of them surrounded with their thick down comfort, they were warm and loving. And Rachel was complete. She had never felt so satisfied, she had never felt so safe. She was blessed as she lay in the arms of the man she had loved so long and so well.

The scream began softly as Josef started to disappear. It was not sudden, it was not a shock. Rather, it was the slow fading of a dream, the inexorable loss of the beloved. Fully experiencing her anguish for the first time since her family had been taken away, the pain was not lessened because it came to her in a dream. It was real and raw and devestating. Forsaken, her shattered life in pieces before her,

85

Rachel tried to hold onto him. But he had become a gossamer spector, a shadow that crossed her life for one lovely and capricious moment, before vanishing on the wings of death.

The silent scream of her dream became real. An instant later, she felt something clamp her mouth shut. Panicked, she opened her eyes and saw Marek's hand over her mouth.

"You were having a nightmare," he said quietly. "I am sorry."

Frantic, Rachel tried to make out the shapes around her, to find her bearings. But there was nothing familiar. Trembling, she looked at Marek, his features murky in the darkness. She nodded, afraid to speak.

He took his hand from her mouth, understanding that she was telling him she would remain silent.

"Try to get some sleep," he said sympathetically. "We have a long journey tomorrow."

Rachel lay awake for a long time. Then she drifted in and out of confused dreams. Overwhelmed by a sense of loss so unspeakably painful that she could not move, Rachel felt unutterably alone, alienated even from Jana who lay sleeping beside her.

How can this be? she thought. How can I be sleeping in the forest with a stranger when only a few days ago I was secure in Budapest, surrounded by crystal and light. I had everything then. It was mine. And I don't know if I can bear this terrible parting. I could die of this severance. Curl up and die. There is nothing here that I know, that I can touch and make mine. Everything is strange and foreign. Everything is a threat. Nothing belongs to me here. Nothing except the life of a small child who loves me. Who trusts me to take care of her, when I do not even have the slightest idea of how to take care of myself.

Holding onto Jana, she managed a desolate smile. I am a stranger to myself now, she told herself. I must learn how to make *that* mine.

In the morning, Marek changed clothes. Under his German uniform, he wore the clothes of a peasant. Stripping the uniform from his body, he buried it, regretting the loss of warmth he would suffer from not wearing so many layers of clothes. But he knew better than anyone the penalty he would pay if he were caught wearing the uniform. He also regretted the fact that he would have to find another German officer just his size so that he could outfit himself for future missions.

They ate their breakfast of sausage and cheese in silence. After scattering the sheltering limbs that bore evidence of their presence, the trio set off once more.

Throughout the day, they trudged over steep and rocky terrain. Every two hours, they stopped briefly for a rest. And then, with a superhuman effort, they would pull themselves to a standing position and begin to walk once more.

Late that afternoon, Marek looked at his two companions. He had prodded them unmercifully, fully aware that he had no choice. Yet he was disgusted with himself every time he was forced to urge them to move faster.

Now, after a day of travelling in the hot sun that is more dangerous in the higher altitudes, the faces of Jana and Rachel were bright red.

"You are not accustomed to the sun in the mountains," he said guiltily, sorry he had not taken notice of this sooner. "You are both burned. We'll take care of that this evening."

Late that afternoon, Marek announced they would set up camp for the night. Rachel was surprised, having assumed that they would not stop until dark.

Marek explained. "I have only a few matches left. At this altitude, the night will be very cold. We must have a fire. This way, I can use the sun to start the fire and save the matches for an emergency."

Once they had made the shelter of branches that leaned against a raw outcropping of rock, Marek instructed Jana to gather some small twigs and dry leaves. Then he put them in a pile on the ground. Using the stainless steel mirror he carried in his pocket, he caught the reflection of the sun and directed it to the leaves. A tiny tendril of smoke rose from the leaves that turned into a tentative flame. Adding kindling slowly, Marek soon had a real fire burning.

"Now," he said. "We shall try to do something

about that sunburn of yours."

He told Jana to gather small pieces of the darkest bark she could find from the trees around them. Then he set about rigging a branch over the fire from which he could suspend Jana's small silver cup.

"We should have a pot to do this properly," he said, "But, for the moment, this will have to do."

Filling the cup with snow and small pieces of bark, they waited almost an hour before the water turned dark. Careful not to spill it, he took the cup and dipped his handkerchief into it. Then he patted the solution gently on their faces.

"It's the tanic acid," he explained. "It will help." And then he added, "Don't worry, Little One, the cup can be polished and it will look good as new again."

On their sixth day of travelling, Rachel was ready to give up. Her feet were blistered and there was not a bone or a muscle in her body that did not send sharp signals of pain as she walked. Her face was peeling and she was filthy. She did not understand how Jana could continue, what drove this child to persevere. She knew that she, herself, was at the end of her rope. She would be lucky if she could continue to walk for the rest of the day. Their pace was slower now, plodding and clumsy as they made their way down rocky inclines and across valleys dotted with streams that had to be crossed and rocks and

89

fallen limbs that had to be climbed over.

The only thing that kept her going was Marek's announcement that they would reach the Partisan camp by afternoon.

The sun was beginning to drop in the leaden sky when Marek stopped them. Moving to an outcropping of rock that was exposed to the valley below, he took out his mirror.

Catching the sun on its surface, he flashed it in the direction of the valley three times. It was only a moment before the signal was returned from the midst of the trees below.

Weary beyond feeling, Rachel looked at Marek, a question in her eyes that she was too exhausted to verbalize.

"We are close now," he said. "This is the most important part of the journey. If we leave a trail behind us, it could cost a hundred lives. The Germans are not the only ones who would like to find our camp. There are the Italians now. And the Chetniks, other guerrilas, fight us constantly. The Ustachi, may their Croatian eyes be plucked from their severed heads, are worse than all the rest combined."

A derelict sliver of fear slid down Jana's spine. She had not heard Marek speak like this and it frightened her. "Who are they?" she managed to ask, "the Ustachi?"

"Evil incarnate," he answered bluntly, without the trace of a smile to lighten his words. "They know only savagery. Nothing else. And they do not like to waste precious ammunition on killing prisoners. So they have devised ingenius ways of butchering without it. You do not want to meet them, I assure you."

Rachel's anger suddenly flared, fired by fear, weariness and the lack of food. "Why do you say such things to a child? she asked. "It's not necessary.

Marek looked at her evenly. "But it is necessary. I tell her such things so that she will not be careless. You also," he added impassively. "This is the last part of our journey. And the most important. One mistake could be the end of us all."

During the past five days, the only human beings they had encountered were peasants. Frequently they had walked on narrow winding mountain trails that were known only to the shepherds who used them to move their flocks to the high country for the summer. Marek had avoided the peasants whenever possible, but Rachel did not understand why until now. He had not wished to frighten his charges with tales of unexpected betrayal and sudden ambush.

Marek did not trust anyone. And the peasants were no exception. They had been squeezed between fear of the Partisans and fear of German reprisals, and it was totally unpredictable which side would be their ally at any given moment. They spent most of their time attempting to remain as neutral as possible. And they accomplished this by being deliberately unobservant where strangers were concerned.

Nevertheless, Marek had found it necessary to ask for help upon occasion. Some offered food and aid gladly; others with trepidation. But Marek trusted none of them.

Now that they were close to the camp, the threat of strangers became more frightening. Jana found herself dreading the encounter with the Partisans. Marek's kindness had not lessened her general fear of strange men. She only made him an exception in her child's mind. She would have felt much more secure if she had been allowed to remain in hiding with Marek and her grandmother. She felt safe with them, immune from harm. And so, with all her pain and exhaustion, she was still not pleased that they had reached their destination.

It took another two hours to move down the mountain. Finally, Marek stopped and pointed to one side.

"Do you see those moss-covered rocks?" he asked.

When Jana and Rachel nodded yes, he then explained their procedure for travelling. Rachel would go first, then Jana, then he. It would be Rachel's task to turn each rock over before she stepped on it. That way, the moss would be protected from their footprints. Jana would follow, stepping on precisely the same rocks. Then Marek would follow, turning the moss up again as he passed each rock. That way, they would leave no tracks for an unknown enemy to follow.

They travelled laboriously in this manner for almost fifty yards before Marek stopped them once again when they reached a rushing mountain stream. He took the lead. Holding Jana's hand, he led her upstream on a path of stones for another fifty yards while Rachel followed.

Scrambling up a rocky bank on the far side of the stream, Marek stopped only long enough to whistle the soft low song of a bird. After receiving an answer in kind, he let his weary, bedraggled companions into the Partisan camp.

There were few overt signs of life, even in the midst of one hundred people. They took meticulous care not to leave any tell-tale indications of their presence. Stukas, constantly searching for Partisan hideouts, might see what foot patrols could not.

It was apparent to the most casual observer that the newcomers that straggled in with Marek were city people, thoroughly unaccustomed to the rigors of the wild. Both Rachel and Jana had the desolate look of the hunted. Jana's face was peeling badly and the white patches of skin exposed in random spots made her look comical in her obvious vulnerability.

Nodding quietly to a group of people who had gathered a few feet away from them, Marek smiled in confirmation of their suspicions. There was nothing he could say beyond the most painful and obvious fact: yes, these were city folk and there were now two more mouths to feed.

Marek walked over to some particularly dense underbrush, then parted the branches to expose the entrance to a cave. He took Rachel and Jana inside and told them they could rest. They both sat down and leaned against the rough, stone wall.

"Wait here," he said, "Serghei will see you later."

"Who is Serghei?" Jana asked in a hoarse whisper.

"My uncle. Our leader," he answered with a touch of awe before walking back out into the waning light.

Rachel and Jana fell instantly into a dark and dreamless sleep, feeling protected—at least for the moment.

Since the first night when she dreamed of Josef, much as she longed for rest, Rachel dreaded sleep. She did not think she could bear such tortured thoughts one more time. Each time she lay down, she prayed that she would not dream.

This was the first time that she was not overcome by dread. Exhaustion took precedence. The only thought that ran through her mind before she drifted off was a curious sense of triumph and accomplishment. Who would ever have imagined, she thought, that Jana and I could have done such a thing; could have climbed mountains and forded streams and hunted for wild berries and nuts to eat. We did it.

"Serghei will see you now," Marek said softly, as he touched Rachel to awaken her. He carried a torch in his hand that cast undulating shadows against the dark walls. "He's outside," Marek added. There was a note of subdued urgency and respect in his voice.

Rachel awakened Jana, then tried to smooth her

hair, sensing this was an important meeting. They hurried out the door of the cave, surprisingly oblivious to the aroma of stew cooking in a huge pot over the fire outside.

Knowing the search planes were loathe to fly in these treacherous mountains at night, the Partisans felt safe about lighting fires. It was the smoke from a fire during the day that would most likely give away their position.

It took a moment for Jana's and Rachel's eyes to adjust to the different light. As if it were a developing picture, Rachel at first saw only the outline of a man behind the fire. Slowly, his features took shape.

Rachel's first thought was of power; that there was an invincible kind of power coiled in the muscles and sinews of the man standing before her.

It was not that the man was excessively large. Rather, his body, taut and alert, carried with it a brazen authority, as if he had absolute confidence in the might of his own command. This was combined with a profound belief in his cause and his unqualified mastery of it. Rachel sensed immediately that this man needed nothing or no one. He was an entity unto himself, complete in his self-generated energy and his carefully controlled passions.

Tito, the leader of all the Partisans, had told his followers that if they needed something, they should get it from the enemy. Serghei had followed this advice with flair.

Wearing German boots and an officer's tunic with the insignia stripped, he sported Italian pants and a belt taken from a Chetnik from which hung several grenades. Over all this, he wore a crude sheepskin coat against the bitter night air and a round fur hat on his head.

His face looked as if it had been hewn from granite and it was covered with a mustache and beard trimmed close to his strong, square jaw.

His eyes were black coals that glowed with passionate conviction in the significance and purpose of his destiny. They were defiant, yet there was a pragmatic serenity behind them, as if he had known beauty intimately before meeting wretchedness and death; and he had refused to relinquish this earlier vision despite what he now knew.

He was a man whose hands could crush the skull of another human being or cradle a newborn baby; a man as unashamed of weeping as he was of laughter; a man who could love and hate with equal passion; and a man always to be reckoned with.

"This is our leader, Serghei Cetkovic," Marek said formally. "And this is Rachel von Weitzman and Jana Horvath," he added.

Serghei nodded with a polite bow of his head. Wasting no time, speaking in crude but passable German, he said, "If you are to stay here, both of you must make yourselves useful. We cannot feed mouths that do not work."

"I understand," Rachel replied in a voice as firm as she could muster. "We shall do our share."

"Here, each of us does more than his share," returned Serghei with an edge of disdain for this city woman's ways.

Rachel nodded, feeling sufficiently chastised.

"My nephew tells me you lived in Budapest. That you were rich. Money is useless here except to buy arms and ammunition. Tell me what you can do."

Replying tentatively, thoroughly intimidated now, Rachel said, "Cook? Bind wounds? I can sew."

"That is good, but not enough." He paused for a moment, then turned to Marek. "You must teach them more. How to hunt. To kill. The child must learn, too."

"Yes, Uncle."

"Then you may stay," Serghei said, looking directly at Rachel for the first time.

She had opened her mouth to reply when she heard Marek whisper from behind her, "Refuse. You must refuse."

He was coaching her in the traditional Montenegrin ritual of hospitality. Although these people were far from home, even in the harsh conditions in which they lived, ritual was to be respected, to be preserved. And in Montenegro, one must never accept an invitation of hospitality without first declining it.

Following her whispered directions without understanding why, Rachel hesitated, then said, "I do not think that we can stay here with you. However, I thank you for your generous offer . . ." her voice drifted off, uncertain of what she should do next.

"Ah, no . . ." returned Serghei with a sweeping gesture of his arm. "I insist. You must stay with us for as long as is necessary. You will be welcome here."

Relieved and obliquely amused, Rachel replied. "Then I thank you for your kind offer. You are most gracious."

"I must go now," Serghei said by way of blunt dismissal. But not forgetting his manners, he added, "Tomorrow your lessons will begin. In the mean time, is there anything you need?"

Rachel hesitated a moment. "Yes," she said firmly. "I need a bath."

His feet spread apart, Serghei placed his hands on his hips and threw his head back, bellowing with laughter.

"A bath?" he said in a mocking voice. "My lady wishes to take a bath? I have heard that city women such as you even use scented soaps. Perhaps we can arrange that, too." Then he stopped laughing and looked straight at her, his dark eyes burning with intensity. "There are no baths here. Baths are a forgotten luxury in the mountains. You should have known better than to ask for such a thing."

Humiliated, Rachel was silent. Then, pulling her body taut, she stood as tall as she could. She met his eyes with her own, and she spoke with a commanding dignity. She did not know how much Marek told his uncle about their journey. But, determined not to sound as if she were weak and self-pitying, she spoke bruskly and evenly.

"I asked for such a luxury because I was raped. And I want to wash him off me."

Caught totally off guard, Serghei swallowed, searching for a response. For a brief moment before he spoke, a hint of guilt flashed briefly in his eyes.

"I will see to it that a bucket of water from the stream is brought to you and warmed over the fire." Then he added, "But do not make a habit of this."

Rachel could not help but feel a creeping satisfaction in his reaction and his reply. Nevertheless, she nodded her head to him in a gesture of thanks. Without another word, Serghei turned and disappeared into the night.

After Rachel had bathed, she sat with Marek and Jana in the cave, each of them greedily devouring a bowl of hot rabbit stew.

Rachel felt better. The bath had done more than wash away the filthy remnants of the German officer. It had cleansed her of her habit of comparing everything she did with how things used to be. Before, she would have remembered the huge tub in Budapest that would be filled by Eva with hot, scented water; the way her silk undergarments felt; the rough texture of the bathtowels and the soft luxury of cleaned and pressed linen sheets. Now, she thought only of the present. For that was what had to be dealt with — not a past filled with luxuries that no longer had any application or meaning in her life.

"I know my uncle's ways are strange to you," Marek said as he sat with Rachel and Jana. "But we are Montenegrin," he said with pride. "We live by *cojstvo*. It is our code. A man must live with honor and dignity. Most important of all is his courage. These mountains are wild and harsh. So are our lives. But we survive because of this code. We have never been conquered, although many have tried. We are warriors. Good ones. And we cannot afford to be soft. Our world does not allow it." Marek paused and looked at Rachel and Jana. "Neither can yours," he added in an oblique effort to warn them of what was to come.

Soon after dinner, Jana fell asleep with her head on Rachel's lap. Marek stayed to talk with Rachel then, as if they had just been introduced. Until this moment, casual conversation had been replaced by walking and sleeping. Neither had spoken much beyond necessary instructions and questions. This was their first opportunity to learn about each other.

Curious about her savior, Rachel asked, "What made you come here?"

Marek stared at the flames of the fire, debating how much he should reveal. Then he spoke, hesitant and unsure, as if he were sorting out his thoughts and motivations as he went.

"There are two reasons why most of us join the fight here. One is because we believe in the cause, that slavery in any form is intolerable. The other reason to fight is that we have nothing left to lose." He stopped for a moment. "I suppose I am a combination of both."

"Why is that?"

"Two and a half years ago . . . I was fifteen then

100

. . . the Nazis had their rail transportation severely disrupted by a series of explosions. Partisan, of course. The high command had already ordered that for every German soldier killed by guerillas — and many died in these explosions — one hundred civilians would pay with their lives. Needless to say, that keeps the civilian population in line." There was bitterness in every word he spoke. "My father, the mayor of our village, and my mother and younger sister and I lived near the railroad. I was gone that day . . . looking after our sheep in the high pastures. When I returned . . ." Marek's voice cracked. Swallowing once, he continued. "When I returned . . . our house was a pile of ashes. My family had been executed, along with the rest of the people in our village." His eyes took on a faraway look then, as if he were revisiting the sight and seeing it all again through a mist of desolation and pain. "In the meadow . . . the meadow near our house was covered with wildflowers. Everywhere, they were in bloom. I always loved that time of year. My sister would pick the flowers and our home would be filled with fragrance and color . . . In the meadow that day, there were flowers everywhere . . . flowers blooming . . . and everywhere these flowers were . . . crushed by the bodies of my friends and family." His voice grew stronger then, as if he had told the worst and could not complete the story. "And that is why I save families. Because no one should have to see what I saw; should have to lose what I lost. I save families. That is what I want to do. It is what I do best."

Reaching over to him, Rachel touched his face, thanking him and loving him at the same time. She wanted to hold him, cradle him. But she knew he would not allow such a thing.

"No," Marek said harshly when he felt her touch. "There is no room in my world for that. No room at all. There is only room for saving lives and killing enemies. That is all."

"You are wrong," Rachel said gently, leaving her hand on his cheek. "There is always room for touching."

Chapter 5

"What's that?" Jana asked, her eyes wide and frightened. She had just listened to an unearthly moan that seemed to be coming from all around her.

"It's all right," Marek assured her. "It's why we're here. Look up."

Shielding her eyes, Jana looked into the twilight sky. There, soaring above, was a large reddish bird.

"It's huge. What kind of bird is it?" she asked, awed by the five-foot wing span.

"An eagle-owl," Marek said. "They hunt at night, beginning at dusk. And when you see them, it usually indicates the presence of mice or rabbits below. That's why I have chosen to set the trap here. The animal droppings tell me where."

Determined to be attentive students and quick learners, Rachel and Jana watched as Marek bent a notched sapling with a noose suspended from the center of its arc, setting a trap for some hapless rodent that would wander helplessly into the noose. At first, Jana had been horrified at the thought of killing an animal. But Marek explained that lack of food was one of the greatest difficulties that the Partisan armies faced. Often, peasants would give them food. But there were days when few would eat at all. Only those scheduled for battle would eat then. The others simply went without.

"Will it hurt the animal?" Jana asked, filled with pity for the doomed creature.

"Not for long," Marek answered flatly. "I know this is difficult for you. But trapping becomes easier when your belly is empty, Little One. I promise you that."

"I hope so," Jana answered dubiously.

When they returned the following day, a rabbit hung lifelessly in the snare.

"Poor thing," Jana whispered, tears streaming down her cheeks as she stroked the limp furry animal. She had eaten breakfast that day.

"I will not ask you to gut it," Marek said. "Others will do that."

Rachel exhaled with relief. She had spent the night tangled in tortured dreams of splitting an animal from breastbone to anus, the blood and guts spilling obscenely from the soft brown fur.

Marek loosened the noose and freed the rabbit. "I shall expect you to set your own traps and tend them every day. It is an important responsibility. For all of us," he said, remembering how painful and gnawing true hunger could be. "But that is only one of the things you must learn," he added as they walked back to the camp.

Marek wasted no time in teaching Jana and Rachel. Every lesson was geared towards one simple thing: survival. He taught them which berries were edible and how to get the nuts from pine cones. He showed them how to start fires with two sticks, how to roast animals over an open fire. "You must roast them quickly over a high flame," he had instructed. "Slow roasting makes tough meat even tougher." He even showed them how to make flour from the bark of trees.

"The scotch pine is my favorite," he said to a very doubtful Rachel, who had trouble imagining scotch pine biscuits.

This crash course in survival took place over a period of three days. It was clear, Marek did not expect the necessity of repeating any lessons. Time was too precious.

On the fourth day, new lessons began, ones which made the killing of animals seem like a kindergarten class.

"Come," Marek said. "I will teach you now about killing. Real killing."

"Of people?" Jana squeaked.

"Of people," Marek confirmed.

Rachel and Jana swallowed hard, then followed Marek to a tree where a dummy leaned against the trunk. Neither of the women had any trouble imagining that this could be a real corpse.

"I . . . I do not think I can do this," Jana said.

"You can do anything you set your mind to, Little One. I realize this is not easy. And it is unlikely that you would have to practice what I teach you. But, on the other hand, it is always better to be prepared. Even a little girl like you."

Marek took a knife from the sheath that was attached to his belt. The blade was five inches long and honed to razor sharp. The handle, made of bone, fit easily into his hand.

"If you use a knife," he began to explain, "you must take care not to allow the blade to get stuck in the ribs. Once the knife is stuck, you have lost your weapon. So the way to prevent this is always to stab upward." Demonstrating, Marek thrust the knife into the belly of the dummy with an upward movement of his hand. "If you stab from above, the knife can graze off the ribs, causing only a superficial wound. So, even if you come from behind, make certain that you grip the knife so that you can stab up . . . underneath the rib cage." He looked at Rachel, his eyes hard, without emotion. There was no room for pity in his expression. There was only determination to teach thoroughly.

"Now, you try it," he said as he handed Rachel the knife.

Her hand trembled as she took it. Reading the acute distress on her face, he relented slightly. "Do not worry," he counseled. "It is not so bad as you think. The first time is the worst. Every time I think I cannot do it again, I imagine a soldier's hand on my sister's breast. Then it becomes simple once more."

Trying not to think of what it would feel like to shove a knife into a real human body, Rachel pushed the blade into the dummy.

"No!" Marek commanded sharply. "That will never do. You must shove the knife in quickly, decisively. You cannot push it in slowly. That maneuver gives the victim too much time to defend himself. Now do it right! Like I taught you! This can mean your life . . . or that of Jana's," he added ominously. With the image of Jana before her, Rachel plunged the knife into the dummy.

"Good!" said Marek. "Now try this." He handed her a piece of wire.

"There are two pieces of wood at the ends of the wire," he said. "They provide a grip for you. Now . . . from behind, you put the wire around the neck, cross it like this and jerk it tight very quickly." He demonstrated on the dummy. "Be abrupt. Brutal. If you are not quick about it, the victim has a chance to slip his hand under the wire. That is why you must cross it. So . . . jerk quickly, pulling hard until you feel the wire slice into his neck. Then pull harder still, choking him at the same time you cut his throat. One way or the other, he will die. And if you are lucky, you will also cut his vocal cords so he cannot cry out. That, of course, is the best way."

Rachel was astonished at the matter-of-fact manner in which he spoke. It was as if he were giving her a lesson in how to prepare chicken paprika.

"I do not think I can do this," she said hesitantly. The thought of shoving a steel blade through the flesh of a man was repugnant enough. Now, considering slicing a human being's neck was too much.

Marek looked at her, his stare commanding full and compelling attention from his student. "Listen to me carefully. In the mountains, women fight alongside men. There is no difference here. We cannot afford to make that difference. We are too shorthanded. Sooner or later, you will be called upon to go on a sortie. And, sooner or later, you will have to kill. That is the way of life here. And you had better become accustomed to the idea now, before your life is threatened. If you hesitate — if you allow yourself to feel pity or sorrow or repulsion — for even one second, you lose your advantage. If you stop for one moment to consider what you are doing, you will be killed. Make no mistake about that. Do not delude yourself with humane thoughts and foolish acts of charity. That does not exist in the mountains . . . it does not exist. I can assure you there is no soldier — German, Italian, Chetnik or Ustachi — who will care that you are a woman, or that you possess tenderness. They will kill you. To a man, they will kill you without a second thought. Oh . . . perhaps later, some might regret it. But then, when it is his life or yours, the decision will not be in your favor. And you will die . . . leaving a small child behind without a relative or a home."

Rachel nodded, too stunned to speak.

Seeing this, Marek continued relentlessly. "If you have trouble doing this, just consider your enemy to be that German Oberleutnant. He not only raped you. In a manner of speaking, he raped Jana, too. Surely you can understand that."

Rachel glanced at Jana. The child stood to one side of the dummy. Her eyes were closed, squeezed tight in her efforts to make the scene before her disappear. Following Rachel's eyes, Marek saw Jana's terror, saw and understood it.

"Jana," he said. "These lessons are for you, too. You must open your eyes. Observe what we are doing. This is life now. This is your life."

Jana opened her eyes, terrified. She expected to see the dummy's head severed, spewing real blood, feeling real fears.

"Here," he said. "I'll hold your hand while your grandmother practices."

He looked at Rachel and nodded. "Remember the Oberleutnant," he said. "Remember. That is who you are killing."

Rachel's imagination swam with obscene visions of arrogance and lust and blood. And, without another word, she slipped the wire suddenly around the neck of the dummy, crossed it with surprising speed and yanked it tight. This was accomplished with a savagery that she did not know existed within her, with a removed brutality that frightened her.

"Good," Marek said, nodding his head approvingly. "That is the way to do it." As he spoke, he could feel Jana's hand trembling in his. "You won't have to do that, Little One," he said gently. "Now that your grandmother knows how to do it, that is enough for you."

By the end of that day's lesson, Rachel was haunted by thoughts of killing, tortured with the image of what it would feel like when knife or wire actually slipped through human flesh. Like slicing veal, she told herself. Or cutting up a chicken. With this, she smiled at herself ironically. Who am I trying to fool? she thought. I haven't done anything like that for years. I had servants, after all; I had servants to do the cutting.

Ten days after Jana and Rachel arrived at the camp, Serghei led twenty-seven men and women on a sortie. Since Yugoslavia was the primary route for Balkan communications between the north and the south, most of the Partisan objectives were concerned with the disruption of railroads, telephone lines and roads. In the process, of course, they made every effort to come back with trucks, ammunition and explosives.

When Serghei's group returned three days later, after successfully destroying large sections of railroad tracks, there were only twenty men and women. Of these, five were wounded, but still walking. One man had crude bandages wrapped around a stump where his foot had been. He had been carried all the way back, over mountains and through valleys, on a litter.

It was dusk when the filthy, exhausted group straggled into the camp. Rachel had been preparing some herb tea when she saw them. Scanning the group quickly, she was relieved to see Serghei, the man who had become a symbol of survival to her. During his absence, she had wondered what would happen to this small band of freedom fighters if its leader were to be killed. The mere thought panicked her, for her terror of being abandoned in these mountains was a real one. If this happened, she knew she and Jana would not survive.

As the litter bearers struggled into the camp at the end of the line, Rachel hurried to them. Her dread of witnessing something unbearable was overcome the moment she saw the seriously wounded man. Pain was carved so deeply into his face that she wondered if the lines would ever disappear.

As soon as the litter was set down close to the fire, Rachel and another woman began to untangle the mass of the dirty bandages that was wrapped around his stump. The problem was not only filth, but the fact that the rags were stuck to the wound. They tried to accomplish the job with gentleness. But that was impossible. When they touched the injury, the man's entire body recoiled, and he cried out with an agony that Rachel had never before heard.

Looking at his face, Rachel noticed then that Serghei was standing next to the man.

"Don't we have any anesthetic?" Rachel asked.

"Yes," Serghei answered calmly, pulling his pistol from the holster. Then with a swift movement, he cracked the man in the temple with the butt of the gun. "Now," Serghei said grimly, "be swift about changing the dressing."

He's a barbarian, Rachel thought, as she hurried to the cave where she kept her satchel. She retrieved a packet of sulpha powder and hurried back to the litter. As she was tearing open the packet, she felt a hand grip her wrist.

"No," Serghei said. "Do not do that."

Rachel's temper flared then. "I'll do as I please,"

she answered. "The sulpha belongs to me. I brought it from Budapest." She did not add that Budapest was where people behaved in a civilized manner, where compassion still had a place in people's lives. At least some of the people, she added to herself.

"I told you not to open that," Serghei repeated.

"And I said that I shall do with it as I please," Rachel answered defiantly.

With one swift movement, Serghei took the packet from her hands. "I am in command here," he told her in no uncertain terms. "And you shall do as I say. If you use this now, there will be none for the stomach wounds when it is far more valuable. Besides, in the morning, this man will be carried to the hospital. There, they have medicines. The British drop them with the supplies."

"Hospital?" Rachel said cynically. "A hospital here in the mountains? Do you think I am foolish enough to believe that? You may as well have left this man to die. Or," she added arrogantly, "you could have shot him like an animal and have been done with it."

Serghei's voice was steely when he spoke. It cut through Rachel as easily as the blade of a razor. "You think we are barbarian here, . . . that we have no feeling, . . . that we are just crude men and women, ignorant and brutal. You think hitting a man on his head is cruel. Well, it is better than conscious suffering. I grant you this: our ways are not fancy. We do not dance to string quartets nor eat our meals from fine china. But we take care of our wounded. Make no mistake about that." His

112

eyes wore the expression of a man who detested having to explain himself in any way to such a woman as Rachel. "You say we might as well have left this man for the enemy. The last time the Nazis discovered a hospital of ours, they had great sport in running over all the amputees with their tanks, chasing them across the dirt as they struggled to escape." He paused then. "That is barbarian, my dear lady. Those fancy, educated, civilized Germans. The ones whose culture is revered throughout the world. The very ones whose language we must speak in order to communicate.

As for our wounded," Serghei continued. "Let me assure you that we do, indeed, have hospitals. They are the best kept secrets in the mountains. They are hidden deep in the forests and, if we must evacuate any area, we take our wounded with us. Always. With no exception. So please, my dear city lady, never, never accuse us of mistreating our wounded. It simply does not happen."

Rachel looked at him, her face burning with embarrassment. But she could think of nothing to say.

"Go now," Serghei said. "Leave the wounded to us. You can brew some tea. It appears that is all you are good for."

Witnessing her grandmother's humiliation convinced Jana that Serghei was a man to avoid. He is no different than the German soldier, she thought as she watched him eat his dinner that evening. His manners are crude. Just look at him wipe his mouth with the back of his hand. He'd not be welcome at my table.

Interrupting her speculations, Serghei looked at Jana and smiled. "Why are you scratching your head?" he asked pleasantly.

"Why does anyone scratch?" Jana asked archly. She saw her grandmother look at her, shocked at the unaccustomed tone of voice in the child. "Because I itch."

"Let me take a look," he said, standing up. "That's a beautiful braid you wear. It falls almost to your waist."

Jana was, indeed, proud of her hair. After the officer had cut the shank from the back of her head, Rachel had shown her how to braid it so that the missing piece would not show. Somehow, in her child's mind, her hair had become a symbol of defiance, of wholeness. She took care to brush it every day and was grateful when Rachel would help her wash it in the chill water of the stream.

Suddenly afraid of this man, of what he would do if he touched her, Jana said quietly, "You can see my braid from where you sit."

He approached her anyway. "I won't harm you," he said in a gentle voice. But when he leaned over her head, Jana shrank visably from his touch.

"No," she whimpered.

"Don't be afraid," he said, touching her head and parting her hair. "I would never harm you."

He stood up, shaking his head. Then he turned to Rachel. "You must cut her hair. Cut it all the way off, close to the scalp."

"Don't be ridiculous," replied Rachel, ready to fight him all the way on his one. She understood

114

Jana's need and her fear. "Jana can wear her hair any way she pleases. And it pleases her to wear it long."

"Then it shall also please her to breed more lice."

"What is lice?" Jana asked.

"Lice?" Rachel repeated. "Surely not. She is not a dirty child."

"Of course she isn't. But look for yourself." Then he added, "I'm sorry."

Jana sat still as Rachel parted her hair. The little white egg sacks clinging to the strands of golden hair were plain to see.

Confronting the obvious, Rachel asked, "Isn't there anything that can be done?"

"Whatever we would do, it would only be temporary. Kerosene would work until next time. When you have one hundred people living in these conditions, lice are impossible to control."

Rachel bowed to the inevitable. Touching Jana on her face, she said, "I'm afraid it shall have to be done, my love. There is no avoiding it."

It was clear to Jana there was no way out. Mute and sad, she sat on a stone next to the fire. She tried to ignore what was happening, but when she felt her locks being tugged in preparation for cutting, her imagination flashed immediately to that hideous day. In an instant, the fire was gone, Serghei disappeared. Only Marek and her grandmother and the German officer were there. Always the soldier. She could feel him, his rough hands grabbing her hair. Her neck and shoulders rigid with fear, her face contorted in the effort to hold back

115

the tears. She could feel the sawing of the knife, the back and forth motion, the terror, the horror, the loss. She remembered seeing the German's hand toss the hair to the ground as he held the tiny leather pouch. She remembered it all. It would not stop, this awful memory film. She felt for a moment that she would be doomed forever to watch it over and over again in her mind. There was her grandmother begging, her grandmother's face filled with pain and revulsion. And the blood. Blood everywhere.

No! she commanded herself. No! I can't bear it. Stop. Stop now! As if she were pulling down a shade over the horror, Jana willed her mind to go blank.

In that complex act of controlling her own personal horror — of creating a way to survive — Jana, like other children forced to endure pain beyond human limits, became a miniature adult. It was a bizarre combination of simplicity and mature comprehension of what must be done in order to survive. She did not understand what she had done. She only recognized the fact that it was a necessity if she were to endure.

And I shall endure, she thought. And when I am a grownup, I shall always wear my hair long. And I shall never allow anyone to cut it. I won't ever allow anyone to do this to me ever again. Now, I must allow it. But never, never again, she vowed.

When it was over, flooded with relief, Jana rubbed her hand over her head, thinking it felt like the teddy bear she once slept with in her soft, secure bed. The sadness of her expression indicated what

116

her lack of tears did not.

When she felt in control again, Jana asked Rachel, "Am I like a boy now? I'm sure no one could tell the difference." Her voice was plaintive, forlorn. "An ugly little boy," she added tearfully.

But it was not Rachel who answered her. She had been so preoccupied that she did not notice the fact that Serghei had sat down beside her.

"You could never look like a boy," he said gently. "Even now, you are lovely as a mountain Vila."

Looking at him, Jana asked, "What is a Vila?"

"Ah," said Serghei, his eyes alive with his own fire. "You don't know what a Vila is? That must be because they live only in these mountains. Nowhere else on earth would you find a Vila."

"Have you ever seen one?"

"Once," he answered, his eyes taking on a faraway look. "Only once, when I was a very young man."

"What was she like?"

"Well . . . they say that you only know real beauty after you have seen a Vila. And that is true."

"What are they like" Jana persisted, forgetting her fear of this man.

"They are nymphs. And they wear white dresses, long to the ground and made of the purest silk. The best time to see them is when you come upon them unexpectedly when they are dancing. They dance under the cherry trees and are as graceful and beautiful as the flight of a swallow at dawn."

"Do they fly? Like faeries?"

"No, indeed. The Vila rides a hart. And they are swift as a streak of lightening in a summer storm."

117

"What do they do?"

"Well now . . . when a child is naughty, the Vila will come and correct him. She knows exactly what to do. And when a man has good fortune, he knows that the Vila is walking at his side. Sometimes, then, he might just catch a glimpse of her. But it is unlikely, since she is so swift and so secretive. But it is said that no man can see a Vila without his heart aching forever after her beauty." There was a wistful note in his voice, as if the remembrance of something inneffable and cherished had lingered with him always.

He leaned over and kissed Jana then. Gently, on the forehead, brushing his calloused hand over her short-cropped hair. "So you see? When I say that you are as lovely as the Vila, it cannot possibly make any difference whether your hair is long or short. Because a Vila is always beautiful, no matter what happens. So you must not worry about how you look. You are special. And nothing that has been done here could possibly change that."

"Do you promise?" Jana asked with a touching innocence and vulnerability. She felt safe with this man now, comforted by the same person she had mentally condemned only a short while earlier.

"I promise," Serghei replied solemnly.

Rachel's eyes met Serghei's then. And she thanked him silently, an enigmatic smile playing on her lips.

By June, admist rumors of the pending Allied invasion of the continent, both Rachel and Jana had made their adjustment to the way of life with the Partisans.

After her first week of being taunted by visions of home, of soft beds, clean dishes, hot baths and loving arms, Rachel had learned to stop asking questions about when they would be able to leave. The first two times she had asked Serghei, her question had been met with stony silence and disdain.

Then the third time, he answered her. It should be enough, she was informed coldly by Serghei, to know that she and her granddaughter were safe. At the moment, passage out of the country was impossible.

"Besides," he added, "in the light of what we are doing, what we are accomplishing, your escape is unimportant."

Angered at first, Rachel slowly began to understand that the work here *was* important.

But this understanding did not happen overnight. She was troubled at first that the leader of the Partisans was a communist. But she gradually began to see that, were it not for this man Tito, the entire country would be crushed under the heel of the Nazis. These people, the ones with whom she was living, were in the dangerous and often fatal process of saving their country.

With that placed in perspective, Rachel settled in for the duration of the war.

Jana's adjustment to this alien way of life came more easily. Once she discovered that she could be genuinely useful, her life took on purpose. She spent much of her days gathering food for the division. Even though death was a fact she confronted with more and more frequency, in her child's mind, it still remained something of a mystery.

Hunger, however, was anything but a mystery. It soon became a fearsome reality with which she wrestled constantly. Jana was no exception when it came to parceling out food. If supplies were short, she went without, just as the others did who did not fight.

Often, she would awaken in the middle of the night, drenched with dreams of food: pots of hot, steaming soup on the stove, platters abundant with veal and children. Memories of sitting at the elegant table in Budapest, shining with silver and crystal, bright with fine linen, haunted her waking hours.

At times such as these, she would work particularly dilligently at finding food. Right after breakfast—if she had breakfast—she would set out. Putting on heavy gloves, she would gather nettles for boiling. Or she would pick wild berries, or spinach or clover. Checking her snares, often she would find a hapless animal trapped, too frequently still struggling for life.

By that time, pity for the creature had been replaced with her determination to eat. The animal represented life, not death. And so she learned to whack it over the head with a rock.

Jana worked hard throughout the day. Then, after diner, she would rest. This was her favorite time. If there was no more work to be done, small groups of men and women would sit by the fire, telling stories and singing to the accompaniment of the *gusla,* the one-stringed harp played by the mountain people.

Although Jana did not understand the words, the music was comforting. Surrounded as they all were by death, illness and danger, the melodies spoke of life, of hope.

Best of all were the times when Marek would sit by the fire with her, his arm around her shoulders in a safe and secure embrace.

Along with Rachel, Marek had become her anchor, one to which she clung with all the trust and innocence of childhood. Everything she knew about living in the wilderness had been taught to her by Marek. Everything she learned about being a child in an adult world of brutality and survival had been eased for her by him. He was the father she missed so desperately.

As for Marek, Jana had become the little sister who had died. And he loved and cared for Jana with a tenderness he had carefully shunned until they met.

In an odd but necessary transition, they became family to each other. It was a bond that transcended their disparate ages, for they found comfort in the presence of each other, in the love and trust they offered.

Towards the end of July, word came to the Partisans that there would be a new drop by British aircraft. This was a relatively recent occurrence, since during the first few years of the war, the British had elected to give their support to the Chetniks, the opposing guerilla group.

The gradual understanding that it was Tito's army that held the real power motivated the British to transfer their allegiance to the Partisans. And with it came the Partisans' increased ability to wage an effective war against their enemy.

News of the drop came with short notice. Most of the unit had not returned from a mission that had begun two days previously. As a consequence, they were shorthanded.

Serghei had stayed behind to wait for the drop. Supplies of ammunition and medical supplies were perilously low and he knew that, in order to continue waging their war, they must receive aid soon.

"I shall want you to come with us tonight," Serghei said to Rachel in a matter-of-fact tone of voice. "We're short of personnel and need your help. The message on the wireless said we should be receiving medical supplies, ammunition and explosives. And we must come back with as much of it as possible."

"But I know nothing about such things," Rachel said, frightened at the possibility of being so directly involved in danger.

"Then you shall learn," he said.

Parachute drops were always a cause of celebration, despite the risk they involved. The women loved it for the parachute silk that could be used to make clothing. The supply cannisters containing arms would later be converted into portable field

122

stoves, a luxury much in demand when they were on the move.

When Jana heard they would be bringing back silk, she asked Rachel a question she had been harboring since the first day they began their journey. "Will you make me a lining for these pants, Buba?" she asked, referring to the itchy pants she had been forced to wear almost every day. "They still scratch." Then, she added, "I never did get used to them like you promised."

Rachel smiled. "If there's any silk left over, I'll do it," she answered, hugging Jana. All the while she was thinking, if I ever return. . . .

And yet she, too, wanted the silk. The delicate underwear she had worn from the beginning, hand stitched of the finest silk, had begun to fray. She knew it would not be long until it fell apart completely from the effects of constant wearing and harsh soap. She wondered if she would ever again feel the luxury of fine silk against her smooth body; if she would ever again know the soft touch of cashmere and linen. Soon she would look like the rest of them: combinations of odd clothing, put together for practicality and warmth, bundled over weary, sun-burnt bodies. She accepted the inevitable. Nevertheless, the possibility of obtaining some silk—no matter if it was of inferior quality—was attractive to her. It did not compensate for her fear of what she had to do to obtain it, however.

Throughout the day, anxiety stalked Rachel like an unwanted shadow. She could feel it gnawing at her, playing with the tight muscles in her stomach, toying with her adrenalin system. By the time she set out with six other men in the late afternoon, fear had become a living presence.

She had become much tougher since she arrived in the mountains. But she was still uncertain of her skills, of her ability to withstand a forced march for five hours to the drop zone. She was frightened that the journey itself would exhaust her, so that her return trip—much more rigorous since she would have to carry supplies on her back—would be impossible to endure.

Although it was daylight when the group started out, they would not reach their destination until close to midnight. That meant travelling over treacherous mountain paths in the dark. The Partisans were accustomed to it. By choice, they conducted as many sorties as possible during the night or in adverse weather conditions. Thus, avoiding the threat of detection by enemy aircraft, they had become intimate friends of the night. But Rachel had yet to make this particular acquaintance. And she dreaded the thought of slipping while she was negotiating a steep, narrow path and falling into a chasm below. Whatever security she had could be permanently destroyed by one foolish step.

When they began, Rachel followed closely behind Serghei. Unwilling to admit her terror, she walked silently, trying to step exactly where he did, concentrating on his every move.

They traveled at a quick, sure pace, and after almost three hours of nonstop walking and climbing, they stopped at a "safe house." It was the home of a peasant, too old to fight, but not too lacking in conviction to help the Partisans in any way he could. He gave them food—hot, spicy soup—and a sheltered floor on which to sit for a few minutes. He also gave them four horses that they would take to their rendezvous so that they could serve as pack animals for the arduous trip home.

It was almost midnight when they reached their objective. Feeling triumphant and relieved, Rachel set about preparing the field.

"We must hurry now," Serghei said bruskly. "There is much to be done."

With two other men, Rachel started to dig a hole in which they would hide any evidence of the drop that they were unable to carry with them. Others unearthed the ammunition dump—empty of supplies—and a treasured wireless transmitter. This was their sole contact with the outside world, and could only be used in selected locations where the mountains did not interfere with their signals. This was the reason they were forced to travel so far to the drop zone.

Working with trained efficiency, every task was carried out with mechanical dispatch. Nothing was left to chance. Every detail had been worked out in advance.

While Serghei patrolled the perimeter of the field, two other men prepared the drop zone itself, fixing five torches to sticks in the X-shape of the St. Andrew's cross, the marker for the plane that would soon come.

At twelve-thirty, they heard the low hum of the

RAF Halifax. This is it, thought Rachel, drawing an oblique comfort from the sound. It was a connection with the outside world, a symbol of hope, of civilization, of the fact that she was not forgotten.

On the ground, the all-clear flash was signalled in a prearranged code. Then, as Rachel watched, ghostly white parachutes took shape against the clear night sky. They floated in quiet majesty, reminding her momentarily of her childhood when she would pick up dandelion puffs and blow them into the wind.

Rachel breathed a sigh of relief as the laden chutes hit the ground with hard, jolting thuds. As soon as they were down, following instructions Serghei had given her earlier, Rachel ran to the chutes. So immersed was she in retrieving the foam-padded containers, she did not register the sound of the machine gun when she first heard it.

With a shock, she felt herself being shoved to the ground. The jolt allowed her to focus on the reality of what was happening: she was being shot at. She could feel the bullets as they whirred over her body; hear their deadly whine. She experienced a moment of disbelief, a feeling of utter preposterousness at being shot at. Desperate, she clawed at the soft earth, certain that she had dug a hole in the meadow by sheer force of will alone. Possessed by the ferocity of the will to survive, she flattened her body and waited, watching the man lying next to her.

Just as quickly as it began, the shooting stopped.

"Serghei," mumbled the man who had saved her

126

life by pulling her down with him.

Unable to speak with him because of their language barrier, she reached out and touched his hand in thanks. He held it tight, indicating that she still should not move. Finally, they heard a whistle. Only then did he motion for her to come with him.

Deliberately, with no regard to what had just taken place, they set about finding all the chutes and organizing the supplies for the journey home. They worked silently and methodically. Only once did a sound interrupt the stillness that clung like a mist to the ridges and valleys. It was the horribly agonizing cry of a man, a sound that spoke of terror, dread, and death. It echoed off the mountain walls, finally drifting and fading into a gurgling halt. Rachel looked questioningly at her companion. But he continued to work as if nothing had happened.

Soon afterwards, Serghei appeared. He wiped his knife on his tunic before replacing it in the sheath attached to his belt.

"Ustachi," he said with defiant disgust, spitting on the ground. "I cut his eyes out before I slit his throat."

Jerking her head towards him, certain she did not understand his words correctly, she asked incredulously, "You what?"

"You heard me," he mumbled, leaning over a chute to free it from the canister.

Stiff with righteousness and conviction, Rachel said, "If you are going to kill a man, you should at least do it as swiftly as possible. You should have some mercy."

"Mercy?" Serghei said contemptuously. "Mercy? For Ustachi?" These men are worse than Nazis. They kill for sport. And you want me to have mercy? I cut out his eyes. May his mother live forever, burdened always with the knowledge that she gave birth to a monster." His eyes flashed with vengeance. "I will tell you this, straight from the mouth of a barbarian: I would have been slower about killing him if we had the time. This death was too good for him. Too easy. May he regain his sight in hell, wrapped in the arms of the damned."

Before she could reply, Serghei walked away to check the horses, making certain the boxes were secure for their long journey back to camp. The death was already behind him, a part of a necessary and brutal past. What concerned him now was carrying as many supplies as possible; and carrying them home without being detected.

Quiet now, trying to concentrate on her task at hand, Rachel remembered something she had learned in history a long time ago. It was no less appalling now than when she first heard it, this story of the Turks. In an effort to quell an uprising in 1804, the Turks built a tower of the heads of Serbian peasants as an example of their conquer's might. This was the tradition out of which Serghei came, a hard and brutal tradition in which mercy goes only to the worthy few. And the man holding the knife is the judge.

Not stopping to rest, the small group set out on their long journey home. Sleep was a luxury they could not afford.

It was a grueling trip back to the camp. Once, Serghei stopped to ask Rachel if she was all right. With only a nod for a reply, she continued to walk, afraid that if she stopped, she would collapse and never rise again. She had never known such weariness, such exhaustion that burned in her bones and tormented every inch of skin. Aches turned to sharp pain and then stayed, unrelieved and unrelenting. But she refused to give into it. Instead, she tried to amuse herself with visions of her past, of how she used to consider a five block walk to the coffee house her daily exercise and how invigorating a game of croquet could be. Once, she laughed out loud when she remembered how she would sometimes complain wearily about how many times in a day she had to run up and down the stairs of her home and how exhausted she was from the duties of running a house.

The sun was just rising in a spectacular show of brilliance and warmth, when they straggled into camp.

Those who had stayed behind ran out to meet the weary travellers, helping them with the unloading. Walking as straight as she could, Rachel struggled over the cave and lay down beside Jana. She was so exhausted that she did not feel the child's arm reach out to her, nor did she see the expression of relief and gratitude that spilled over Jana's face when she knew, finally, her grandmother was safe.

The fear of being left alone in the world, considerably intensified during Rachel's absence, had left

Jana in a state of mute anxiety. Trapped with peasants who did not speak her language, she spent the night covered with a mantle of fear and dread.

Her only solace during these confusing times was Marek. More and more he took on the guise of savior. Even though he, too, was gone during the frightening night she was forced to endure alone, Jana believed totally in Marek's invincibility. He had once saved her life and Jana had no doubt that, were his own life threatened, he would manage to do the same for himself. He knew how to fight, how to negotiate treacherous mountain passes, how to find food and make shelter in the wilderness. He would survive.

And so Jana consoled herself with this fragile knowledge, believing with the naive trust of a child that if anything happened to her grandmother, Marek would take care of her. He'll look after me, she told herself. And when I grow up we will marry. We shall be family. And we will have each other on long lonely nights. At least we'll have each other.

Despite the confusions and anxieties and terrors that hovered over the warm summer months, by autumn, Jana had become a true child of the wilderness. She was an expert at gathering and trapping food, and she was no longer haunted by the fear that she would lose her way and be unable to take care of herself before she could find her way back to camp. Landmarks were now familiar and her strength had increased remarkably. Her muscles had adapted steadily to the long walks and hard climbs. All this was now a natural part of the rhythm of her life, an integral part of her being. Her surroundings, once threatening and awesome, were now beautiful. The mountains had at last become her friends.

Rachel was deeply proud of Jana's growth. It comforted her to know that the child had become a survivor, a tough but necessary state of being in these harsh conditions.

Rachel, too, had come to love and respect the mountains. Their beauty never failed to offer her a kind of natural serenity. Sometimes she even wondered if she might make a life here for herself and Jana, forsaking her dream of America for a more immediate haven. This consideration was always overshadowed by thoughts of her family in Budapest. They would come to her at odd moments, in unexpected places. And she knew that she could never abandon the quest to find them once the war was over.

Jana's thoughts of city life had begun to fade. But her memories of her parents grew in direct proportion to this. She was tormented with the need to be held once more in her father's arms, to be comforted by her mother. She longed for their good-night kisses. Sometimes, when she was alone and certain that her grandmother would not hear her, she would talk to her parents, carrying on conversations with her father and telling her mother what she had done that day. It never once occurred to her that she would not experience this again.

Consequently, her thoughts were not as dispairing as her grandmother's.

Rachel clung obsessively to the belief that her future would once more include her beloved husband. She told herself this daily in order to combat her increasing dread that he had been sent to a death camp. Even here in the mountains, stories circulated of Nazi terrors, of their treatment of the Jews. And she would flinch with guilt at the fact that she had escaped this fate, that she had survived.

This guilt took on an even harsher form one warm evening in August when she was sitting outside by the fire and drifting with the music that the assembled group quietly sung. It happened at the moment when she look at Serghei. He had returned earlier that day from a brief reconnaissance mission and was tired and filthy.

That evening, it was if she were looking at him for the first time. There was a nobility about him, a pride that she had not seen before. He wears his stench and filth like a king wears velvet and ermine, she thought. Like a king.

At that very moment, he looked at her. The enigmatic smile in his eyes startled her. She felt strangely vulnerable and naked before him, as if he had exposed a hidden nerve, a nerve that signalled warmth and femaleness, a nerve that spoke of longing and passion. It was only an instant. For immediately afterwards, with an elusive nod of his head that she found herself hoping was directed only to her, he stood up slowly and walked away.

The languid insolence of his gesture, barely recognizable and extremely tempting, stayed with her. Disturbed by the insistence of Serghei's intrusion in her thoughts and the guilt that it engendered, she tried to conjure up images of her life in Budapest. But, try as she might, for the first time, Rachel could not make her past come alive. She could not grasp hold of the images, could not touch the feelings. There was only loss, terrible loss combined with a bare wisp of hope.

Separated from her past by an impossible distance created of violence and survival, Budapest had become a collage of misty images, a cherished phantom — a phantom that had been abruptly dismissed by a smile that promised nothing.

Chapter 6

Had its origin been unknown, the sound of the breaking mirror might have been musical. Hundreds of tiny shards, reflecting the sun in random patterns, created a crazy quilt of light.

Oberleutnant Fritz Walther stood before the broken mirror, one piece clinging stubbornly to the wall. He could not bear even that. Taking the butt of his pistol, he hit it until that piece, too, fell to the floor. Snarling, he kicked it aside.

A nurse, meek and perfunctorily concerned, entered the hospital room, summoned by the noise that could be heard all the way to the end of the hall.

"What is it?" she asked, scurrying over to Walther.

Restraining his urge to hit this ignorant female, he answered with disdain. "Can you not find the answer to that imbecilic question in my face?"

Uncertain how she should respond, the nurse took a step backwards, avoiding the blow of his words.

He was a difficult patient, this Oberleutnant, and she hoped he would be leaving soon. His nasty disposition colored every day she was on duty. He did not ask, he demanded; he did not speak, he sneered.

Certainly, she had worked with other men whose injuries had left them with faces far worse than this. But she had never been required to deal with such naked malevolence as a result.

He is wicked, she thought to herself as she trotted down the hall to find an orderly who would clean up this mess. She did not wish to risk doing the job herself. Every time she did something in his room, she had the feeling that the Oberleutnant might hurt her.

When Walther first arrived at the hospital, he was not overly concerned about the injury on his face. His plan was to pass it off as a dueling scar in the future; a scar which would provide him with a social status he had never known. Thus, he took his wound in stride, making — as usual — the best of any difficult situation.

This acceptance was brutally destroyed when he learned that his facial nerve had been irreparably severed; that the left side of his face would always droop, forever unresponsive to what the other side did. On those rare occasions when he laughed, his face looked exactly like a combination of the classic theatrical masks depicting comedy and tragedy.

This crazed appearance was intensified by the unscrubbed hands of the doctor who sutured his wounds. An infection had set in that required four months to cure, leaving both his facial and shoulder scars even more hideous than they might otherwise have been.

Every time he looked at himself in the mirror, Walther was reminded of the nurse's comment he had overheard two months previously. "It's a pity," she said to a co-worker. "So handsome on one side of his face and so repulsive on the other."

Unwilling to accept this at first, he had tried his luck with women, hoping it was his own exaggerated imagination that made him feel so hideous.

He flirted with the prettiest nurse he could find and he received perfect politeness as a response. When even the ugliest nurse rebuffed him, he knew, finally, what his future held in store.

The only women he could have now were the ones forced to inhabit the whore house that the army thoughtfully maintained for the pleasure of its officers. No other woman would have him now, he thought bitterly. That was what he had been thinking when he picked up the water glass and hurled it against the mirror that reflected the horror of his own image.

Taking a perverse satisfaction in watching the orderly begin the task of cleaning up the kaleidoscopic mess he had created, he stood there for a moment before turning abruptly and picking up a box that lay on the table near his bed.

Without a word, he left the room.

Striding down the hall, a hint of a crooked smile on his face, he pulled his body stiffly to its full height. Power, at least, was still his, and he had learned to utilize it in every way possible. He was aware that the manner in which he held his body could make a definitive difference when dealing in that alluring commodity; a commodity he sought with a rapacious skill.

Entering the sun porch where the majority of the burn victims gathered in their feeble attempts at comraderie, he stood quietly by the door. There was a stir in the room, as if new life had been injected into the stale, sad air.

Tentative and elusive, nevertheless Walther could feel it: that erotic, seductive quality of having control over other human beings. When he first recognized that power could be his, Walther carried on a love-hate relationship with it, uncertain how to use it. Finally, understanding that men who have been beaten will give their wretched allegiance to one of their own who manages to beat the system, he took full advantage of his position. And he was totally successful.

"Ah, Walther," said one of the less intimidated young men, whose entire face was an obscene scar, "What invigorating activities have you scheduled for us this afternoon?"

"Something new," Walther replied. "But not for this afternoon. For tonight."

"Like what?" came the question from a gaping hole that was trying to pass as a mouth.

"Like games and laughter. Revelling for all," he answered.

"And you? Shall you be master of the revellers?"

"He's always master," came the words from the

hole. "Master of anything and everything. He would not have it otherwise."

"And where are we to do this merrymaking?" asked a disembodied voice.

"In the city," Walther replied.

There were audible objections from every man in the room. None of them wished to be subjected to the humiliations of rejection that they universally received when they encountered the whole faces of the uninjured. At best, they could hope the reaction to their appearance would be one of pity instead of revulsion and shock. In either case, they avoided these painful meetings.

"This time it will be different," pronounced Walther, completely certain of his position.

"Yes. You are right. I will not go," replied one of the soldiers.

"Will you go if you are wearing one of these?" Walther asked, reaching into the box he carried and pulling out a jumble of colored objects.

Slowly, passing them out as if he were the Pope offering his blessings to his subjects, the objects began to take shape. Each one was a mask. A clown, a devil, a monster. And each one would cover the entire face of the man who wore it.

"Where did you get them?" asked one of the men, slow comprehension creeping into his voice.

"I have my sources."

"Is there anything you can't get?" he asked, attracted and repelled by the ingenuity of this Ober-leutnant.

"Nothing," replied Walther, creating truth out of

his lie. "Absolutely nothing. All you have to do is ask."

Walther's mask was different from the others. He had designed it himself. In a stroke of inspiration, he had a mask made that covered only the injured side of his face. Leaving the good side exposed, the mask was created in the visage of a gargoyle. No one could possibly believe that this is the way I really look, he thought bitterly to himself when he slipped it over his face. A monster in a monster's mask.

Through one of his many connections, Walther secured a truck to take them to the beer hall in the middle of the city. All of them were in high spirits, grateful to their leader for creating this opportunity for them. This was the first time since their injuries that they could venture into the general population with a light heart and laughter. And they were appropriately indebted to the man who had arranged it.

The beer hall was one huge room. Long and narrow, the walls were made of rough plaster and the planked floors were covered with sawdust. Long tables ran from front to back, with benches alongside them. There, strangers sat together, singing and drinking their beer.

On this night, the hall was filled with people intent on forgetting that they were still living in the midst of hunger and battle. And when they saw the masked revellers enter, their response was universal and immediate. The music picked up tempo, songs were sung with renewed enthusiasm. Everyone was ready for a party, desperate for one. The need already existed. Only focus was lacking. And that was what Walther's party of playful grotesques brought with it.

Ordering drinks for all his comrades, Walther made an appropriate show of his generosity. He was, indeed, master of the revellers, just as he was master of a significant segment of their lives. Without any effort on his part, his control extended to most of the people in the room. After all, the participants thought as they looked at the handsome half-exposed face of the merry Oberleutnant, the least we can do is join him in his celebration.

A pretty young woman, long accustomed to living off the desire and generosity of soldiers, approached Walther. She had learned long before to approach the man in charge. The benefits were much more rewarding.

Smiling invitingly, she reached up and touched Walther on his face. She must have touched the last of his humanity, for tears sprung unexpectedly to his eyes. He did not need to beg for her attention. For one moment, he was a man again; a desirable man. And he lost no time in running his trembling hands over her supple, smooth body.

He felt himself harden, experiencing a sense of elation and well-being that was oddly combined with somber relief. Since that morning months earlier when he had been with the Jewess, he had wondered if he were still capable of being fully aroused by a woman. Compelled to find out the answer immediately, he whispered to the woman:

140

"Take me to your room. Now."

Leaving his comrades, but not before buying them another round of drinks to keep them happy Walther walked out into the cool night air. This is how to use power, he thought.

They climbed three flights of stairs to her tiny, squalid room that was tucked away under the eaves of a two hundred-year-old building. Once inside, they were both eager.

Delighted at the possibility of snaring this handsome officer, the young woman flirtatiously smoothed the covers on the narrow cot. Then she sat down coyly on the shabby coverlet.

"It's time to take off your mask," she said provocatively.

"Never," he replied in a playfully stentorian tone of voice. "It is more fun this way. There is much you would have to do in order to have all of me."

He unbuckled his belt as he spoke, feeling a new surge of potence sweep through him. Then he leaned over and pulled the girl's blouse over her head, exposing her full, rounded breasts. He stroked them eagerly, admiring, lingering briefly over the soft voluptuousness of her young, supple body.

He could wait no longer. Pushing her down onto the bed more roughly than he intended, he pulled up her skirt, a vague flash of a similar scene momentarily invading his consciousness. He liked it this way: taking, demanding. He was totally in control now. Powerful. She would do his bidding. The vision of the beautiful Jewess misted before his eyes again and he remembered the bitter aftermath. This

141

time I will finish, he told himself. I will finish it in any way I wish. She is mine to do with what I please.

The woman made perfunctory noises of desire and lust, although this was not what she wished at all. But her noises sent the officer into a frenzy of desire and she was aware this could mean extra money for her when it was all over.

She tried to accommodate his needs, to urge him on. For she wanted this to be over soon. There was something in him that frightened her. It was the way he pushed so hard, pinned her so helplessly beneath him.

Attempting to hurry the process, she placed her hand on the officer's back, stroking him, urging him to completion. She could see he was excited, that he needed to do it this way.

Thinking he would want to expose all of himself at this moment, she reached towards his face. He was not even aware that she had touched him there, that she had removed his mask. He only realized it when he looked at her face beneath his. Her expression changed abruptly from desire to shock. Then a look of horror and repulsion spread over her, staining every part of her with dread.

She screamed in shocked terror. Furious, Walther silenced her with one swift blow of his hand. Then, his hands pinning her shoulders to the mattress, he continued, aware she was too frightened to utter a sound. Her fear became an aphrodisiac as he continued to thrust himself into her. He was unaware of the stream of spittle that oozed uncontrollably from one side of his twisted mouth and dripped like acid onto the appalled face of his victim.

Finally, he finished. He looked at the girl who lay beneath his sated body and grinned obscenely. She meant nothing to him now—nothing, besides a vehicle for confirmation and relief.

When he saw the glaze of fear that had coated her eyes, the trickle of blood that had begun to cake at the corner of her mouth, he felt a peculiar and heady sense of satisfaction. Her fear became a visible manifestation of his power; a derelict symbol of his instinct to survive.

He did not even hear her sobs of relief when he stood and pulled his pants up his strong, powerful legs. Instead, he rationalized that she had enjoyed the experience of being subjugated by such a powerful man.

She had been raped after all, by the master of the revellers. The king of grotesques, he thought to himself with a twisted smile as he walked out the door.

The following evening, cracks of doubt began to mar Walther's assured facade. Listening to Deutschlandsender Radio, Walther learned of the attempted assassination of Hitler. Walther's confidence that he would survive as a master in a victorious Germany began to crumble. Defeat had no place in Walther's plans.

But flexibility did. And he began to prepare for the worst, for a world in which he could be at the

143

top of the most repugnant heap imaginable. No matter what the state of the bodies underneath, Oberleutnant Fritz Walther vowed at that moment that he would be breathing the freshest air.

He had already become deeply involved in the black market that thrives so readily in any location where there is too much deprivation and not enough amenities to make life bearable. Using the brooch as bait, he always managed to pay for the goods with something other than his treasure. It had become a symbol to him, a talisman to insure victory in the midst of pain.

His plan was to accumulate a store of small, expensive, negotiable goods. Instinctively understanding that mobility would be essential if escape became necessary, he only held onto large quantities of goods for a very limited time. Always he returned to jewels and gold.

As summer drew to an end, he appreciated more and more his accurate assessment of the increasingly dire military situation. The Russians had begun their summer offensives in the middle of July. With a series of stunning and alarming victories, they had reached the Vistula near Warsaw by the middle of August. And by the end of that month, they captured the Polesti oil fields in Rumania. This was Germany's greatest source of oil, the destruction of which would spell certain defeat.

When Walther learned that Paris had fallen with no more than a perfunctory German defense, he understood the war was lost. The Allies were moving inexorably east and there was little, besides worn-out and ill-equipped troops, to stop them.

Yet Hitler refused to give up. This was the first time since the Napoleonic Wars that Germans had been forced to defend their honor on their own soil, and der Fuhrer had no intention of going down to an even more humiliating defeat because of this fact.

Firmly believing that women should be left at home to tend to children and kitchens, Hitler refused to ask them to help keep industry alive while the men in factories fought. Instead, in an act of maniacal desperation, he mobilized young boys and old men and any other male who could possibly hold a rifle and point it in the correct direction.

Boys without fuzz on their cheeks fought alongside feeble old men with heart conditions. None of them had been adequately trained, beyond which way to march or direct their gunfire.

As the battles continued in both the east and the west, desperation led to mass desertions. Thus, it was made very clear to those men still fighting that if they deserted, their relatives would pay with their lives for the soldier's cowardice and treachery. This was clearly a persuasive reminder to those considering defection.

In September, his wounds finally healed and well on his way to becoming a rich man, Oberleutnant Fritz Walther received orders to move north to Poland. There, he was to command a rag-tag unit of last chance soldiers.

Encouraged by the news of the temporary subsiding of the Allied advance in the West, Walther complied with the orders. But he did not comply without first considering the personal advantages in the situation that he might reap for himself. He was fully aware of the fact that the more chaotic conditions became, the easier it would be for him to profit.

After a grueling journey, Walther arrived in Warsaw. What he found there genuinely appalled him. Nothing had prepared the officer for the turmoil and complexity he now had to face. The men he was to lead into battle were more than a sorry lot. They were miserable, lost, and already defeated.

Few of them were healthy, mentally or physically. And those that were fell into the category of adolescence or senility. Fewer still had received any adequate training. They had simply been taught how to fire a rifle and become cannon fodder.

That's all they are good for, Walther thought at his first meeting with the men he was to command. This is a nightmare. He surveyed the men, standing at attention in a wavy line. They are defeated before they begin, he thought.

Walther spoke to an old man who was tired, frightened and hungry. Whenever the officer asked the man a question, the feeble gentleman would glance sideways, avoiding the horror of his commanding officer's face.

"You must look at me, old man," Walther ordered in a politely menacing voice. "It is not courteous to look away when you are addressed by an officer."

Walther smiled then, making matters worse. His

left eye and the side of his mouth dropped even more. When contrasted with the other side of his face, he did, indeed, resemble the gargoyle mask that he once wore.

The old man nodded and looked at Walther. But as soon as his eyes beheld the grotesque face of his leader, his gaze wandered away. As if it were an involuntary reflex over which he had no control, his watery blue eyes would waver then drift away.

Enraged, Walther grabbed the old man's head between his hands, knocking off his cap and winding his fingers in the thinning grey hair.

"Now," he said, forcing the head into a position so that he would have to look directly at him, "I do not like it when you glance away. See? I look at you. And you, old man, with your flaccid skin and sagging jowls, are as ugly as I."

The old man nodded, terrified, his head locked in a vise. Walther then took one hand and placed it under the quivering chin.

"I am the officer in charge here. And when I tell you to look at me, you will look at me. And when I tell you to look to the left," he said, jerking the man's head in the appropriate direction, "you will look to the left."

"And," he continued through gritted teeth, "when I tell you to look to the right, you will look to the right."

Jerking the man's head in the opposite direction, Walther heard a crunch, then a sharp crack. "From now on, you shall do exactly as I say. Do you understand?"

It took Walther a moment to realize that he was holding up the full weight of this pitiful used-up body. Suddenly letting go, the old man folded like a puppet whose strings had been cut. As if in slow motion, his neck askew, he fell lifeless to the ground.

Surprised, Walther stepped back. Looking down, he understood what had happened. But it was an understanding with no trace of remorse.

Turning to the shocked soldier standing next to the body, he said in a crisp military voice, "Go inform the medical officer that this old man has had a heart attack. It is a shame, a deep shame, that they have drafted such old, weak men into our glorious army."

It is difficult to determine whether this indifferent act of savagery had been born of his newly acquired deformity, or whether Oberleutnant Fritz Walther's nature had always been a dark abyss that had quietly sheltered itself until it could match the obscenity of the physical appearance. One fact, however, was certain: with this single unspeakable act, Fritz Walther became a monster. Like Grendel, maimed by Beowulf, he became a boundry stalker, skulking across the corners of the night; derelict and cunning, he moved to the outer edges of humanity where the grotesques reign supreme.

Standing before his men, silently daring one of them to dispute his word, Walther knew one thing: he would not have any trouble from his men. They were his.

Dismissing the stunned soldiers who stood before him at rigid attention, Walther watched them scuttle away like mistreated dogs with their tails between their legs.

As they disappeared, he thought ironically to himself that he was, indeed, a leader of misfits. And this time it was official.

Chapter 7

In the middle of September, Marek left for points unknown on another family-rescuing mission. Eighteen days later, he returned.

It was dusk, and those Partisans who were present at the camp had begun to settle into the quiet of evening. The sky, rich with garlands of clouds after a cool autumn rain, had turned mauve in the waning light. The air itself was pink, casting a gentle glow even on those unwilling to stop for a moment and admire its beauty.

Jana, with the child's impatience at stopping whatever project in which she was involved, had walked to a large rock outcropping from which she could watch the soft coming of night.

Feeling the unusual peace of the moment, she was frightened at first when she saw the weary stranger emerge from the shelter of the trees below. His face was covered with a halfhearted growth of scraggly beard and his gait was awkward as a result of simple exhaustion.

The familiarity of his body soon brought recognition. It was Marek. She had worried continually since he had been gone, fretted in the middle of the night, looked for him during the day, and prayed for him constantly. And now he was home.

Running to him, her arms outstretched with joy and relief, Jana was scooped up in Marek's suddenly revitalized arms.

"So . . . Little One . . ." Marek said with a broad smile. "Have you been a good girl in my absence?"

"Oh, yes, Marek," she answered, her arms tight around his neck. "I've trapped lots of rabbits and helped Buba make flour and . . . oh . . . all the time I've been waiting for you to come home." Leaning back slightly, she rubbed his beard gently with her hand.

"Well, if that is, indeed, the case, I have a surprise for you."

Her eyes lit up as he set her down gently on the ground. He was too weary to hold her any longer. Instead, they held hands as they walked back to camp.

"What's the surprise?" Jana asked immediately. "Tell me!"

"Not yet," he replied as he leaned over and kissed her on the forehead. "If I told you, then it would no longer be a surprise."

Let it be the brooch, Jana thought. Please, God, let it be the brooch.

Skipping beside him, her eyes shining with anticipation, she laughed from the sheer pleasure of his presence.

When they returned to camp, Jana could barely

contain her excitement as she waited for Marek to complete his report to Serghei. Then, when they were finally settled near the fire, she hugged him enthusiastically. In the harsh life she lead, a present was almost as rare as the sighting of a Vila. Afraid she would annoy Marek by asking too many questions, she wiggled and squirmed beside him until he had no choice but to put a stop to it.

Smiling once at Rachel, Marek looked at Jana. "Now . . . let me see . . ." he teased. "Let me see if I can find it," he said, feeling dramatically in his pockets, a consternated expression on his face. "I don't know . . ." he fumbled. "I hope I didn't lose it."

"Oh . . ." Jana mumbled, bravely trying not to show the disappointment she felt.

"No, wait!" he exclaimed, his eyes lighting up when he reached into an oversize pocket in his coat. "Here it is."

Pulling his hand out carefully, he held up an object that was wrapped in dirty rags. Peeling them away very gently, like the unveiling of a precious work of art, he held his prize aloft between his thumb and forefinger.

"Oh . . ." Jana shrieked, forgetting about the brooch. "An egg! I had almost forgotten what they look like."

"Careful now," Marek cautioned. "Handle it gently. Shall I help you boil it?"

"Oh, yes. And then I'll share it with you and Buba."

"This is all for you."

"Never," she answered. "You must have some."

"Then, because of your generosity," he replied as he reached for a tin container, "I have something else for you."

Unscrewing the top, he offered it to her.

"What is it?" asked Jana, slightly dubious about drinking something she could not see."

"Milk."

She took the container greedily between her hands and tipped her head back, taking several long swallows. Then she offered him a drink.

"No," he answered, nodding his head firmly. "That is all for you. I want to see to it that your teeth remain sound while you're in the mountains. It's very important."

Jana sipped the milk slowly, savoring every drop. Then she dutifully went to the stream and rinsed out the container as she waited for the egg to boil in a small pot over the fire.

When the egg was ready, she asked her grandmother for the special pearl-handled knife that she had carried with her from Budapest. This egg could not be cut with just any knife. It was too special.

She peeled it with extraordinary care, and set it on a tin plate. Debating how to divide it into three pieces, she marked it gently with the knife before making the definitive slice.

Then she offered Rachel and Marek their share, holding out the plate with solemn formality.

Before taking her first tiny bite, she turned to Marek and thanked him once again.

* * *

Ten days later, after a breakfast of watered down stew made of squirrel and a few wild herbs, Rachel looked at Jana and saw that her hands were trembling.

"What's the matter?" she asked her granddaughter.

"Nothing much," she replied with an unusual listlessness. "My head hurts a little. That's all."

"That is all?" Rachel asked. "Then why are you shaking?"

"Because it is so cold. I don't think my coat is warm enough."

Rachel reached over and touched Jana on her forehead. It was hot and dry. "You have a fever."

"Surely not," Jana replied. "I'm just cold. Besides, I must go check my snares."

"The snares can wait," Rachel said firmly. There was a lump of fear in her throat as she spoke.

By evening, Jana's fever had increased. There was no thermometer, of course, but a simple touch was enough to tell Rachel that Jana was very sick.

She lay on her straw pallet in the cave, her eyes glazed and her hair matted to her head from sweating.

Kneeling next to Jana to bath her face with cool water, Rachel was so involved that she was startled when Marek sat down next to her.

"I heard Jana was sick," he said. He had spent the afternoon sorting some rifles that had been taken from an Italian unit just the day before and had only heard about Jana when he returned to camp.

"Yes," Rachel said. "I think she must have influenza. But I can't imagine where she picked it up."

Marek looked down at Jana and smiled. She licked her parched lips and tried to respond. But her effort got lost somewhere between the intention and the deed. Her head ached unbearably, and her back and legs felt as if they were carrying heavy weights.

Marek and Rachel stayed with her throughout the night. They took turns bathing her, and speaking in soft, soothing tones when she cried out. In the morning, she seemed slightly improved.

But by that evening, the fever had risen once more. It became clear that Jana was desperately ill. Gaunt with worry, Rachel had not left her granddaughter's side. When Marek saw Jana that evening, he said simply, "I'll go get Serghei. I think we should take her to the hospital."

But Serghei was not there. He had gone to the valley to investigate a rumor about some explosives that could be purchased by a man willing to help the Partisans; but also a man intent on making a profit from his offer.

Throughout that night, Marek and Rachel tended Jana, bathing her with cool cloths that had been dipped in the stream and urging her to take sips of water.

When Serghei returned the next morning, Marek told him how sick Jana was.

Rachel felt an immediate sense of relief when she saw Serghei. Having faith in the judgment and wisdom of this division leader, she was touched when

155

he came to the cave and knelt down beside Jana.

He felt her brow. Then, very gently, he pulled the blanket from her and raised her sweater, looking carefully at her abdomen. It appeared to be slightly swollen. When he pushed on her belly, low on the right side, Jana cried out weakly.

Stunned, Rachel whispered, "Appendix?"

Ignoring her question when he saw the raised red spots on Jana's chest, Serghei shook his head. Pushing the spots, they momentarily disappeared, then returned to their full color when he took his hand away.

He covered her gently, then stood up, pulling Rachel up with him. Marek was there beside them, worried that Jana would have to have surgery.

"It is not appendix," Serghei whispered. "I have seen this before."

"And?" Rachel asked, fearing the answer.

"I think it is typhoid. Although I cannot imagine how she could have gotten it."

There was a long pause. Then, sick with dread, Marek uttered, "The milk."

"What milk?" asked Serghei. "We have no milk here."

"I brought it to her," he said. "When I returned last week. The old woman promised me it was fresh."

"I'm sure it was," Serghei muttered with disgust. "Fresh and contaminated. Did anyone else drink it?"

"Just Jana," Rachel said, sick with the irony of the gift. "We saved it all for her."

"I'll take her to the hospital," Marek said with

156

determination as he leaned over to pick up Jana. As soon as he moved her, she cried out in pain. Rachel kneeled down and stroked her face, mumbling the comforting noises that mothers have always known.

"Look at her," said Serghei. "It is half a day's journey to the hospital. I don't think she could withstand the trip. We'll have to take care of her here. I will send for a doctor. Perhaps . . ." he said, his voice drifting off. He knew how extraordinary it would be if a doctor were to travel to them. His authority replacing his doubt, he took over, giving Rachel and Marek very specific instructions about what should be done.

"The first thing you must do is to burn the bed and the coverings. Scrub everything. Boil everything that can be boiled. Clean. Everything must be clean. If we are to prevent this from spreading to the others in the camp, you must do everything you can to clean. And you must be particularly careful in the disposal of waste. Bury it. Far away. And you," he said as he reached over to touch Rachel on her face, "You must use that precious soap of yours. Keep yourself meticulously clean. Jana, too." He stopped, not knowing what else to say, except, "I'm sorry."

"I'll help, of course," Marek said, tormented with guilt that he had brought contaminated milk to Jana. "We'll begin right now."

Stunned with foreboding and fear, Rachel nodded mutely.

"Rachel?" Serghei said. "I want you to listen to me. It is important. We will do everything we can.

Have you any aspirin saved?"

Numb, she nodded in the affirmative. "I have been giving it to her."

"Do not use any more. Save it. A few days from now, she will need it even more. Try to control the fever until then with cool water. The night of the crisis . . ."

"Crisis?" she asked.

"Yes. There will be a crisis," he said in a soft voice. "It will get worse until then. Probably at night. You will know. And if . . . when . . . she passes that, she will get better. Until then, keep her clean. Clean her tongue and teeth and lips or they will become crusted. Water. Make certain she gets lots of water. She will need it. And I will make sure we have broth for her. You must force her to drink it."

Working together, Marek and Rachel boiled, cleaned and scrubbed everything they could touch. Tireless, they nursed Jana with infinite patience, putting exhaustion aside until another time.

Everytime she saw Serghei, Rachel asked about the doctor, if it would be much longer until he came. "I do not know," he said, the last time she asked. "I sent word to the hospital. And the message I received was that a unit to the south has taken a horrible beating. Forty wounded and still coming in. The doctor said he would try to get here . . ." Serghei's voice drifted into an inconclusive end. He knew that no doctor would travel a full day in order to save the life of one child if he had to jeopardize the lives of numerous others.

158

When Rachel heard this, she knew that it was futile to protest. The die had been cast and Jana had lost.

For endless hours, Marek sat beside Jana and told her stories. He sang to her, soft songs of loving and faraway times; happy songs designed to make children smile. But he never once received a real response from Jana. She was too weak.

There was no warning when the crisis began. The first thing Marek noticed was a slight twitch in Jana's wrist. For one hopeful moment he thought she was trying to move. But the twitch became worse. He tried to still her hands, to hold them tightly, but it made no difference. As if her fingers did not belong to her, she picked aimlessly at the bedcovers. They did not stop. Fumbling, touching, continuously picking at the covers, it was as if she were intent on pulling them apart thread by thread.

Marek woke up Rachel. Holding a candle close to Jana's face, they could see that her eyes were uncommonly dark; that they were oddly dialated as she stared vacantly at the ceiling of the cave. Semicomatose, she saw nothing, heard nothing, except her own inner voice.

"Papa?" Jana mumbled. "Help . . . Mama . . ."

"What?" Rachel asked, leaning close to the child's face. But what she heard made no sense. They were only nonsense noises that contained an occasional intelligible word. As the night progressed, the sounds became unbearable cries of pain and loss. Around midnight, Jana awakened half the camp with a cry of such agony that no one slept for the remainder of the night.

"MAMA!" she screamed. "No . . ."

Delerious, crazed with a perilously high fever, Jana spent the night tossing restlessly, sometimes jerking in uncontrollable spasms. There was no helping her.

At one point during the evening, Serghei appeared. "Are you using the aspirin?" he had asked.

Rachel nodded affirmatively, too weary to speak.

By morning, the fever had abated slightly. But Jana's delirium continued, her eyes wild with the hallucinations that come with such an assault on her mind and body. By afternoon, the fever shot up once more. Her body felt as if it had been scorched by the hand of the devil.

Marek and Rachel worked tirelessly, bathing, cleaning, and wiping Jana's mouth free of the crust that formed on her tongue and lips. When she was quiet, they coaxed her to sip some water. Occasionally one of them would fall into a fitful nap, confident that the other would care for Jana. Often they would work side by side, as if they were one person.

That evening Jana's fever began to drop. Slowly, fitfully, her body cooled down.

Marek was holding her in his arms when she opened her eyes. He rocked Jana gently, stroked her face, bathed her forehead with a cool cloth.

"Jana?" he whispered when he noticed that she was looking at him. "Can you hear me?"

"Mmmm," was her only reply. But both Rachel and Marek understood it was a deliberate response, not an involuntary sound.

At this moment, Serghei entered the cave. When he saw Jana, he smiled. "The crisis has passed," he said.

Rachel's mouth quivered in her effort to speak. But there were no words to express what she felt. Instead, she began to cry. Weeping shamelessly, her entire body shook with fear and relief. Understanding her need, Serghei wrapped his arms around Rachel and held on.

Out of control, anguished sobs tore through Rachel's body. Sobs of terror and loss. Sobs of rage at the capricious fates who had toyed so mercilessly with Jana. Rachel realized then that Fate was a rapacious scavenger who picked at strangers with arbitrary greed.

Until six months ago, Rachel's life had been simple. For over forty years it had been eased with the illusory balms of money and status. Even when her family had been torn from her, she managed to escape. And with that escape had come the false knowledge that she would survive, that she would endure; that it would be Jana who would carry the torch to light the remainder of her life.

And now Rachel had come perilously close to losing that light. She knew then that youth was no more sacred than age. Everyone was vulnerable. No one escaped. There was no guarantee. There never had been. She simply did not understand that until this moment. Safety was an illusion spawned by need. It had nothing to do with reality.

Now she knew reality: The die was cast into the arena of life with fickle whimsey. It favored no one;

161

it only appeared that way. We are all condemned to balance between the abyss and safety, never knowing from one moment to the next which way we will fall.

The only way to survive, Rachel learned, was to live on the edge with grace and to laugh when there is nothing left to lose.

"I thought we could get the money," Rachel overheard Serghei saying. "If I knew where the dump was, I'd just take some men, clean it out and be done with it."

"Excuse me for interrupting," Rachel said as she approached Serghei timidly. He was speaking with two other officers and she had always been cautious about interfering with the business of the camp.

Looking up, Serghei asked gruffly, "What is it you want?"

"Well," she began with a tentative smile. "I could not help overhearing what you were saying. Is it money you need? For something important?"

"Explosives are always important."

"Then perhaps I can help," she said evenly.

"How would that be?"

"I have some stones . . . a diamond. I will give it to you to purchase explosives."

"You have diamonds?"

"Yes."

"Show me," he said. Then he turned to the two men with whom he had been speaking. "I will go with her. And you," he fixed his eyes on them with a hard stare, "You will forget what you just heard. I have no doubt that there are those who will ask where we suddenly got the means to purchase explosives. We just got it, that is all. If I hear of anyone . . . anyone . . . sniffing around this woman's belongings, then I will know you told. And if this happens, I will tell you this: you will wish you have been caught in the act by Ustachi instead of me. Because what I will do to you will make those swine look like babies. Do you understand?"

"I understand," said one man, swallowing hard.

The second, too frightened to speak, simply nodded.

Walking beside Serghei to the cave, Rachel felt herself pulled to this man by invisible ties. She had never indicated her feelings, understanding the very clear code by which these people lived. There would be no liasons between men and women in the Partisans. It was not tolerated. Few people attempted to find out what would happen if they indulged in such frivoloties and were caught. Sex and love were simply put aside until the war was over.

Inside the cave, Jana slept on her straw mattress. Her recovery had been slow. The strength she had lost in her bout with typhoid had been considerable. It had taken almost two weeks for her even to feel capable of taking a short walk.

Every day, Marek visited. Sometimes he would bring her a small bunch of wildflowers that he had gathered in the meadow. Other times, he brought a colorful feather or a stone that had been washed smooth by the cold, mountain waters of the stream.

As her health returned, Marek would put her on his shoulders and take her for a walk. Each time, he would set her down a farther distance from the camp so that she could walk home. In this way, Jana's strength increased steadily.

Marek also tended her traps and often came in the evening with a rabbit in his hand, eager that his contribution to the meal would aid in her recovery.

Her convalescence was slow but steady. Even now, three weeks later, Jana still took long naps in the afternoon, too weary to make it through a whole day without the rest.

Jana awakened when she heard Rachel in the cave. She opened her eyes and was surprised to see Serghei there, also. Although he had visited often when she was sick, it was not his habit to come into the cave. Sometimes, Jana had the feeling he was avoiding them.

Jana watched silently as her grandmother bent over the satchel and cut the threads of the handle with her knife. The child had learned long before not to ask unnecessary questions that might get her in trouble.

Rachel felt the diamond drop into her hand. Then she stood and held it up to the light that filtered in through the mouth of the cave. A shower of color sparkled over the walls before Rachel handed the stone to Serghei.

"It is very beautiful," he said with an edge of surprise as he scrutinized the diamond. "Until now, I could not understand why people placed such value on them. But the light . . . the fire inside . . .

is extraordinary. How much is it worth?"

"What the market will bear," Rachel answered wryly. "Although, if a war were not being waged, if you are not forced to trade it, it would probably be worth an entire ammunition dump."

"That's nothing compared to the one that Buba gave the German soldier," Jana interjected with the enthusiastic naiveté of youth.

"You gave one to the German?"

"It was necessary," Rachel said coldly.

"It was a diamond ten times that size," Jana blundered on. "With pearls. From Charles Lewis Tiffany himself," she said, unconsciously mimicking her grandfather when he would tell her about the purchase of the brooch. There was an unmistakable air of pride in her words.

Serghei looked closely at Rachel, uncertain whether he was angry or just curious. "Why did you give it to him?"

"It was necessary," she repeated with cool firmness, clearly indicating that this was a subject he should not pursue.

Staring at the diamond he held in his hand, he tried to imagine what one ten times that size would look like, how it would feel. Then he asked softly, "Do you have more?"

Rachel hesitated only for a moment. "Yes. I have more."

"I see," he mumbled.

"And," she said, inhaling deeply, "they are yours if you need them."

"I would not do that. You will need them in the

future."

"Yes. But I might not have a future if it weren't for you, for the people here. We never know what we must do until the time comes that demands something new of us. The diamonds are yours. If you need them, just ask. I owe you our lives."

"Consider this payment in full."

Serghei looked directly into her eyes. Even in the dim light of the cave Rachel was transfixed. She could not speak. It is impossible, she told herself, not for the first time. Impossible.

"I must go now," Serghei said hoarsely. His voice was far away, his eyes connected to hers, still speaking silently. He turned to go, then hesitated. "After I see to the purchase of these explosives, in a week or two, we shall be going down to the valley for a big operation. We shall need everyone. Including you and Jana."

Rachel started to object about including Jana in anything that would involve the child in danger. But Rachel did not have a chance. Before she could utter a word, Serghei was gone.

During the next ten days, Jana and Rachel saw very little of Serghei. He remained at camp, but his time was taken up in quiet meetings and planning sessions with his most trusted officers.

When Rachel did see Serghei, it was just in passing. On those occasions, he would smile or nod, then hurry away as if he had important business to take care of. Even in the evenings, he was not to be seen. And Rachel began to feel a sense of loss—a loss of something she never really had.

In the late afternoon of the tenth day, Rachel saw him again. This time, however, he stopped to talk with her.

Throughout the day, the air had been thick with tension. Conversation was quicker, movement more brusk. It was as if an invisible conductor had increased the tempo of everyone's life.

"Tomorrow is the day," Serghei said to Rachel. "Until now, we have not had the quantity of explosives necessary to carry out this new objective. Thanks to you, we do."

"What is the objective?" Rachel inquired.

"One of the largest railroad bridges between north and south Yugoslavia. We plan to attack at night. Half the division will wage a diversionary battle two miles away. The other half—with me leading—will blow up the bridge. You and Jana will come with us. We will travel the night before, then wait through the day. After eliminating the guards, we shall set the explosives and blow up the bridge.

"We will take pack horses for ammunition and explosives. Jana will be allowed to ride. It will be her job to care for the horses before and during the battle. We cannot afford to leave an able-bodied person behind to do this. We will need everyone. But do not worry. She will be out of the way of the battle."

"Thank God," Rachel whispered.

Serghei looked down at the ground then, hesitating about his next words. "I must ask you to do something for me. For you. I want you to write down the names of your relatives that you mentioned, the ones who live in New York. I have left instructions that . . . should anything happen . . . Jana will be sent there after the war. Do you understand?"

"I understand," Rachel answered, her heart lurching into her throat. "But can you be certain that this will be done?"

"I can be certain. She will be flown with the British to Bari in Italy. There are Americans there."

There was no question of Rachel refusing to go. It was not even considered as a possibility. In these conditions, everyone was expected to do his part. There were no exceptions in this harsh world.

"We shall leave tomorrow night," Serghei said bruskly. Then he walked away, disappearing into the dimming light.

It was dark when Serghei returned. He had gone to the stream. The water was icy and numbing, and he was shivering with the chill of evening. Nevertheless, he had taken off his clothes and washed himself with a tiny sliver of soap he had saved, cursing when he was forced to put the same dirty clothes back onto his body. All this just diminished the stink, he thought wryly, it didn't eliminate it. Better this than nothing, though.

Returning to camp, he found Rachel washing tin plates that she and Jana had used for dinner. She was still hungry, since dinner this night had consisted of a thin gruel. At least we shall eat tomorrow. It's the only advantage of battle, she told herself as Serghei approached.

He sat down beside her and waited silently until she had finished her chores. He cleared his throat, as if he were gathering courage. Finally he spoke. "I have asked Marek to look after Jana tonight."

Stopping her work, Rachel looked at him. He's bathed, she thought as she saw his clean hands. "Why is that?" she asked.

Serghei spoke softly. "I have asked Marek to look after Jana if . . . you will come with me."

Rachel could feel her face flushing. Caught off guard, she did not answer immediately. She set the plates down. Then she said simply, "Yes, I will go with you."

"Meet me at the stream as soon as you can." He stood and walked casually away.

He was waiting in the shadow of a tree. She did not see him at first. Looking around, she wondered what to do. Then he stepped from the darkness and moved beside her. He had a down quilt rolled under one arm. His other hand was free, but he did not touch her. "Come," he said.

They walked silently for fifteen minutes. Rachel could feel him, feel the current running through the air from her hand to his. But she made no attempt to span the distance. She was too nervous. And frightened, she thought. Because this was the first time since . . . then.

Finally, he stopped walking. He spread the blanket on a bed made of pine needles, then turned to her. He was shaking when he touched her face, stroking it lightly with the back of his hand. Then he leaned over and kissed her ever so gently on her lips.

"I have wanted to kiss you since the first moment I saw you," he said.

Without thinking, her arms moved around his back. And they stood for a long time just holding each other.

"We need not hurry tonight," he whispered, his lips moving on hers. "We have time to . . . create our own memory."

It was awkward at first. Even funny. It was too cold to remove all their clothes, at least in the beginning. When they finally lay under the blanket next to each other, they could not stop touching, kissing, exploring. They were like children in their joy of discovery, in the pleasure they took in everything they did.

Their hands roamed over each other's bodies. Then, with a shock of recognition, she felt his hand moving up her thigh. There was no warning, just a flash of the German officer. The ground beneath her spun as she fought against the image that took hold of her. She felt as if she were suffocating. She wanted to scream, to cry out. She bit her lips in her effort to quell her fear.

The night was clear and cool, the light from the stars above filtering through the trees. She closed her eyes tightly, squeezing back the tears. Then she felt Serghei's hand on her face, gently smoothing the furrows of her brow.

"Was it so bad? With the German?" he asked. "Is it happening all over again?"

She could not speak.

"Will it be all right?" he whispered.

"I . . . don't know," she managed to say.

He put his arms around her then, held her close. "Until you know, we will do nothing. We can spend the night together, like this. That will be good."

Relieved and grateful, haunted by the mixed images of her past, she moved closer to him, fitting herself to his body as if she were the missing piece in a magical puzzle of love. They lay quietly together. Then, very slowly, she began to touch him all over. This time her caresses were fresh, unencumbered, only for Serghei. Slower still, he returned her touches, never moving on until he received the silent permission of her increasing desire.

Somehow, in a tangle both erotic and amusing, they took off the last of their clothes. Naked under the quilt, with no witness this time except the eyes of their own passion, they made love with perfect grace. There was no German officer, there was not even Josef. They belonged to another time. There was only this moment, this isolated instant that was captured by purity of feeling and nobility of desire. There was nothing else for them. There could not be. There was only now.

She was aching for him when he finally entered her. She thrust herself to him, taking and giving with renewed life. She was greedy now, greedy to experience the fullness of passion, the essence of loving that this man offered so freely. She floated in a continum of loving she had known all her life.

She refused to close her eyes, eager to take all the

171

moment, to make it hers. She watched his face tighten, the expression alone taking her to the edge. Her mouth open, gasping for air, gasping with pleasure, she was his. And he was hers.

They lay together loving throughout the night, clinging to each other as if their touches alone could hold back the dawn. In the still darkness of early morning, Serghei spoke.

"We must go now. We must. But I want you to know that no matter what happens in the future, where ever we go, I shall remember this night until the moment I die."

Chapter 8

It was dusk when they started out. The wind had blown strong throughout the day and the slate sky hung thick and low, hovering over the tops of the surrounding mountains.

Fifty-three men and women and one child travelled that evening. Silent and single file, they made their way cautiously down to the valley, then up the mountain on the other side.

Their objective was a bridge spanning a high gorge, its steel girders forming a lacy support for the railroad.

Having received permission to lead the pack horses, Marek kept a wary eye on Jana. Although she had taken a long nap that afternoon, by midnight, she was nodding and swaying as she tried to stay seated on the horse she rode. Stopping for a moment, Marek took a sleeping bag and rolled it in front of Jana, securing it to the saddle. Then, tying her to the horse by means of a rope passed around her waist and under the animal, he showed her how to lean forward and sleep while he led her horse.

It was a difficult journey, but not one single person complained. They knew what had to be done. They knew that if they accomplished their goal, they would effectively disrupt railroad traffic from north to south in this area for the remainder of the war. And if they failed, they would most likely die.

Around two in the morning, they stopped at a *katuni*, a crude hut built by shepherds in the high meadows for shelter during the summer months. There, they rested for twenty minutes and picked up additional supplies of food that had been stored there previously in preparation for their journey to and from the bridge.

Around four in the morning, they came to a precipice that looked down upon a winding mountain road. Serghei, in the lead, was startled when he saw an undulating snake of dim lights in the distance.

"Transport trucks," he whispered to his second in command. "We cannot afford to pass up this opportunity."

Serghei grabbed a pack, then motioned to five men to follow him down the steep side of the mountain. They scurried over the rocks and ledges as if they had taken lessons from mountain goats, every step sure, every movement instinctively calculated.

The men understood precisely what they had to do. No questions were asked, no instructions given. Within minutes, they had scattered three dozen sharp steel spikes on the road at a precipitous hairpin turn.

Rachel watched from above, anxious and frightened, as the men climbed back up the side of the mountain. She willed them to return to safety before the trucks hit the spikes and their tires exploded. She knew when that happened, the vehicles would careen crazily all over the road. Then, from those trucks that did not go over the edge, scores of armed men would appear shooting at anything that moved.

When Serghei finally returned, he walked past Rachel and whispered, "It is all right. Distances are deceiving in the mountains. It will be half an hour before the trucks reach the turn. By then, we shall be safely hidden."

Rachel felt as if he could read her mind.

"I'm glad," she exhaled in relief. "I'm glad it's over."

As if he did not hear her response, Serghei continued. "Ah how I wish we could be there when the trucks hit the spikes. There is probably a lot of ammunition in them. Ours for the taking, were it not for the fact that it would give away our presence. This is one gift we shall have to pass up," he said, regret in his voice.

He hesitated for one last moment, watching the lights of the trucks below as they snaked methodically towards their destiny. Then he turned to the rest of the group and motioned for them to hurry on.

They walked for another hour until they came upon an overgrown mass of trees and bushes. Moving to a particularly high pine, Serghei parted its full lower branches and disappeared. Then others followed silently behind him.

"This is a special hiding place," Marek explained in a whisper to Rachel. "Many of the peasants have clung to these secret places for generations. Each family has a different refuge, carefully guarded, totally hidden, where they can flee in times of trouble. Serghei has known about this one for a long time, saving it for the moment when we came to the bridge."

As they emerged on the other side of the trees, they passed through a narrow opening in the rocks. On the other side, pristine and unsullied, was a tiny valley. No more than thirty feet deep, it was a box canyon, surrounded on all sides by high stone walls.

"It is beautiful," Rachel whispered as she stood at the entrance.

The sun was just rising, casting dull purple shadows across the floor of the valley. Evergreens rose tall at its edges, forming a natural shelter for those who sought refuge.

"We must stay under the trees," instructed Serghei. "No one is to go out from under the branches and risk being seen by a plane. We will stay here for the day and move out after dark. The bridge is only two miles away."

The group settled down quietly and spread their blankets for desperately-needed sleep. Several of the men and women passed around bottles of plum brandy.

"For warmth," Marek said to Rachel after he took

a swig and passed her the bottle. "And for sleep."

Rachel took a generous gulp, appreciating the clear fiery liquid that warmed the inside of her mouth, then left a hot trail all the way down to her stomach after she swallowed.

Rachel and Jana slept most of the day, awakening only to eat their early dinner of stew and biscuits.

At dusk, Serghei gathered the group around him and explained what had to be done.

"There is no way we can set the explosives and blow up the bridge without the guards seeing us. It is watched from above as well as below. There are sentry posts at either end of the bridge," he explained as he drew a picture in the dirt with his knife. "Because of that, we shall have to eliminate them first. The longer we can maintain silence, the better chance we have for surprise. We must kill silently and swiftly."

Serghei pointed to three men. "You know where the telephone wire is. We must cut it first. And remember to bring the wire back with you so that communications cannot be restored too quickly."

During this monologue, Jana snuggled safely in Marek's arms. Marek sat next to Rachel and translated for her from Serbo-Croatian to German.

After he had completed his instructions and answered questions pertaining to various tactical technicalities, Serghei approached Jana. He touched her face gently, wiping the wisps of hair gently from her brow.

"I have a special job for you," he said. "You must stay here and look after the horses. I have a bag of grain for you to feed them. Do not allow them to become restless, to make any noise or to pull away from their tethers. Just take care of them quietly and we shall return by morning."

Rachel watched the color drain from Jana's face.

"Serghei," Rachel said softly. "You cannot leave her alone all night in the dark. She will be terrified. It is cruel."

"War is cruel," Serghei replied, his voice hard in the dismissal of Rachel's plea. "She will do what she must do. Like the rest of us."

Rachel accepted his response without question. It was not possible to do otherwise. Serghei was their leader and they were bound to do what he said. And so she turned her attention away from her own anxiety and set about giving Jana encouragement.

Rachel smiled at Jana then. "You can do what he asks," she said. "Serghei would not ask you to do a job unless he believed in you."

Jana nodded, then said in a squeaky voice, "I shall do what I must do." Lions and tigers, she thought. They will come and get me in the night. And ghosts, too. Please, Serghei, she pleaded silently. Please change your instructions.

"I love you, Jana," Rachel said. "You are very brave to do this for us. Just remember that we will return to you in the morning."

"Buba?" Jana said in a quivering voice. She appeared small in her fear. "I love you, Buba. I will always love you."

Jana looked at Marek. She felt safe in his arms, protected from all the demons that haunted her in

178

the dark. "And I love you, too," she whispered into his ear.

Marek hugged her and then stood up. "We must go now, Little One," he said gently. "But before we are off, I want to tell you something to remember the rest of your life."

Jana nodded mutely. Her face was pale and her eyes were wide with fear.

"When we return for you in the morning, you will be here and you will be very proud of yourself. You will have done something very brave and you will know for all the days of your life that there is nothing you cannot do, nothing that you need fear any longer."

"Marek?" she said meekly.

"Yes, Little One."

"I'm already afraid. I'm . . . afraid of the dark."

Marek thought for a moment. He walked over to a pack horse. He returned with a flashlight and handed it to Jana. "I'll tell you what I'll do. I will leave you my lucky torch. You may keep it with you while I am gone. But you must only use it if there is an emergency. And, if you do turn it on, put your hand over the end like this," he said, demonstrating, "So that just a tiny bit of light escapes."

"Is it really lucky?" Jana asked, ready to believe anything that would remove some of the stark dread she felt.

"Indeed it is. So you must use it very carefully. Its magic is powerful. Do you promise to treat it with respect?"

"I promise," Jana answered solemnly.

Marek put his arms around her and hugged her fiercely. It could be the last time, he thought. Then he stood up and joined the single file of men and women who had already begun to move out of the hidden valley.

As Serghei passed Jana, he smiled and ruffled her head of short hair. "I'll bring you a medal in the morning. A medal for being so brave."

Jana waved once before they all disappeared, struggling to prevent the tears from flowing to the surface. "Your tears must be saved until we are safe in America," she remembered Rachel telling her. It seemed years since they were in the hiding place in Budapest. And then — with the coming of the dark — it suddenly seemed to Jana as if it had only happened yesterday.

Rachel and Marek shouldered their share of the explosives that the horses had borne until now. This burden, combined with the darkness and the danger of the steep and narrow path, made the movement of the Partisans slow. Marek spoke only once as he walked in front of Rachel.

"Serghei asked me to stay with you until this is over," he said. Then he was silent.

They could hear the water rushing in the river long before they saw it. When Rachel reached the top of the gorge through which the river flowed, she shuddered when she looked down. She could not see the bottom clearly. Occasionally, a wispy poof of white water would make a brief appearance in the darkness, then disappear.

A faint light from the sentry posts at either end of the span made the bridge look like a gossamer web, far too delicate to withstand the weight of a train laden with arms and ammunition and troops.

Before moving down the side of the gorge to a more advantageous position, Marek cautioned Rachel that even a falling rock would alert the sentries; that she must be extraordinarily careful in her descent.

Having received their detailed instructions beforehand, they moved towards their objective in perfect silence. Terrified, Rachel clung to the rocky side of the gorge as she inched slowly toward her destination. Behind her, she could feel Marek's hand touch her occasionally in a gesture of comfort.

They were close now, almost fifty men and women clinging to a small abutment above the bridge. Without a word, fifteen of them continued on down the side of the gorge, three to cut the telephone wires and the others to take care of the guards.

Rachel and Marek stayed behind with the rest, fanning out to take their positions, ready to fire if the plan went awry.

With her rifle propped securely on a rock in front of her, Rachel watched Serghei make his way down to the sentry post. She prayed for his safety, willed him to take care of himself, not to forego limited success for the possibility of a risky but total victory. She knew this was a futile form of wishing, but she continued to do it anyway.

Serghei had barely spoken to her since that last moment together in the woods. She understood, however, that this was the way it had to be. What they had shared only the night before had belonged outside time. This is what is real, she thought, as Serghei disappeared from her sight.

Rachel sat quietly and waited. She did not know how many minutes passed before chaos exploded down below. She had lost track of time. It seemed only minutes earlier that the men had gone down to set the charges on the bridge. And now, with the first blinding explosion, she returned to the present. The noise, unnatural in its abruptness, echoed off the steep walls of the gorge. Red and white tracers streaked toward her.

She took aim at the sentry post nearest her, and sighted carefully down the long barrel of her rifle. Then she pulled the trigger.

There were few stars to comfort her. Nor was there moonlight to shine down into the tiny hidden valley where Jana was more alone than she would most likely be for the rest of her life. Just a sliver of a new moon and an occasional star that shone through the curtain of clouds bore testament to the fact that light and illumination were still part of her world.

She clung tenaciously to her magic flashlight. Even at her age, Jana understood the risk she would take were she to give in to her fear and slip the switch silently forward on the flashlight. Discovery could signal the introduction to an abomination for which she could have no defense. She had learned she could no longer expect concessions because she was a child. She was playing a grown-up's game and would surely pay a grown-up's price if she were discovered.

Walking among the horses, she spoke softly to them, patting their soft noses and offering them grain she carried in a canvas bag. She dreaded the possibility that one of the horses might neigh, the sound alerting strangers lurking in the dark to her brave but vulnerable presence.

The more she thought about discovery, the more terrified she became. Even worse, she grew increasingly convinced that no one would ever come for her, that she would be lost forever in the mountains. Then, abandoned to the elements, she would die alone.

Time stretched across a chasm without end, a yawning abyss that held no hope beyond darkness. She could feel her shoulders tighten, could feel her tormented nerves committing painful tricks upon her unsuspecting body.

Hallucinations born of terror swept across her vision. Each time a shadow moved, she wanted to scream. Each time a bird cried out or a horse stirred, she quivered with fear. But through it all, she refused to turn on her flashlight. For she truly believed she would use up the only magic she possessed, that there would be none left for something even more terrifying that was yet to come.

Desolate and alone, her insides writhing with fear,

she finally backed herself into a shallow crevice formed of boulders. There, she sat down and prepared to continue her vigil, ever alert for a wolf or a lion. Or worse yet, a vampire.

Desperately drowsy, her eyelids drooped. She had not been asleep for more than a few minutes when she heard the first shot. The returning volley reverberated through the mountains, bouncing off walls of sheer rock and green valleys. She knew the battle had begun and she prayed for the safety of those she loved.

Looking toward the sound of the battle, she could detect an occasional flash of light in the sky. Even though it offered her no additional illumination, the very sight of the light was a comfort. Strangely beautiful to her parched senses, she recognized the irony that the end result of this lamentable beauty was death.

Death, itself, was no longer a stranger to Jana, an abstract concept to be casually dismissed. She had killed enough animals to know its meaning; she had seen enough dead and dying Partisans to understand its vengeance. The one area in which she managed to maintain total denial was in her blind conviction that Rachel, Marek and Serghei would come through the battle unscathed. To think otherwise would have destroyed her.

Jana knew she was virtually helpless against an attacker. That single thought, boiling inside her, nauseated her. Her stomach churned with anxiety, increasing until she vomited, spewing forth all her fear in a foaming mess. Terrified that she was losing

184

part of her insides, that she was literally spilling forth the organs that kept her alive, Jana gripped the flashlight with horror. When she finished vomiting, she began to shake uncontrollably.

She sat clutching her knees, trying to fend off visions that came increasingly her way; visions of torment, visions of death.

She tried to think of Budapest, of home, of her parents. But these things were gone. She felt herself slipping, being pulled into that dark lonely place where the sun never shines.

Instead of marching forward, time seemed to spin in a self-perpetuating funnel, creeping neither forward nor backward. Suspended between two ticks of the clock, she felt herself moving to embrace death. Just as a soldier in battle learns to function normally by resigning himself to dying—and thus discovering a place where he can live—Jana slipped into the alien comfort of being nowhere, of sensing nothing. There was a blessed deliverance in this absence of life, an acceptance of circumstances without question. For the first time that night, she could finally take a deep breath.

Thus, she endured the night, the significance of her own survival having totally lost its meaning.

Just before the first pink shadows of dawn insinuated themselves into the hidden valley, the Partisans returned. Lost in a dreamless sleep, Jana was not even aware of it.

She had not heard the final explosion, the one

185

that destroyed the bridge. Although Rachel would tell her about it later—about how the delicate span seemed to hang in space after the explosion, suspended by some insolent magic—she was not even aware of this fiery finale.

Marek was the one to find Jana nestled in the small crevice of the rock next to the horses. Her head resting lopsided against the rock, she clutched the flashlight in her lap as if it were a life preserver.

Leaning over to awaken her gently, Marek touched her cheek and whispered, "Wake up, Little One. We're back."

Jana's eyelids fluttered with the confusion of emerging from nothing, and it took her a few moments before she could focus on Marek. She blinked once and stared uncomprehendingly at him. Then she said, "I did not use it once. Not even once, Marek. I saved all the magic for you."

She handed him the flashlight in a mechanical manner. He took it and set it aside. Then he picked her up. He was frightened at her lack of animation.

"Did you feed the horses?" he asked in an effort to evoke a genuine response.

"Yes."

Her voice was dull, detached, as if she had travelled through uncharted territory to a place where darkness and light meet in a bewildering ether. The sound of her voice alarmed Marek. He had heard it before, that terrible dullness born of terror and dread; that dazed response, as if life and animation have been surreptitiously sucked from the victim and replaced with a reasonable facsimile.

186

Marek understood that Jana had simply run out of feeling. In one unspeakable night, hope had been annihilated and loneliness had been ground into abandonment. She had endured for as long as she could before finally caving in under the weight of her own terror. Then she just went to sleep. Her circuits overloaded, she sought the solace of oblivion, too young to understand that this was the closest she could come to the final delivery of death without actually crossing over into its waiting arms.

Marek understood instinctively that the longer this wretched state was allowed to fester within her, the longer it would take to recover. But he did not know how to exorcise it. He did not know how to make her feel again.

Fate knew, however. Unfortunately, fate knew.

The first people to straggle back into the hidden valley were some of those who had come through the night unscathed. They walked slowly, sluggishly, without hope, without dread. They simply were.

Behind this group came the walking wounded.

Jana watched them come through the parting in the trees. Her expression was that of a curiously disinterested onlooker. It was as if she were watching a film of the action, rather than being directly involved in it. She was vaguely aware that she was waiting for her grandmother. But her anticipation had been diluted by the terror of the night, and she was incapable of calling up any passion or interest from her depleted emotional reserves. It never even

187

occurred to Jana to ask about Rachel.

Behind those who could walk came more wounded. They were carried on litters by those who were capable of bearing this additional burden as they climbed the steep paths back to their temporary refuge.

When Jana finally saw Rachel walking alongside a litter, she was reminded of the time she first ventured out on the street with her grandmother after they had been ordered to wear the yellow star on their clothing. She remembered the way her grandmother walked then, the proud carriage that refused to indicate her pain, the dignity that refused to acknowledge this order as a humiliation.

Jana saw something of this now in Rachel. Somehow, she knew her grandmother was hiding something, that her stance was a deliberate overlay that covered deep pain. But still Jana could not respond. Instead, she merely blinked her eyes in a subdued reaction, focusing on the object of her security with bland relief.

Jana watched quietly as the litter next to Rachel was lowered gently to the ground. She watched as her grandmother bent over the figure lying so still, her shoulders hunched now, already rounded in the posture of mourning.

Jana stood up, curiosity drawing her back into life. Taking Marek's hand, she walked silently towards the litter.

She looked down at Serghei. The expression on his face was like nothing Jana had ever seen: a pagan agony had transformed Serghei's features into a kind of splendid nobility, as if any moment he would jump from his bed and, with one sweep of his powerful arm, banish death forever from this hidden valley. His eyes were open, burnished with defiance. There was even a hint of a smile as Jana came into his line of vision.

Serghei's lips moved, but no sound emerged. This strengthened Jana's impression that she was, indeed, tangled in the midst of a horrible silent movie.

Rachel bent over Serghei then, her ear close to his lips.

"In my hand . . . for Jana," he whispered hoarsely.

Looking down, Rachel saw that he clutched something in his fist, something he had carried throughout this last, agonizing journey. Rachel touched Serghei's hand. He opened his fist, and a small, heavy object fell to the ground beside him.

Picking it up, Rachel stared at it and was puzzled.

"He promised Jana a medal," Marek whispered, his words choked with tears.

Marek leaned over and picked up the medal that had been ripped from the uniform of the enemy just hours earlier. The cloth from the coat still clung persistently to the back. Then, in a silent gesture that carried the full gravity of the moment in every move, Marek kneeled and pinned the medal solemnly in Jana's coat.

"A medal for your bravery," he said.

Jana looked down and moved her hand to touch it. Understanding how difficult it must have been for Serghei to have taken it, Jana was touched by his promise and its fulfillment. She pulled the jacket away from her body so she could see it more clearly. Suddenly tears stung her eyes. She gasped for air. As if her oxygen supply had been cut off during the endless night, she inhaled in great sobbing gulps, the impact of her pain hitting her with full, undiluted force. Then, turning to Marek, she buried herself in the safety and love of his arms, a flood of feeling and loss overwhelming every nerve ending in her tiny, fragile body.

She did not see Rachel bend over Serghei. She did not see how her grandmother placed her lips on Serghei's ear and whispered, "I love you."

"Yes," he managed to say. "Love. We were . . . good together. It was . . . a lifetime in a night."

"A lifetime," Rachel repeated, struggling to maintain her facade of calm in the face of Serghei's agony. "Hush now," she whispered, only to him. "Hush now, my love. I'll stay with you."

Rachel sat on the ground next to him, holding his hand, wiping his brow. She would not leave him. When the others dressed his wound and the stench of entrails permeated the clean, crisp mountain air with a putrid smell, she put her face close to his and tried to distract him from his pain with soothing words of encouragement. She was a mixture of a mother soothing her child and a woman saying good-bye to her love.

Throughout the day she remained at his side, fearful that if she left him even for a moment, he would die alone.

But it was a long dying, one in which agony was

ambushed by Serghei's lust for living and loving. The man would not give up. It was as if he were determined to hold on to Rachel for as long as he possibly could, to hold their loving above death in an act of life-affirming defiance.

In a battle with death worthy of a legendary hero, Serghei refused to bow to the inevitable.

Once he spoke. "I'm sorry to die in front of you," he said to Rachel, his voice barely audible, his eyes softening when he was able to focus clearly on her. "A man should never die in front of the woman he loves. It spoils what went before."

"Never," whispered Rachel, tears glistening in her eyes.

Near the end, Marek took Jana over to Serghei. They bent to him in silence and kissed his deeply lined face. Then they left. As if by mutual consent, everyone in the camp drifted away from Serghei and Rachel. The aura around them created the effect of an exclusively shared intimacy, as if in some way they were making love and should be accorded the appropriate privacy.

Rachel felt her reserve crumbling, felt another part of her dying as she touched this extraordinary man beside her. Once, when she could not bear the pain of his departing for one more minute, she looked at him, begging him with her eyes to stay, begging him to find a miracle and be with her always.

In the late afternoon Serghei looked at her. For an unguarded moment, the mist cleared from his eyes, making room for such ineffable regret that Rachel thought her heart would shatter at the sight of it.

"Ah, Rachel," he said clearly, only to her. "I'm leaving you now. And . . . I . . . do . . . not . . . want . . . to . . . go."

Then a strange cry swept away the illusion of life from his eyes, clearing the air with its lingering power. A brazen protest, it was the anguished lament of a man spitting in the eye of death. Barbarian and profound, it was the defiant cry of a rogue.

It was the sound of Serghei dying.

Chapter 9

There were at least ten men in the company—perhaps even more, had circumstances favored them—who would happily have shot their commanding officer in the back had they seen his departure.

As it was, with the chaos of the Russians breaking through the line, the constant interference of the refugees attempting to flee the battle, and the desperate efforts to save one's own life, that particular opportunity was denied the soldiers.

Leutnant Walther simply did not follow the men he ordered into battle. It was that simple. He waited for the right moment and walked away. Wearing the long, tattered overcoat he had procured earlier to hide his uniform, he joined the writhing mass of refugees and disappeared.

It was as easy as that.

For his journey home, Walther travelled light. He carried gold, diamonds and food. That was all. He walked quickly on the Autobahn, for it was a bitter cold winter, and he did not want to be on the road any longer than necessary.

Grateful his home had been spared during the

long war years, Walther looked forward to the two tiny rooms in the middle of the city where he could sleep on a soft bed and warm himself close to the cast iron stove.

He did not know it at the time, but most of the swelling mass of refugees who crowded the road on which he travelled were heading towards the same ill-fated city as he was: Dresden. The entire country now looked to that fabled city for safety. It was a place the Allies could not possibly construe as a center of industry, which would make it an automatic target for bombs.

All of Germany felt that since Oxford had been spared the terrors of the Luftwaffe, the Allies would do the same for Dresden, a city vast in culture and treasures, museums and cathedrals. The citizens also presumed that this grand city would be the postwar capitol of Germany, an additional reason for its being saved from bombing. Thus, hundreds of thousands of refugees fled to this peaceful haven, swelling the population to the bursting point.

Indeed, the German General Staff felt so secure about Dresden's continued immunity from the horrors of war, it ordered the flak batteries to be moved to other war zones where they could be more useful. As a consequence of this foolish decision, the city was entirely defenseless.

When Walther arrived at his home after five days of walking in treacherous cold, he began to have doubts about whether he would be able to find enough food to sustain himself. But, fingering the gold chains in his pocket which he could cut in pieces when he made a purchase, he knew he at least had the means to buy the necessities.

He sighed deeply as he placed the key in the lock of his parent's apartment door, fearful his face would frighten his mother.

But his mother was not there. Instead, he confronted a stranger.

The woman was so involved in trying to start a fire in the stove with only two sticks of wood, she did not hear him enter.

"Who are you?" Walther demanded in his most imposing military manner.

With a shocked cry, the woman turned to him.

"I said 'Who are you?' " repeated Walther.

"Gretchen. My name is Gretchen," she uttered.

"What are you doing here?"

"I might ask you the same question," she answered with more than a touch of insolence.

"This apartment belongs to me."

"Oh . . . you are the Walther's son," Gretchen said, nodding her head.

"Where are my parents?"

"Dead," she answered matter-of-factly. "They couldn't get enough fuel and food, I'm told. Anyway, my aunt and uncle live next door and managed to get me in here."

"Then go back to your aunt and uncle," Walther ordered.

"I'll do nothing of the kind. This is my place now. I've been living here since January. Almost fifteen weeks. You weren't here. So it is mine."

Walther looked at her. She wasn't so bad, he

thought. Could be worse. She had thick blonde hair grimy from lack of washing, which she wore in a single braid that hung almost to her waist. Her skin was too fair and pink for his taste, but she had a well-formed nose and mouth. It was her eyes that bothered him: They were small, set too close together.

"You may stay," Walther said abruptly.

"*I* may stay?" she said, her arrogance gaining momentum. "I am the one who should say that to you."

"Be my guest," he said with a crooked smile.

She looked hard at him. "Can you pay?" she asked.

"I can pay," he answered, disgusted with himself. He wondered why he had not thrown her out immediately. He knew, of course, that he wanted a woman and that this was probably the only opportunity he would have.

"Can you pay with food?" she asked. "I'm hungry."

Walther looked at her, his eyes burning into her insolence. "The question is not whether *I* can pay," he said. "The question is, can *you* pay?"

"Yes," she whispered, her eyes narrowing as she looked at the floor. "Yes," she repeated. "I can pay."

Around ten o'clock on the night of February 13th, the third air raid sounded in the streets and alleys of Dresden. The first two air raids — the previous October and January — were considered Allied mistakes, for there was simply no reason to bomb the city. And so the citizens continued to live in the illusion that they were safe.

Thus, in February when they heard the sirens, there was no great rush to the shelters. Even though the radio urged them to take cover, the people could not believe they would be harmed. How could they know that they were the target for the most wicked and inhumane bombing raid ever deliberately conceived in the mind of man. It was unthinkable.

But the unthinkable had begun. And it was no mistake. Everything that happened that night and the following day was planned. The destruction of Dresden was carefully planned in advance, taking into account previous experience and scientific principle. In fourteen hours, a monster was created by Great Britain and America that would make Hiroshima look like an act of mercy.

Gretchen was naked, lying on the bed next to Walther, when the alarm sounded. He was still partially clothed, having just enjoyed pretending he had taken her against her will. But the plain fact was that these two had reached a business agreement during the past ten days.

"Fritz feeds and Gretchen fucks," was what she would say to him, insinuating her hips persuasively.

Grateful to have a full belly for the first time in a year and a half, Gretchen made it her business to discover exactly what this maimed clown wanted. Then she proceeded to give it to him. The fact that he was brutal meant little to her. Although she might have preferred gentler sex, when Walther ordered her on her hands and knees, she did it. She already knew that hungry was something she never wanted to be again. Bruises were a fair trade as far as she was concerned.

"I suppose we should go to the basement," Walther said laconically as he listened to the wail of the siren. They dressed slowly, then left the apartment, making certain they carried all their valuables with them.

On their way down the stairs, Walther stopped and looked out a window on the landing. He was mesmerized by the scene. The entire city was lit up in green and white light. Just moments before, the first wave of planes had flown over the city and dropped illuminated parachute flares. There were no bombs. Then, as Walther watched, Mosquito marker planes followed, dropping red flares to indicate particular targets that should be bombed. Had this not been so serious, one might have mistaken this Shrove Tuesday for Mardi Gras. It was, indeed, beautiful.

But when Walther saw the flares, an alarm went off in his head. He knew, beyond doubt, that the city was in for it. Yet, he still insisted on watching, especially since he could not see any red markers near his own house.

Walther sent Gretchen to the basement. But he stayed by the window, awed by the supernatural beauty of the moment. He clutched the brooch in his fist, feeling invincible as long as he held onto it. Then he watched horrified as the Lancaster bombers moved in on the city.

He knew Dresden was helpless, that there were few planes for defense and absolutely no anti-aircraft guns. It was a city swollen with refugees, hundreds of thousands of people crammed into its boundaries for safety.

He did not understand the purpose of the raid; could not fathom why the Allies would want to destroy it. Nor would he ever understand it.

Understanding did not matter, however, when he felt the impact of the first eight thousand pound bomb explode. He ducked just before the window in front of him shattered, spraying glass everywhere.

For one stunned moment, he did not know what to think. Then, in a flash of understanding, he knew: fire storm.

That knowledge sent him scurrying to the basement. Even though he loathed the thought of being trapped in a small airless room, he had no choice.

The basement was filled with less than fifty people when he arrived. The room was eerily quiet. Grateful this was a small apartment house so he was not jammed in like a sardine, Walther immediately sought out Gretchen and took her to a spot next to the wall that formed a common wall with the basement in the adjoining building.

Much of Dresden was comprised of attached houses stretching for blocks in every direction. The only real preparation the city had made for a bombing attack was to insist that every common wall between basements be thinned. That way, these wall breaches, as they were called, could be broken down. If one were trapped in a basement, the solution was to break through the wall into the basement next door and thus escape. It was possible to travel the length of an entire block in that manner, eventually finding an exit.

Walther knew that, in the event of a full-fledged fire storm, this would be their only hope.

He had first heard the term "fire storm" after the Allied bombing of Hamburg. This first storm had been accidentally created. But the Allies learned their lesson well. The theory of this kind of bombing raid is simple: the first planes drop illuminated parachute flares to light up the city. The second planes mark the targets. The next planes drop high explosive bombs in order to break windows and roofs of houses. The next wave of bombs to be dropped is comprised of incendiaries. Falling on the already exposed houses, the incendiary bombs immediately set fire to the drapes and rugs in exposed areas. The object of this is to start so many little fires that the fire brigades cannot possible control them. Gradually, these small separate fires come together to form one massive inferno that covers several square miles. It is at this point that the true fire storm begins.

Once the fires have come together, all hope is lost. The fires of hell could be no worse. Because out of this unbelievably massive furnace, a literal tornado of wind and flame is born. The rising heat, like a giant chimney, requires such an immense amount of oxygen that it sucks all the oxygen from the cooler air nearby. This suction is so powerful that it causes gale force winds. Hence, the name fire storm. But this storm does not only suck oxygen: the winds are so intense that they suck in whatever else is in the area: children, adults, furniture.

The major death toll, however, comes not from this hideous suction; it comes from asphyxiation from carbon monoxide fumes. Death in this manner causes side effects so bizarre that the human mind cannot imagine it. The scene after the storm looks as if it had been created in the mind's eye of a mad surrealist painter; for the fumes cause the bodies to turn bright colors, transforming them into orange, blue, and green.

However, this manner of dying, so obscenely colorful, is preferable to being trapped in a shelter. In the basement there are no flames. But the heat can reach the unbelievable temperature of 1000 degrees farenheit. In such heat, bodies do not simply die. Some are carbonized without a flame ever touching them, and they simply disintegrate into mere heaps of ashes. Others melt into undulating globs of viscous human liquid.

Two hours after the first waves of bombing stopped, Walther could feel the heat beginning to build up alarmingly in the basement where he had sought shelter. Incredibly, he felt somehow bound to these people with whom he had spent the last several hours. Without understanding what was happening, a tiny spark of humanity kindled within him, a phoenix of feeling rising from his emotional ashes.

He called the people in the basement over to him and tried to explain what would happen to them if they were to stay in there. But the horrors he outlined were so hideous that not one person in the room could bring himself or herself to believe this ugly, grotesque man.

"You're no expert!" shouted one frightened woman. "Who are you to tell us things like this?"

A man joined her. "Look at you! You've nothing to lose if you go up there. We do."

"I'll never go up there," Gretchen whispered hoarsely. "Never!" She shuddered, fearful of more bombs falling on the city.

"Can't you feel the heat?" Walther asked contemptuously. "Can't you?" he repeated, grabbing her arm. "Don't be a fool!"

"Yes. I feel the heat. But it's not so bad that I can't stand it."

"Listen to me!" he said desperately, grabbing her by the arm. "If it continues to get hotter in here, you will eventually be roasted like a pig on a spit."

Gretchen looked down at her arm. "Let go of me," she said.

When he refused to do it, she spit at him.

At that moment, the small spark of humanity that had flared so briefly in Walther died. There was no warmth left inside him and there was no way it would ever be rekindled. He simply let go of Gretchen's arm, turned his back on her and picked up an axe. Then he swung it against the wall. When he had broken through, he did not even bother to look back before stepping over the rubble into the adjoining basement.

Walther travelled the distance of four houses in

202

that manner until he felt the air grow slightly cooler. In the last house, with no one following him, he made his way out the basement and up the stairs to the ground floor.

Then, with dread, he opened the door to the outside. He was assaulted by an unearthly roar. It sounded as if a train were going to burst through the house at any moment. For a moment he could not focus. Then, when he could see, all his fears were confirmed: At the very moment when he put his head out the door, a woman holding onto a baby carriage flew past him with a hideous whooshing sound. For a frozen instant in time, he could hear the baby's cry before it flew past and was sucked into the huge furnace that was no more than fifty yards away.

Understanding there was no going back, Walther got down on his belly and snaked his way down the stoop onto the sidewalk. The suction of the fire tugged at his body. But he held tight. Gripping the iron railings that lined the houses on the block, had made his way down the street away from the fire.

Everything seemed unreal, as if he had been pitched into a hideous fantasy. The air raid sirens had been silenced. There was only the roar, the hideous incessant roar.

By this time, other citizens of Dresden had begun to crawl out from under the flaming rubble. Those who could, fled from the flames like ants from a water-logged ant hill. It had been three hours since the attack had begun, and the people, stunned by the extent of the damage and the shock of the

Allied betrayal, assumed this was the end of the bombing. But they were wrong.

The Allies calculated correctly that, by this time, the few German fighters capable of combatting an attack would be on the ground refueling. Furthermore, the fire brigades in the city would be fully occupied; The original bombing runs had seen to that. Finally, after three hours, the city should be burning well enough so the fire would light the way for more planes. They would not need to expend any further effort on the use of flares.

Walther did not hear the planes coming. Few people did. The roar of the storm obscured the sound. Therefore, the Lancaster bombers—which had flown for ten hours to reach Dresden—could drop their blockbuster bombs and thermite incendiaries (whose sole purpose was to scatter more fire) with impunity.

It was only when Walther heard the explosion and felt its impact that he knew the city was targeted for even worse terror. Looking around, Walther had only one thought: If I die and go to hell, it cannot possibly hold any surprises for me.

Since Walther had managed to make his way to the edge of the existing fires, he was dismayed to see that the British were intent on expanding the parameters of the inferno. Methodically, with the light from the burning city illuminating their way, the massive bombs continued to be dropped around the edge of the existing fires.

It is said that some of the pilots and crew of those bombers felt abject pity for the Germans trapped below. But they did their duty and dropped the bombs. From the air, the city was a flaming holocaust. Rainbow hues of light were cast for a distance of two hundred miles. Every Englishman in the planes above knew exactly what was happening to the helpless civilians below. Some begged forgiveness before dropping their bombs.

As soon as Walther heard the new wave of bombs, he began to run, scrambling over the rubble as fast as he could. He knew his only chance was to outdistance the widening perimeter of the fire. Flaming embers fell on him, burning his clothes and searing his skin. He screamed, his twisted mouth opened in what appeared to be a silent cry.

Frenzied, Walther stumbled on, not knowing where he was going, what he was doing. The hideous noise of the bombs, the terror of the fires stalked him mercilessly.

With luck once more leading him, he eventually reached the Grosser Garten, the large park of Dresden. It was untouched by the surrounding fires. There were bomb craters everywhere. But for some reason — most likely its lush greeness — it was not burning. Screaming with relief, Walther dived into a deep crater near the zoo and huddled his body into a ball. It was there he spent the remainder of the night.

It was dawn when he opened his eyes. Looking up, Walther was awed to see a column of smoke almost three miles high snaking its yellow finger into a black, defeated sky. He was covered with ashes and bits of pieces of paper. Strange, unearthly sounds punched holes in the eerie air. It took him a moment to realize that these were the screams of trapped zoo animals and frenzied people. There was little distinction between the two. Already the smell of death surrounded him, its stench more pungent and sickening than he had ever known.

His legs shaking, he stood up. There was nothing but devastation in every direction. The carnage was complete. A strange sound assaulted his senses and he looked towards it: a flock of vultures, escaped from the zoo's destroyed aviary, swooped down from the smoking sky and landed on a black panther. Then they began to pick huge hunks of bloody flesh from the body of the wounded animal. Screaming in protest, the panther writhed. But it was helpless and could not prevent the birds from continuing their gory feast.

Chunks of flesh and pieces of paper continued to float down from the sky. One piece interested Walther. It was the valid identification paper for a man. Walther picked it up and folded it carefully, then slipped it into his overcoat pocket. With a smile, he took a lesson from the vultures and set out in search of food.

The first shop Walther passed still contained some food. The dazed survivors had not yet gutted the shelves. Nobody wished to risk being shot for looting. Walther circled around behind the store and entered it from the alley. Then, from a storage room out of sight from the street, he filled his pockets with tins of meat and fish, the protein he knew he would need for the journey ahead of him.

Walking through the annihilated city, Walther watched details of British and American prisoners of war as they stacked bodies like cords of wood in the street. These heaps of humanity would later be burned when the pile could go no higher.

Many of the POWs were so dazed they could barely function. The handkerchiefs tied over their noses did nothing to keep out the unbearable stench that assaulted their senses. They vomited as they labored, unable to prevent themselves from adding to the hideous mess in which they worked.

Walther watched, fascinated, as two men tried vainly to pry up a body that had literally been glued to the street from the intensity of the heat. As they were attempting to slip their shovels under the body, a dismembered hand fell from the sky directly on top of one of the men. By the time he stopped screaming, the man had retreated into madness.

Most of the rescue squads had been liquored up with schnapps in order to get them to open cellar doors and dig under the ghastly rubble of human flesh.

The men who were forced to open the cellars underwent the most hideous shocks: in some places, the bodies had merely been carbonized into heaps of ashes. But in others the men were ordered at gunpoint to wade into the thick soup that was nothing except the congealed remain of melted human bodies.

The carnage was unspeakable, the destruction complete. It was impossible to travel quickly through this chaos. But, by noon, Walther had managed to move to the outer perimeter of the destruction. And he joined the thousands of other refugees who were fleeing the city. The road was crowded, a writhing mass of suffering humanity walking out of hell. There could not have been one sane person in all the thousands of tormented people who were fleeing.

Walther thought he was hearing things, seeing things. Because when he first heard the hum of airplane engines, he told himself it was not possible. There was nothing left to bomb. He looked up. But he could see nothing, for the entire sky was obscured with smoke. The noise continued, so he stepped off the road away from the other people. He listened carefully. Then he knew: it was not his imagination. The noise he heard came from planes, and they were perilously near.

Functioning on instinct, Walther dived into a ditch and crawled under a slight overhang. He was just in time. From out of the clouds of smoke, a swarm of American Mustangs descended on the refugees. Like angry hornets, they came in low, understanding there would be no resistance from the helpless people at whom they aimed their automatic weapons.

Thus began the third and final stage of the meticulously planned destruction of Dresden: the straffing and bombing of unarmed escaping civilians and the meagre rescue units that were moving towards the city to offer aid. In a scheme that matched concentration camps in its inhumanity, the civilians were picked off like clay pigeons. The refugees did not have a chance. The practiced skills of the well-trained American pilots were not necessary. For this was like shooting gnats with elephant guns: they simply could not miss. One by one, innocent survivors were mowed down as if they were grass. There was no escape, no way they could avoid their preplanned fate.

Only Walther, with the luck of the wicked, survived in his immediate vicinity. He stayed in the ditch for over three hours before finding the courage to stand up. Barely able to think, he only knew one thing: he must stay off roads.

Stepping over the dead and dying — ignoring the maimed bodies and pitiful cries for help, for mercy — he crossed the bloody road to the other side. He stopped for a moment to get his bearings, then reached into his pocket.

He felt the pleasant rattle of loose diamonds in his pocket, tested the weight of the tins of food he carried. Then he wrapped his fingers around the brooch, still safe in its doeskin pouch.

My lucky charm, he thought vaguely to himself. As long as I have this, luck will be with me.

Then he started walking west.

PART TWO
(1945-1959)

Chapter 10

"Look, Buba! She's holding a torch!" Jana cried. The Statue of Liberty looked soft and ethereal wrapped in the mist of New York harbor. "Maybe it means I won't have to be afraid of the dark anymore."

"I'm sure it means that," Rachel said, injecting a confidence into her voice she did not feel. She was frightened, lonely, and dreadfully wary of meeting the relatives of Jana's father for the first time. The Horvaths were Christian. And, although Rachel had been friends with many Christian women in Budapest, this was different. This was America, she thought. Alien. Remote. Powerful. And totally unknown.

She sought comfort by reminding herself the mountains had been far more alien than America. But she had survived there, survived under unthinkable conditions and against enormous odds. Rachel's thoughts drifted to Serghei, how much she missed him, how important to her the brief time with him had been. She wished more than anything that he was at her side to guide her through this new phase of her life, to be her strength when she doubted its certainty. To be her love in the middle of the long, dark nights.

After Serghei's death, a tangible vitality had been cut from the heart of the Partisans who had fought so valiantly in the Dinaric Alps of Yugoslavia. Rachel was no exception. When Serghei died she lost the source of her inspiration and strength.

It was fortunate that the war was drawing to a close, that the battles were waning. For Rachel had little confidence they would survive the sustained rigors of deprivation which they had known for so long. She could feel the difference in the spirit of the people she lived with. They had not been defeated but they had been diminished. They were battle weary, fatigued to the point of ennui. And they simply no longer had the heart for battle, for risk, those essential qualities that not only kept them alive, but justified their very existence.

Jana, too, was deeply affected by the change. As a consequence of the decaying spirit and the devastating loss of Serghei, she had come to depend heavily on Marek as her link to life. He became her anchor, her sustaining light. In spite of this core of stability, she suffered greatly. She had seen too much to believe in a viable future; she had laughed too little to seek it. She merely lived from day to day, her child's sensibilities invaded with a deep and profound cynicism. And yet beneath it all, buried by fear and dread, the little girl of her past — innocent, childlike, and vulnerable — still lived.

After Serghei's death, Marek turned inward. For

weeks, he could barely bring himself to work. Nevertheless, guided by sensibilities that had been formed in the crucible of massacre and mayhem, he persisted halfheartedly in his missions, moving through the motions of his life with an increasing lack of conviction and conscience.

This spiritual listlessness led to the inevitable: he became careless. Once, when he entered Belgrade for a brief mission, he had been caught and detained for five days by Nazi agents. Only his skilled lies and his native cunning saved him.

That particular mission should have been easy. In fact, Marek thought it would be so easy that he made the mistake of telling Jana the day he would return.

When he was two days late, Jana told herself that he had simply been delayed by bad weather or some minor problem. But, by the fourth day, she was frantic. She fabricated stories that Marek was late because he was searching for the brooch. The Tiffany jewel took on new meaning to Jana then, a meaning that persisted long after reality told her it could not be so. As if it were a living thing, the brooch became the symbol to her of safety, of the restoration of her past, of her parents. The brooch meant wholeness and life. Slowly, in her child's imagination, it took on the mystical properties of a talisman, one which was imbued with the power she was unable to find in herself.

When Marek finally returned from his five-day detention, Jana threw herself at him as if he were the Messiah. Once he was settled, she waited for her surprise, eagerly anticipating what it would feel like

215

when he reached into his pocket and, with his wonderful smile of conspiracy, held out his hand and presented Jana with the gift of the brooch.

In fact, the last thing Jana ever saw in Marek's hand was not the brooch, but a dirty, brown handkerchief. He used this tattered piece of fabric to wave good-bye to her. She could still see him standing alone on the airstrip, tears streaming down his handsome face as he waved farewell. He grew smaller and smaller as the plane lifted off and circled once before heading west to Italy. Slowly and painfully, Marek became a speck that dwindled to nothing.

In the coastal town of Bari, Jana and Rachel waited for months as the American authorities processing endless papers wrapped in tangled lengths of red tape that officially assured those in charge that the two displaced persons would be sponsored in the United States by relatives of the child's father. After what seemed an interminable period of waiting, Jana and Rachel set sail for America.

The crossing had been uneventful. And now, dressed in a navy blue coat, a wide-brim straw hat and white knee socks with black patent Mary Janes that were two sizes too large for her, Jana watched the fabled Statue of Liberty take shape before her eyes. The medal Serghei had given her was suspended on a ribbon around her neck. She wore it under her dress, because she knew that she should not be wearing it at all. Nervous, she tugged at the ribbon and gripped the medal in her small fist as the statue loomed, massive and intimidating, over them, a formidable goddess of freedom reaching out to the desperate and homeless.

A sting of tears glistened in Rachel's eyes as she held tight to Jana's hand. They had arrived. The long, arduous journey was over. Neither Jana nor Rachel had any way of knowing that their real ordeal had just begun.

The day was steaming hot. Jana felt herself sweating under the wool coat they had picked out of a bin of donated clothes. The coat was too tight, adding to her increasing discomfort. And the shoes were beginning to rub a blister on her heel. The heat and confusion were overwhelming. Endless lines and harsh questions from immigration officials blurred past her. Rachel's hand gripped hers more firmly than necessary as they were caught up in the mass of humanity seeking a new beginning, a new life. The pushing and shoving unnerved them, expectation and disappointment dogged them.

After hours of chaos, Rachel and Jana were finally delivered into the vast main hall of the hot, dirty building. They each gripped a suitcase. It was their understanding that they would be met by Stefan Horvath's relatives. But the two weary and bedraggled refugees did not know what they looked like.

"Do you see them, Buba?" Jana asked anxiously.

"Not yet, my love," Rachel answered gently, masking her anxiety about what she would do if they were not met, if they were suddenly plunged into America with no anchor, no home. She comforted herself with imaginary scenes: warm greetings from strangers soon to be friends; exchanges of names that would have to be repeated later on when they were settled; the relief of being gathered into the welcoming and comforting bosom of relatives. Love. Home. Hope.

As they walked together toward the end of the vast building, Rachel saw a uniformed man standing to one side of the human flow of traffic. He held a hand-lettered sign in front of him. Two names had been printed on a piece of shirt cardboard: von Weitzman - Horvath.

Rachel stopped and looked at the man.

"Excuse me," the man said. "Are you perhaps Rachel von Weitzman and Jana Horvath?"

"Yes," Rachel nodded. Her heart fluttered erratically.

"My name is Johnson. Mr. and Mrs. Horvath sent me to fetch you."

"I see," Rachel said, disappointment written clearly on her face.

The driver understood. "I'm sorry the Horvaths couldn't be here," he mumbled apologetically. They were . . . detained. But they will be waiting for you at home."

"Thank you."

"Let me take your luggage," he said, reaching for the battered suitcase that had been given to Rachel at the displaced persons camp. Jana's little satchel was the same one she carried out of her attic over two years earlier.

"Follow me, if you will," Johnson said.

They walked slowly to the end of the building.

Above them, motes of dust danced in the oppressive, summer air.

When they emerged into the sunlight, Johnson said, "This way," and walked directly to a new 1946 Cadillac limousine that was parked by the dusty curb.

Once they were settled inside with the glass partition separating them from Johnson, Jana asked in a whisper, "Is he Mr. Horvath, Buba? He's a very strange man."

"No, love," Rachel whispered with a smile. "He is the Horvath's driver."

"They are rich, then?"

"It appears so," Rachel commented wryly. Then they both turned their attention to the new city unfolding before them.

The streets, lined with long rows of tenements, teemed with vitality. The sense of life was palpable. It seemed to grow, excited and agitated, out of the cracks in the sidewalks. The pulse of the city beat in a staccato rhythm, fast, hard, compelling. A dramatic sense of life pervaded everything. It could be seen in the way people walked, in the way they spoke with animated, passionate gestures, in the color and confusion of the traffic. Yet there appeared to be an order to it all, a kind of playful master plan that governed the people as they went about their daily activities.

As Jana and Rachel travelled farther east, the streets became less congested and the buildings began to speak of money and substance. The car turned left and rode uptown past Grand Central Station and onto Park Avenue. They passed the

219

famous Waldorf Astoria and St. Bartholomews Church, both dressed in the unmistakable cloaks of wealth.

The Horvaths lived in a huge apartment building located on the corner of 70th and Park Avenue. Johnson pulled over to the curb where a uniformed doorman awaited them.

Another uniform, Rachel thought. Stand-ins for the Horvaths. She felt an ominous sense of foreboding as they were whisked up to the ninth floor. They stepped out of the elevator into a small entrance hall. To one side was a table with fresh flowers set on it. To the other was a door, the only door on the ninth floor.

With a bang, the elevator closed behind them.

Jana felt trapped. "What do we do now?" she asked.

"We knock on the door," Rachel said, trying to sound positive, cheerful. Then she added, "Please try to remember to speak in English, my love. I know it will be hard, but I doubt if these people will understand Hungarian or German."

Since the day Jana and Rachel had arrived in Bari, Rachel had been teaching Jana English. Although she was far from mastering the language, Jana could make herself understood when she tried. But the effort made her self-conscious. Now, among strangers, she was afraid.

Rachel took a deep breath as she looked down and smiled at Jana. She adjusted her hat unnecessarily and tugged at her coat. Then, with a small burst of courage, she knocked on the door.

The door was opened by a uniformed maid.

"We've been expecting you," the maid said with a pleasant smile. "Come in. The family is waiting for you in the library."

They were taken immediately to a richly paneled room that was lined with hundreds of books. An elaborate Bokarrah carpet lay on the floor, a profusion of deep colors dominated by crimson and midnight blue. For a moment, Jana thought she was home again.

At the end of the room was a fireplace. The mantle was ornately carved in rich mahogany. In front of it stood a man, a woman and a twelve-year-old boy.

"Welcome," the man said, stepping toward Jana and Rachel, his hand extended. "I'm Stephen Horvath." He was handsome in a cold sort of way. Rachel could see a distinct resemblance between Stevan Horvath and her son-in-law in their square, chiseled features and ash blonde hair.

Rachel took his hand. "I'm Rachel. And this is Jana."

Stephen leaned over and kissed Jana awkwardly on the cheek. She stiffened at his touch. But she knew what was expected of her and stood still.

"And I am Gilliam Horvath," the woman said. "And this is our son, Christopher." The smile on Gillian's face was strained, as if she were bravely doing her Christian duty. No more. No less.

She was an attractive woman, in a preserved kind of way. Her dark hair was drawn away from her face and secured in a chignon at the back of her head. Her eyes, round and brown, looked as if they had not shed a genuine tear in years. It was a face in the process of losing the last of its youth, a face that reflected little depth or passion.

Jana endured an additional kiss from her aunt and the perfunctory handshake of her cousin.

"How old are you?" the boy asked.

"Almost ten years old," Jana answered in her best English. Of course, that question and answer had been practiced many times. But her accent was still heavy, and she was not certain the boy had understood her.

"I'm twelve," he said, as if this fact alone was a magnificent achievement, something Jana should revere.

Jana could not think of anything to say to Christopher or the grown-ups, so she sat down carefully on the end of a leather Chesterfield sofa. Her memory of the afternoon was one of doubt and confusion. She sensed the tension in the room and she felt like she was drowning in her own uncertainty and fear. It was clear to her that she was not wanted. Even though these people were cousins of her father, they did not feel like relatives. Relatives opened their arms to you, welcomed you into their homes with hugs and kisses and the scent of cinnamon and wine. Strangers greeted you politely like the Horvaths had done.

Jana sat stoically through a formal dinner. She tried her best to speak English, but she saw the boy smirking at her efforts, so she reverted to Hungarian, which Rachel then translated. This increased Jana's growing sense of alienation, her sense that America was not a place she wanted to be.

Rachel and Jana shared the guest room that night. It was the first time they had been given any privacy in almost three years.

The room was decorated with forest green velvet drapes and bedspreads that picked up the green leaves in the pattern of the cabbage rose wallpaper. The sheets, expertly pressed linen, were not white, as expected. They were pale pink.

"It's beautiful," Jana sighed, gingerly touching the drapes.

"I find it hard to believe we ever lived this way," Rachel commented.

"Did we have perfumed soap like this?" Jana asked, returning from the bathroom with a bar of pink soap in her hand.

"Yes, my love, we even had that," Rachel said, hugging Jana to her. "It's been a long time."

"I remember our house . . . some of it, anyway," Jana said, a faraway sound in her voice. "But now it seems like a dream."

"Yes . . . it does," Rachel agreed. "A very beautiful, very luxurious dream."

At breakfast, a palpable strain hung over the table. The newness of everything overwhelmed Jana. She had been absent from civilization too long. When Christopher handed her a banana, she hadn't the slightest idea what it was.

"What is it?" she asked in her careful English.

"A banana," Christopher said, not bothering to hide his disdain at her ignorance. "It's fruit. Go ahead. Eat it."

With that encouragement, Jana bit into the banana. Instinctively, she spit out the bitter peel on her plate.

"No, no!" Christopher laughed, derisive, unbelieving. "You have to peel it first!"

Jana's face turned crimson. Her humiliation cut deep as she watched Christopher peel the strange fruit.

"Shall I slice it on some cereal for you?" he asked, kinder now. After his temporary lapse of manners, his sense of duty had taken hold. After all, he was a well-brought-up boy.

Jana nodded, not understanding his rapid-fire New York English.

She watched carefully as Christopher instructed the maid to bring his cousin a bowl of Rice Krispies. When it was set in front of her, she waited silently as Christopher sliced the banana on the cereal. Then he poured some cream over the top.

"Listen to the snap, crackle and pop," he instructed. Jana understood nothing except the word listen. And so she did just that. The cereal made noises! Furthermore, it was not cooked. To her, cereal was hot, like oatmeal or groats. She had never heard of cold cereal, much less a cereal that made noises. She was afraid to eat it.

"Take a bite, my love. It's all right," Rachel coaxed in Hungarian.

Jana felt so uncomfortable she barely tasted the strange food she ate. She felt foreign in a way she had never known before, set apart from the events taking place around her as if a wall of glass had descended between her and the others.

Over the next three days, the feelings didn't diminish. Nor was it helped by Gillian Horvath's

224

announcement that, in spite of the housing shortage, her husband had pulled some strings and located an apartment for them in a place called
Greenwich Village. She informed them she had
taken the liberty of furnishing it for them. Clearly,
she was doing her duty.

And, just as clearly, it was her duty to purchase
some clothes for the two bedraggled refugees. She
was embarrassed by the appearance of her relatives
as they walked in and out of the exclusive Park
Avenue building. And so Gillian took Rachel and
Jana shopping. Not to Fields and Thomas, the place
where Gillian bought her clothes. They went to
Macy's. It was practical and moderately priced.

After the deprivations of the mountains and the
spartan living conditions in Bari where used clothing was handed to them with little regard for fit,
Jana could not believe the sights she encountered in
Macy's. It was a fairy-tale kingdom. And she did,
indeed, feel like princess when she tried on a new
dress—a navy and red plaid cotton pinafore with a
sash at the waist. She could not believe her image in
the mirror. Who was this pretty, clean little girl
wearing a dress that actually fit?

She smiled tentatively at Gillian. Gillian smiled,
too, this time with genuine warmth, as if a slight
thaw had begun to take place.

"It's lovely. Perfect for you," Gillian said. "And,
when it gets colder, you can wear a sweater under
it."

"Thank you," whispered Jana. "It is very beautiful."

Rachel felt uncomfortable accepting such overt

225

charity, but she had no choice. They needed the clothing too much. She would need a dress to wear when she applied for a job. She still had seven diamonds, the emerald and sapphire, and the diamond ring. She would sell the smallest diamond in order to have some money for food and transportation until she got a job. But the remaining stones were for an emergency. New clothes weren't an important enough reason to part with them. Instead, she informed Gillian politely that she would make every effort to repay her for the clothes and furnishings as soon as possible.

"That's not necessary, my dear," Gillian said, dismissing the thought with a wave of her hand.

"I insist," Rachel said proudly.

With this understood, Rachel felt free to choose as good a dress as she could find. And when she stepped out of the dressing room wearing a simple deep blue jersey dress with padded shoulders and an A-line skirt, she was stunning. It was at that moment Gillian Horvath realized she was dealing with an equal.

"It suits you perfectly," Gillian said sincerely.

Rachel, too, thought her smile was warmer.

Two days later, Rachel and Jana moved into their one-bedroom apartment on Cornelia Street, just two blocks away from Washington Square Park. The furnishings were plain but adequate, and Rachel made a mental note to find out how much this kind of furniture cost. She was determined to repay her benefactors, for she knew without a doubt that she never wanted to be beholden to them. She was grateful to the Horvaths for all they had done. But she could not think of them as family. In fact, they were not her family. They belonged to Jana. And as long as Rachel accepted their charity, she would feel inferior.

After they moved, Rachel and Jana spent the next week discovering the streets and alleys that criss-crossed Greenwich Village. A wisp of familiarity touched Jana's senses when she heard so many people speaking Italian. It reminded her of Bari.

Jana walked with Rachel as they found the fish-monger, the butcher, the greengrocer, the market. And they enrolled Jana in P.S. 3, the public school that was six blocks from home.

Along with the housing shortage, jobs were diffi-cult to find. But Rachel was determined to find work as soon as possible. She knew there were few suitable jobs for her, because she wasn't trained for anything. Women of her status naturally assumed they would always be cared for. There was only one area in which Rachel was skilled: needlework. From an early age, she had been schooled by her mother in every kind of sewing, from elaborate embroidery and lace-making to the creation of the finest dress.

Rachel's first step to employment was to ask Gil-lian Horvath for the name of the best store in New York, the one with the finest clothes and the most exclusive reputation.

"That's simple," Gillian said. "Fields and Thomas. I do all my shopping there," Gillian said proudly. "Perhaps I can introduce you . . ." she said vaguely, suddenly wondering why Rachel wanted this information.

"That won't be necessary," Rachel answered politely. "I'll manage."

The introduction was, indeed, unnecessary. For when Rachel presented herself to the store personnel department and told them she was a skilled seamstress who spoke four languages, she was hired immediately. There was always a need for bilingual help in an establishment that catered to the international set.

The evening Rachel got her job, she took Jana to dinner to celebrate her achievement. They ate at the Grand Ticino, a pleasant basement restaurant where they could get a complete meal for one dollar.

When Rachel's wine was served, she poured a small amount into Jana's glass.

"L'chaim," Rachel said, touching her glass to Jana's.

"L'chaim," said Jana.

Chapter 11

It was a warm, bright September morning, but Jana felt the chill of the unknown creep through her body as she walked reluctantly down Bleecker Street.

She wore her new plaid pinafore. Her hair was long enough now for short pigtails and it glistened gold in the morning sun.

"But I've never been to school," she said to her grandmother. "Why can't I just get a tutor like I had in Budapest?"

"Because children in America go to school," Rachel answered tolerantly.

"What will it be like?"

"I'm not sure," said Rachel, wishing she could be of more help to Jana. "Just do as the teacher says and you will be all right."

"I took a bite out of the banana when Christopher told me to. And that wasn't all right." Jana could still hear her cousin's derisive laughter.

"That was an honest mistake. After all, you have never seen a banana before."

"And I've never seen a classroom before, either."

"Then it's time you do."

The school building was dark and oppressive, foreboding in its old-fashioned construction and massive, uninviting design. In direct contrast to the architecture, the excited screams and yells of children greeting classmates they hadn't seen since June created an atmosphere of uncontrolled exhubrance. Nobody paid attention to the little girl with the older woman. Nobody at all.

After what seemed to be an endless procession of people and rooms and long hallways punctuated by caged stairwells, Rachel located Jana's classroom and introduced her to her teacher.

Miss Linsey was an older woman nearing retirement. Wisps of grey hair escaped from her bun, curling in soft tendrils around her plump face. Her eyes, a soft blue-green, had deep crinkles at the corners and her mouth was full and generous. It was clear from the outset that the children loved her. She had an ample bosom for hugging and a formidable voice for controlling. And she used both with judicious concern.

"Welcome to P.S. 3," Miss Linsey said, leaning over to Jana. "We're so glad you're going to be with us. Where were you in school before?"

"She's never been to school," Rachel said.

"Never?" Miss Linsey was shocked. "How can she be entering 4th grade, then? She'll be behind in her work."

"I assure you she reads and writes beautifully," Rachel said. "She can add and divide and she knows her multiplication tables through twelve."

"And all without school," Miss Linsey exclaimed.

"That's quite admirable."

"There's only one problem," Rachel said.

"Yes?"

"Her English is . . . rudamentary."

"Oh. What is her native language?" Miss Linsey asked.

"Hungarian. But she also speaks fluent German."

"Then I'm sure she'll learn English in no time. I know a little German, and I'll try to help her in every way I can."

"Thank you."

Rachel looked down at Jana. There were tears in her eyes. Fear was etched on her face. She could sense Jana's terror, and felt guilty because she had to leave her in such strange surroundings.

"Now don't lose your keys," Rachel admonished gently, speaking to her in Hungarian. She checked to see that the keys were still on the ribbon that hung around Jana's neck. "Remember to lock the door when you come home. I'll be there by six o'clock. Be a good girl and I'll bring you a treat."

Jana flung her arms around Rachel's neck, clinging to her last vestige of security.

"Don't leave me, Buba," Jana begged in Hungarian. "Please don't leave."

"I have to leave, my love. Remember, I have a job now. I must take the subway uptown and go to work. Your teacher will take good care of you. I know that."

Rachel leaned down and kissed Jana on the forehead, then smoothed her furrowed brow with her hand.

231

"I believe in you," Rachel whispered. Then she was gone.

Throughout the day, Jana floated on a cloud of fear and dread. Darkness closed in on her and she felt isolated and totally alone. She listened carefully to the teacher, but only understood about half of what she said. Nothing made sense. Nothing connected in her brain. Instead of trying to figure everything out, she simply followed what the other children did. The chaos of recess assaulted her. The harsh bell that rang periodically to indicate recess and lunch made her jump. Nobody talked to her. And nobody asked her to play. All day long, she felt as if she were drowning.

When three o'clock came, Jana almost wept with relief. She followed the other children in a line as they walked noisily down the caged, concrete stairs. Only Jana was silent.

Outside, Jana gasped for air as if she had not breathed all day. And then set out for home, running all the way.

Relief surged through her as she raced up the three flights of stairs without pausing, stopping only when she reached the door of her apartment.

It was dark inside. The sun had long since abandoned that tiny corner of the city. She turned on the light and walked over to her small, narrow bed at the far side of the tiny bedroom and lay down. She stared at the ceiling, unmoving, uncaring until she heard Rachel's key in the lock. Only then did she breathe easily again.

"How was school?" Rachel asked brightly.

232

"Fine," Jana lied. She didn't want to make Rachel sad by telling her the truth. "Actually it was a lot of fun. I think I'm going to like it."

Rachel's face lit up, and Jana knew she had said the right thing. "I'm so glad to hear that. I worried about you all day."

Jana's second day of school got off to a dreadful beginning. That's because when she leaned over the water fountain to get a drink of water, one of the fifth grade boys grabbed her pigtails.

"I'm going to cut them off!" he teased, brandishing a pair of school scissors that were barely sharp enough to cut a piece of manila paper. But the kind of scissors didn't matter to Jana. All she understood was the threat. And that threat was no different than the German soldier's.

In an instant, the boy's laughter turned from taunting to evil, his freckled face became adult, his tease became a deep and powerful threat.

Jana looked at him and tried to form some intelligible English words. But they got caught in her throat. She finally managed to choke out a desperate "No!"

"Yes!" he laughed in the manner of every fifth grade boy who ever teased a girl.

"NOOOOOOO!" Jana screeched, her face mirroring her terror.

Blindly, instinctively, Jana applied what she had learned in the mountains to the boy's arm. She twisted away from him and grabbed his arm, just as

Merek had taught her to do. With a quick jerk, the boy screamed in pain and dropped the scissors.

"Where did you learn to do that?" a girl in her class asked with wide, blue eyes and a distinct note of admiration in her voice. Dark, curly hair framed her delicate face, and her cheeks were flushed with excitement.

Still frightened, Jana looked at her.

"Are you all right?" the girl asked. She spoke with a clear English accent.

"Look," said the girl, stepping closer to Jana. "Miss Linsey said you come from Europe and English is difficult for you. Do you understand me? Are you all right?"

"Yes," Jana whispered at last. "I am all right."

"I doubt that boy will ever bother you again. You really showed him!" The girl paused a moment. "My name's Margaret. Margaret Pym. What's yours?"

"Jana."

When Rachel got home from work that evening, Jana didn't have to lie when she was asked how school was.

"I have a new friend," Jana said almost shyly.

"How wonderful," Rachel said. "What's her name?"

"Margaret Pym. She only lives three blocks away in the MacDougal Street Gardens and her father is a professor at New York University. Could I go to her house after school?"

"Just ask her mother to call me so we can make arrangements," said Rachel with a smile. "And, of course, we must invite her here, too."

By Christmas, Jana and Rachel had settled into a comfortable routine. Jana's friendship with Margaret blossomed immediately. They declared themselves "best friends" and spent hours telling each other their most private secrets, making plans for spending the night with each other or going to the movies.

Jana still harbored a dread of the dark, a fear she confided in Margaret. She even told about the secret hiding place in the attic. Her fear would diminish with time, of course, but in her childhood it still held a terrible power over her. Rachel's gift of a flashlight helped. Nevertheless, Jana fought the battle against this unseen enemy almost daily. And slowly, painfully, she gained on it.

Rachel was delighted with Jana's progress. Each morning, she walked Jana to school and then caught the subway for the trip to 40th and Fifth Avenue where she worked. After just three weeks at Fields and Thomas, it was apparent that Rachel was a talented and knowledgeable seamstress. Soon, the most difficult alterations and repairs were automatically referred to her. Although her wages were low, she was often allowed to bring home scraps of fabric from which she would skillfully fashion clothes for Jana and herself. They lived a simple life. But it was increasingly satisfying to both of them.

The only minor blemish in their comfortable routines was the monthly dinner at the Horvaths. Rachel tolerated it. Jana despised it. Because Christian Horvath had become her nemesis. As a twelve-year-old-boy, he had developed an interest in girls. And no girl was as pretty, as delicate, and charming as his cousin, Jana. He wanted her attention in the worst way. And that's the way he went about trying to win it.

"Stop it!" hissed Jana. "Cut it out right now, or you'll be sorry."

"And how are you going to make *me* sorry?" Christian said. "I'm bigger than you. Stronger, too."

Jana looked him straight in the eyes. Her mouth formed a thin, determined line as she weighed what she would say. The only person who knew about the mountains was Margaret Pym. It had been a deliberate decision not to tell Chris. There was something deeply private about the experience. And she did not want to share it with her cousin.

"If you ever grab my hair like that again," Jana said slowly, deliberately, "I'll make you pay."

Chris smiled scornfully. "Don't make me laugh."

Jana stood her ground. "I know how to kill a man."

"Spare me," said Chris. "Would you hit him with your great big fist? Ohhhh . . . I'm scared."

"No," said Jana as she reached for the cord from the Venetian blind. In one deft move, she looped it around Chris' neck from behind. "I'd choke him like this." She tugged gently on the cord.

Chris grabbed for the cord, trying to slip his

fingers under it.

Without a word, Jana let go of the cord, then turned her back on him and walked away.

She didn't see the expression of pure rage wash over Chris' face.

Chapter 12

Six months after the airlift began, Oberleutnant Fritz Walther stood at his window and watched the cargo planes fly to and from Templehof Airport. The monotonous drone of planes hung heavy and incessant over the besieged city where the low, vibrating hum had become a permanent sound in the ears of the citizens. Day and night, wave after wave of planes flew over West Berlin, unloading food and equipment to the waiting citizens of the beleaguered city.

The city of Berlin is situated one-hundred and ten miles inside East Germany. Then, as now, it stands as a bastion of freedom in the midst of a communist-dominated world. This was, of course, unacceptable to the Soviet Union because too many East German citizens immigrated to Berlin, lured by the bright lights of freedom. In June, 1948, Russia tried to bring Berlin to its knees by cutting off all water, rail, and road traffic to the city. It was the Russian hope that the blockade would force Berliners to submit to communist domination. But Soviet hopes were dashed by the fierce Allied determination to keep the city free from communism.

The response to the Russian political piracy was overwhelming: if America, France and Britain could not send food and equipment to the city by land, they would fly in the supplies. For eleven months, twenty-four hours a day, Berlin survived quite handsomely with these airborne gifts. At the height of the airlift, an Allied plane landed at Templehoff airport every forty-five seconds. Without the airlift, the two million citizens of the city would have starved.

In the midst of this organized chaos, admiring and disdainful of the free world's efforts to circumvent the blockade, Fritz Walther lived in decadent splendor.

Fleeing Dresden after the bombing, he had made his way west. When he reached Berlin, a city of magical reputation even in its war torn ruins, Walther decided to stay. With the communists cracking down on half of its citizens, he figured West Berlin would be the perfect place for him. Black market trade was brisk between East and West. Opportunities, both illegal and immoral, were rampant. And Walther missed few of them.

As he stood by the window, transfixed by the drone of the planes and the brightness of the late afternoon sun, a woman sideled up behind him and slipped her arms insinuatingly around his waist. Her face was ruddy from too much beer and she had crossed the line from pleasingly plump to fat years earlier.

"Come inside before dinner," she said, pressing her body hard against his. "I have a treat for you."

Walther smiled.

"And what must I pay for this treat?" he asked.

"Not what. But how," the woman said tantalizingly.

"How, then?" he asked, marginally amused.

"Let me wear the brooch tonight," she said. "Just this once, let me wear the brooch. It's my birthday. And I want my friends to see me wearing something special. I want to impress them."

Walther slid his hand in his pocket. His fingers slipped reassuringly around the worn leather pouch. He traced the outline of the Tiffany brooch with his index finger.

"I don't know," he said, his voice slippery with teasing. "Will you be a good girl?"

"Yes," she said submissively, hating the fact that she was selling herself for a momentary glimmer of respectability.

"A very good girl?" he asked.

"I promise. You can do anything. And I'll wear my silk."

"Then we'll see," Walther said, reaching behind him and grasping the woman's rump. "But you must be very good."

"Anything," the woman said, trying to keep the humiliation she felt from creeping into her voice. "Anything."

After three years in the alterations department of

240

Fields and Thomas, Rachel was promoted. She was now Supervisor of Alterations. It was her duty to see that all the alterations were done properly, that the staff was happy and the customers were pleased.

The Christmas rush was in full swing in 1949. The store was crowded with shoppers and the alterations staff worked late into every night. Frayed tempers threatened to come apart. Leisure time was low and tension was high. That's when the French Ambassador's wife chose to create a scene.

"You've ruined the gown!" Madame Joue said contemptuously to the seamstress named Millie. Her heavily accented English was barely understandable.

"But that's what you asked for," Millie answered. "See?" she said, holding out the alterations ticket. "Remove the sash on gown. It says it right here."

"Ruined!" the Madame Joue cried. "The ball is tonight. The gown was purchased especially for this event. I have nothing else to wear. Impossible! This is impossible! All because of your incompetence," she added venomously.

Seeing that the situation would soon explode, Rachel stepped from behind her desk.

"What seems to be the problem, Madame Joue?" Rachel asked in impeccable French.

"The problem is that your alterations lady has ruined my gown by removing the sash," Madame Joue said imperiously.

Exhausted, Rachel had the urge to put her hands around Madame's long, aristocratic neck and strangle her. Instead, she spoke calmly and politely.

"As I recall, Madame, it was at your request that

the sash be removed. Because it was such an integral part of the gown, I supervised the work myself."

"But it is horrible! I won't pay for the gown!"

"It may well be horrible," Rachel said, trying to keep her voice neutral. "Nevertheless, the removal was done at your request."

"How can I wear this tonight?" Madame Joue lamented. "Please put the sash back on."

"I'm afraid that's impossible," Rachel said. "As you know, the sash was pieced together quite uniquely. It frayed badly in removing it."

"Then match the fabric!" the woman demanded.

"The fabric can't be matched, but perhaps I can help," Rachel said soothingly, knowing that she was dealing with one of Fields and Thomas' best customers. In spite of her own personal opinions or feelings, it was Rachel's job to keep the customers satisfied. After all, it wouldn't look good on Rachel's record if this woman were to refuse to pay for an expensive designer gown because of unsatisfactory alterations.

"Nothing will help this," the woman said contemptuously.

"Wait one moment," Rachel said confidently. "I know just the thing. Your dress will be stunning."

Madame Joue looked down at the ice blue satin of her gown. Everything else seemed to be satisfactory except for the sash.

Rachel returned in one minute. In her hands she carried a magnificent piece of bright pink Chinese silk embroidered with gold threads. The fabric rippled and shone in the light.

Caught off guard, Millie gasped when she saw the silk. But Rachel quieted her with a glance and a subtle nod of her head, signaling to her to say nothing.

Madame Joue looked at the silk. In spite of her irritation, she could not resist reaching out and rubbing it between her fingers.

"Isn't it lovely?" Rachel asked soothingly.

Madame nodded begrudgingly.

"Here," said Rachel. "Let me tie it around your waist. You'll see how beautiful it is."

Rachel fussed with the silk, making a dramatic show of tying the sash just so. She was aware that Madame Joue was watching her every move in the mirror. She was also aware that Jonathan Duer, the president of Fields and Thomas, had been watching the entire episode. It was his habit to wander unannounced through the store, checking employee performance, customer satisfaction, and general atmosphere. Believing he could run a better establishment if he knew what was going on inside it, Duer scrutinized what went on behind the scenes as thoroughly as what went on in front.

It made Rachel nervous to think she was under this important man's scrutiny. One mistake and she could get fired. She couldn't afford to lose her job. She had gotten a substantial raise with her promotion, and knew that she didn't have enough credential yet to earn a comparable salary at any other store.

Spreading the loops of the bow, Rachel stepped aside so that Madame Joue could see the full reflection of herself in the mirror.

"See how beautifully the pink shows off the dress?" Rachel said with an air of practiced assurance.

"I even have pink shoes," the French woman said begrudgingly.

"Then all the more beautiful. Stunning. And you'll never have to worry about finding another woman wearing your dress."

"Of course, I can't pay for the sash," Madame Joue said. "After all, the dress must have a sash. It is incomplete without one."

"I agree entirely," Rachel said with a smile that never reached her eyes. "Of course, Madame does not have to pay for it."

Rachel turned to Millie and spoke in English. "Would you please help Madame Joue with her dress and see that it is perfectly pressed for tonight?"

"Of course," Millie muttered. "The sash, too?"

"Yes," Rachel said firmly, looking straight into Millie's eyes. "The sash, too."

It was only after Madame Joue departed that Millie turned to Rachel.

"You let that horrible woman have the sash for Jana's dress! It's taken you weeks to make that dress. What will you do?"

"I don't know," Rachel said. "All I know is that this job is more important to me than the dress. It must be."

"Excuse me," said a deep voice.

Rachel turned to look straight into Jonathan's

244

Duer's eyes.

"Yes?" Rachel took a step backward, as if his very presence presented a threat.

"You handled that situation marvelously. Madame Joue is not an easy person to deal with."

Wondering if he knew that from personal experience or her reputation, Rachel smiled. "Thank you." She nodded politely and started to walk to her desk. But Duer's voice stopped her.

"Your French is impeccable," he said.

"I spent some time in France as a child," Rachel said modestly.

"Do you speak other languages? Your native language, for instance. What is that?"

"Hungarian. And, yes, I do speak others. German and Italian. Yiddish. And a little Serbo-Croat."

"That's marvelous," Duer said with a smile. "And impressive, too."

Rachel was startled to realize that while she was trying to manage a polite exit, he was trying to make a real conversation.

Suddenly his brow furrowed. "You're in alterations?" he asked.

"Yes."

"Why?"

Rachel pulled herself taller. Her voice was a mixture of pride and defiance. "Because I have to make a living. And I was never trained for anything. Sewing is something I know well."

"I didn't mean any offense," Duer said kindly. "I was merely curious why a woman as obviously educated and cultured as you is working in the alterations department. With your qualifications, it seems limiting."

Rachel couldn't think of anything to say and so she responded to the compliment with a nod.

"I feel I must ask you," Duer said, "Where did that magnificent pink sash come from?"

"I had it in the back," Rachel said. "It's all right. I just happened to have it. I was happy I could soothe Madame Joue,"

"At whose expense?" Duer asked. His pale grey eyes looked into hers.

Rachel glanced away. There was something disturbing about his eyes, unsettling. He didn't feel like a stranger at all.

"Who is Jana?"

"My granddaughter," Rachel answered in a low voice. "I was making her a Christmas present."

"That was very special fabric. Can you get more?"

Rachel smiled. "I don't think so."

"Then find her a dress in the store. Charge it to me. I'll be certain to alert my secretary so that there won't be any misunderstanding."

"That's very kind," Rachel said.

"You're very kind," Duer smiled. "Just make certain you choose a very expensive dress."

Jonathan reached out and shook her hand. Rachel felt his warmth and, for a moment, wished she were wrapped in it. Don't be foolish, she admonished herself. Don't be foolish.

Three months later, Rachel was promoted to the post of assistant to the Director of Customer Relations. Her naturally aristocratic manner, her command of several languages and her easy ability to deal with difficult people made her a natural for the job. Jonathan Duer knew she would be. Six months later, when the director of customer relations quit her job to be married, Rachel was promoted to the position.

"Will you have lunch with me to celebrate the promotion?" Jonathan asked Rachel.

"I don't see how I could turn you down," Rachel said. "After all, you *are* my boss."

"That's not why I'm asking you," said Jonathan. His eyes searched hers for something beyond a polite response. Much as Rachel tried to hide it, Jonathan found what he was looking for.

In March of 1950, Senator Joseph McCarthy announced that he personally knew of eight card-carrying members of the communist party who were currently working in the state department. As Rachel sat quietly by her Philco radio and listened to the Senator speak, a chill of foreboding crept relentlessly up her spine.

At first she did not understand why she was so deeply frightened. But as Rachel listened to the Senator from Wisconsin rant on and on, it came to her: she was listening to the voice of a fanatic. It was Adolph Hitler all over again, raving about enemies of the state, pointing his finger at imagined offenders, separating and accusing minorities for society's woes.

Even though she and Jana had become American

citizens a year earlier, Rachel began to feel insecure. What if they come again? she thought. I spent time in the mountains with supporters of Marshall Tito. I could be accused, too. I could be accused of being a communist. Or even a communist sympathizer is bad enough for this maniac. Just one finger pointed at me, and Jana and I could be homeless again. Never! she thought. Never.

"It won't happen in this country," Jonathan said calmly when Rachel told him how frightened she was. "This is America. A democracy. You're safe here."

But McCarthy's diatribes grew worse. And Rachel grew more anxious.

"It frightens me," she said. "He's too much like Hitler."

"You've nothing to fear from him, my love. Nothing," he whispered softly, reassuringly.

When Jonathan spoke to her that way, Rachel wanted to curl up in the soft sound of his voice, to allow herself to be folded into the warmth of his being.

Yet, much to her distress, she could still hear Jana's voice after she first met Jonathan.

"He's a very nice man, Buba. Is he Jewish?"

"No. But neither was your father," Rachel answered, just a shade too defensively.

"But *I* am Jewish," Jana said, "Regardless of who my father was. That's who we are. That's who we come from. We didn't flee from our home because we were Christian."

"That's true," Rachel said. "You're almost fourteen years old, Jana. At your age, you still haven't learned that there are times in life when we must compromise. Many times, alas. Perfection is not human. And I'm not even certain it is desirable. I understand why you ask me these questions. Of course, I wish he were Jewish. I wish many things. All I know is that this man is fond of me and I am fond of him. He has been a good friend. What is more, he makes me laugh." And he makes beautiful love to me, too, Rachel added to herself. A glimpse of the joy they experienced together crossed through her consciousness, and the gratitude she felt for every loving moment they spent together brought tears to her eyes.

"Do you feel guilty?" Jana asked.

Rachel thought about Jana's question. "Sometimes," she answered honestly. "But I'm not certain whether my guilt is because I feel I am betraying Josef or because I am betraying my heritage. When your mother got married, Josef and I had friends who refused to attend the wedding. Some never spoke to us again. But who was I to tell my daughter she could not marry your father? He was a good and loving man. He made her happy. Very happy. At least she had that."

"And that's how you feel now? That at least you have Jonathan?" There was no hostility in Jana's question. Only curiosity motivated by love.

"I'm not certain how I feel. I do know that I would never marry him. I could not do that to Josef. Because I never knew for certain that he died, I never really said good-bye to him."

Rachel looked at Jana, her eyes trying to measure the depth of her granddaughter's disapproval. "Do you dislike him?" Rachel asked. "Or are you just worried that he is not Jewish?" It was at that moment Rachel realized how important it was to her for Jana to approve of Jonathan. He was a part of her life now. An important part. And she did not want to be placed in the middle between Jana and Jonathan, each tugging at her for time, for attention.

"Oh, Buba. I don't dislike him at all. He's very nice. And it's not important to me that he's Jewish. I just worry for you, that's all."

"Thank you for your concern," Rachel said, giving Jana a hug.

But Rachel could not dismiss their conversation. For weeks after they talked, she thought about what Jana had said. Yes, I am a Jew, she told herself. Do I compromise my heritage by being involved with a gentile? It was a question that Rachel could answer either way, depending on the day. But it never stopped her from loving Jonathan Duer.

It didn't take Jana long to become accustomed to Jonathan's presence in her home. She liked him very much. Perhaps it was because he talked to her as an adult. Or perhaps it was because she sensed that he was genuinely fond of her. Besides, she told herself, he makes Buba happy.

In just a short period of time, Jonathan had become a regular visitor at the tiny apartment on Cornelia Street. In the beginning, Rachel had been self-conscious about the ordinary appearance of her home. After all, Jonathan lived on Fifth Avenue. He had servants and rooms to spare. But after his wife died, it didn't seem like home anymore, he said. He used to tell Rachel that he preferred her apartment because it was filled with life and warmth.

At first, Rachel thought he was only saying those things to be polite. But it soon became apparent that Jonathan was serious. He did like her apartment. And he liked her.

"I want to buy a home of my own," Rachel announced to Jana and Jonathan one Saturday afternoon after the three of them had returned from seeing the fascinating new movie, *All About Eve.* "A home that can't be taken from me by men like Joseph McCarthy."

"A home? Here? In New York?" Jonathan asked.

"Yes."

"I've saved my money. And I have some stones I can sell. That should be enough for the down payment. I have a good job, so I can pay the mortgage."

"Oh, Buba!" Jana exclaimed. "May I have my own room?" Then a dark cloud crossed her face. "We wouldn't move far from here, would we?"

"No, love, not far from here," Rachel said with a smile. "I know you don't want to move away from Margaret. Not everyone is fortunate enough to have a friend like that."

"Have you looked at any real estate?" Jonathan asked.

"Yes," Rachel smiled almost shyly. "And I found

251

something: A wonderful, two-bedroom apartment on Washington Square."

"Then, by all means, let's go see it," Jonathan said. "And afterwards, perhaps I can persuade you two beautiful women to have dinner with me. After all, this is an occasion that calls for champagne."

Rachel saw the joy on Jana's face. Then she looked at Jonathan, at the love in his eyes. "Yes," she said. "This occasion *definitely* calls for champagne."

Chapter 13

In September of 1950, Jana and Margaret Pym began their ninth-grade classes at the High School for Art and Design. Both of them had been thrilled to be accepted.

Margaret had her heart set on being a graphic designer. And Jana, following the path her grandfather had laid out for her so many years ago, intended to become a jeweler. But she also wanted to design and execute her own work.

By this time, Jana had become an extraordinarily beautiful young woman. In contrast to the fashion of the times, her thick, honey-blonde hair flowed in an abundant cascade past her shoulders. Her large, dark blue eyes flashed with intelligence. They also indicated something else: fear.

Not only had fear of the dark become an integral part of her life, she had now reached the point where she was attracting the constant attention of boys. But just the fleeting memory of that hideous spring morning when her grandmother was raped was enough to convince Jana that she should stay away from men. That didn't stop them from trying to attract her attention, however. And that included her cousin, Christian Horvath, who still thought Jana was the prettiest girl he knew.

No matter how much Jana tried to be nice to him, the mere thought of him touching her sent shocks of disgust throughout her body. There was something frightening about him, untrustworthy, unbalanced, as if his oily desire for her would contaminate her entire body if he were to touch her.

Unfortunately, the more Jana turned away his attention, the more intense Christian Horvath's obsession became. He asked her to go out with him on more than one occasion, but Jana always turned him down.

"Ah, come on, Jana. I'll take you to see *From Here to Eternity*. Don't you want to see that?"

"No I don't," Jana said. She and Margaret had seen the movie just the week before, but she didn't tell her cousin that. She didn't want to give him the satisfaction of knowing she had gone to such a movie. The fleeting image of Burt Lancaster and Deborah Kerr lying in the sand, the waves washing over them as they kissed, passed disturbingly through her consciousness. "But thanks anyway," she said with stilted politeness.

"Then how about the theatre? You like musicals, don't you? I can get house seats to *The King and I* anytime I want."

"I've seen it," Jana said, although she would love to see it again. She adored the music. She and Margaret listened to it for months after she first bought the record.

Although it was excessive, Christian's persistent

attention didn't come near to preparing Jana for the boys at her new school. Once they caught sight of her cool blonde beauty, the boys swarmed around. The more elusive and indifferent she became, the more desirable she appeared in the lustful eyes of her suitors. But not one boy, no matter what he did or how hard he tried, was ever successful.

After a two-year detour in Paris, Walther wanted a change. He had moved from Berlin to Paris expecting beautiful women and glamourous, glittery nights. What he found was the deep Parisian disdain for Germans, any German. This was not helped by his hideous face.

Even the renowned French whores disdained him.

"Allez-vous en!" they cried when he approached. "Go away!"

Occasionally, of course, the lure of a handful of francs waved in front of her face would convince some hungry woman to go to a nearby room with him.

But she wasn't one of the beautiful whores, one of the ones with elegance and class. She was old and used up. Good only to please a desperate man.

And Walther was desperate.

It was after a particularly painful rejection by a common French tart who would not allow herself to be abused by him that Walther moved to Hamburg. It was the largest seaport in the world, rife with opportunities in the black market. And at least there, he reasoned, I'll be accepted by my own countrymen. They won't turn me away.

Walther was correct. In Germany, the disfigured leutnant was considered a hero. Nevertheless, even the heartiest and most compassionate soul had trouble looking at him without flinching.

As he became more and more embittered, his once ugly face turned hideous. The sagging of his eye and mouth was even more pronounced, the sight of his face more shocking.

In spite of its reputation as a sailor's haven, Hamburg was a beautiful city built around a beautiful blue lake. In the summer, sail boats slid gracefully through the water as patrons in the lakeside cafes looked on. Although much of it was bombed during the war, the city still retained an air of quiet grace.

By 1952, business was booming once again. And where there were sailors from every country in the world, business opportunities of Walther's kind were abundant.

Although he had a large stash of money and could have afforded to live in a nicer section of the city, Walther settled in an apartment near the Reeperbaun, the dark part of the city where prostitutes legally plied their trade.

Walther's apartment had a shabby elegance about it. Large and light, it was on the fourth floor of a building that had seen better days two decades earlier. Years of neglect were turning it slowly into a tenement. Its faded red velvet drapery was dusty with age. The furniture had begun to sag. Nevertheless, it was a respectable place to live; a place he could entertain women without shame. A place, in his poverty of human contacts, he would eventually call home.

He was comfortable in his world of sailors and whores. He fit in with the transients and the misfits of the world. Nobody questioned him. Nobody noticed him, either. He could be anonymous, the wisest way for a criminal to live.

Every day at five o'clock, Walther visited a tavern near his house. There, he would sit and watch the customers, longing to be included in the comraderie that surrounded him. And he would talk to Ingrid, the barmaid.

Then, around eleven, if he was in the mood, he would stroll up and down the Reeperbaun, window shopping for a woman.

At the windows, women leaned on the sills or stood provocatively in the light. Some showed off their bodies, clad in scanty lace and silk. Others showed their specialties, dressed in leather and holding whips and chains.

Sometimes, Walther would just shop. Other times, he would nod to a woman. Then she would smile and beckon him to enter the house where he would take his hasty, furtive pleasure and then leave.

"Ingrid," said Walther one night to the barmaid at the tavern as they were laughing over some inconsequential joke. "One night soon we should have dinner together."

Although it sounded like a casual invitation, it had taken Walther weeks to gather the courage to issue it. Because all he really wanted was to find a nice woman, not a whore, and take her to his home. Although she wasn't that bright, to Walther, Ingrid was a "nice woman." She clearly did not mingle with the patrons of the bar. Perhaps that's what Walther found so alluring about her. That, and her unmistakable beauty. Her lush copper hair reminded him of the Jewess he had possessed so many years earlier.

"Sure," Ingrid said. "We should do that one night."

It was easy for Walther to mistake her politeness for willingness because he was a pitifully desperate man. And so a week later, with the courage of a glass of schnapps burning in his belly, he asked her to have dinner the following night.

Ingrid's politeness froze on her face. She smiled. "I'm sorry . . . but I'm busy."

There was no mistaking her this time. Ingrid had no intention of dining with him. Not the following night. Not ever.

Walther put his hand in his pocket. He grasped the brooch for reassurance. At least he had that to remind him of a beautiful, elegant woman.

"Then fetch me a schnapps," he said. "A double."

In their senior year of high school, Jana and Margaret were still inseparable. Since they had met in fourth grade, their close friendship had been Jana's salvation. She told Margaret almost everything. The only significant story of her past she omitted was about Rachel's rape. Somehow, she could not bring herself to talk about it.

Academically, Jana was at the top of her class. But her social life was different. In contrast to Margaret, Jana wasn't ever really popular at school. She longed to be one of those shining girls, the ones everyone wants to be with. But she didn't know how to make it happen. Other than her friendship with Margaret, she kept pretty much to herself. She participated in school activities, joined the French club and the art club, but she did it as an outsider. She was part of the action, but not involved in it.

One quiet autumn afternoon, Jana and Margaret sat drinking a cup of tea in Jana's bedroom that overlooked Washington Square. Rachel had allowed Jana to redecorate the room on her last birthday. It was quite sophisticated for a schoolgirl, with a color scheme of mauve and pale blue. Two small easy chairs were placed by the window separated by a round glass coffee table. Jana placed only one thing on the table: a small, silver baby cup, the scratches and dents adding character to the highly polished connection to Jana's past. This was the girls' favorite place to talk.

"I wish I understood myself better," Jana said. "It's hard to put my finger on it. Sometimes when I start to get involved in something, I feel like I'm looking at myself from the outside, that it's another person doing the work or playing the game. It's as if I can't allow myself to care, to really become involved with other people."

"I don't understand," Margaret said. "You and I are certainly close friends."

"But you are an exception," Jana said, trying to pull her feelings from a massive tangle of memories and fears. "With most people, I think I'm afraid I'll lose them if I start to like them. Other than you and Rachel, I have lost everyone in my life I learned to love."

"But those were the war years. Things are different now," Margaret said. "Much different."

"I know," Jana said. "But that doesn't seem to make any difference. I'm still scared."

"Maybe you should practice getting involved," Margaret suggested. "Practice somewhere you don't know anyone so there's nothing left to lose."

"Where?" Jana asked.

"How about a hospital?"

And so one afternoon a week after school, the two young women volunteered their time at St. Vincent's Hospital. Jana liked what she did. In reaching out to people, she felt useful. The girls worked hard at cheering up the patients, and between visits to the rooms where they distributed books and magazines, they chatted about school.

"The counselor said she was sure I'd get into Parsons," Margaret commented as they pushed a cart of magazines and books down a long hallway of the hospital. "They're the best for graphics."

"I don't want to go to school anymore," Jana said.

"You don't?" Margaret looked at Jana as if she'd lost her mind. She was shocked that her friend didn't want to go to college. It was always just assumed they would go.

260

Thud! In her distraction, Margaret had shoved the cart right into a man who was waiting for the elevator.

"Oh!" Jana cried. "Oh, golly, we're really sorry."

Margaret ran around the cart and inspected the man for damage.

"Are you all right?" Jana asked.

"I'm sorry. I really am," said Margaret.

She noted the white jacket and the stethescope in his pocket. His nametag read Joseph Dakin, M.D.

Oh God, I've hit a doctor, Margaret moaned to herself. We'll probably get kicked off the volunteer list for this.

The man smiled at them. He wasn't handsome, but there was something very appealing about him. Even though he was only in his twenties, he had crinkles at the corners of his eyes. Humor and warmth radiated from his face.

"Yes. I'm all right. No harm done," he assured them. He looked at the two young women. Although Jana's cool beauty was more striking, it was Margaret's gamine face surrounded with unruly dark curls that appealed to him.

Too young, he thought, dismissing her. Much too young. Pity.

"Are you certain?" Margaret asked. "I wasn't paying attention to where I was going. I'm really sorry."

He liked the slight trace of an English accent that Margaret still retained. She was delicate yet strong. With her flushed cheeks and porcelain skin, she looked like a china doll.

Margaret looked into Joe Dakin's eyes with the

intent of seeing if he was, indeed, all right. Instead, she fell in love.

"It's too bad he's so old," Margaret said later. "Why does he have to be so old?"

In the long run, age didn't make any difference to either Margaret or Joe. Love was the only operative word in their emotional vocabulary.

As Jana watched the drama of falling in love unfold before her, she felt a painful stab of envy in her heart.

Will I ever feel that? she asked herself wistfully. Will I ever experience that kind of love, that kind of joy?

At her high school graduation, Jana delivered the valedictory speech. She was radiant that day, filled with eagerness and vitality.

Standing before the audience robed in the traditional cap and gown, her golden blond hair cascading from under the mortarboard, Jana was astoundingly beautiful. Perhaps it was her elusiveness, her skittishness that made her so appealing. Perhaps it was her elegance or her mystery. But whatever it was, there were men at that graduation ceremony who would carry the image of her beauty in their hearts for the rest of their days. Christian Horvath was no exception.

After the ceremony, Jonathan invited Jana and Rachel, the Pyms and the Horvaths and Joe Dakin for a celebration dinner at the Metropolitan Club. Nobody could know what a bitter pill this was for

Gillian Horvath to swallow.

For years, she had longed to become a member of the Metropolitan. But her husband had never been asked. It required more than money to belong to that club. It required family. Old family. And social status. The Horvath's had neither. They could only aspire to them.

Here was her immigrant relative who was barely off the boat, Gillian thought. A woman who *worked* for a living, yet she was involved with one of the most socially prominent men in New York city. And Jana . . . Who does she think she is, ignoring my son that way? Doesn't she think he's good enough for her?

Much to her parent's disapproval, Margaret Pym married Joe Dakin the August after she graduated from high school. The Pyms tried to talk their daughter out of it. Then they tried to bribe her by offering to send her to England for a year. But nothing they could say or do made any difference.

Margaret and Joe Dakin were married in a simple Episcopal ceremony in the small chapel of St. Bartholomew's Church. Jana was the maid of honor. She was happy for her friend, happy that Margaret had found the man she wanted to marry. But she knew their special friendship would never be the same.

After the wedding dinner, Jana went home with Rachel. When she got into bed, she wept like a child. Since the day in the mountains when she was left to guard the horses, Jana had never felt more alone.

"We'll always be best friends," Margaret said when they were having lunch. She had just returned from her honeymoon in Bermuda, and she was tanned, relaxed and exceedingly happy.

"Of course," Jana said. But she didn't really believe it.

"I know what you're thinking," Margaret said, poking her friend on the arm. "You don't have faith in the longevity of human relationships. That feeling comes from all the terrible things that happened to you when you were little." It was clear, from Margaret's comments, that she had tuned into her husband's medical specialty of psychiatry. "But that doesn't mean those things apply now. Love *can* last. So can friendship, Jana. It's time you learned that."

"I know," Jana answered. "I know it in my head at least. It's my gut that's having a problem."

The two women smiled.

"I know it's hard," Margaret said. "But keep the faith. And, while you're doing it, tell me about your new job."

Jana was apprenticing with a jewelry maker in Greenwich Village. He had a small shop on Mac-Dougal Street and had agreed to take Jana on as an assistant.

"I love it," Jana said. Her face lit up as she began to tell Margaret about it. "We're starting to make things for Christmas. And already Conrad is allowing me to design and execute my own ideas." Jana hesitated, as if she could not believe what she was saying. "He says I'm good, Margaret. Really good. Jonathan and Rachel think so, too. The other day Jonathan said I could be famous if I wanted to be, that I have what it takes to really be a success."

"I'm not surprised." Margaret smiled at her friend.

"And you know what?" Jana asked almost shyly. "This is the best part. Jonathan says if I continue to do this well, he thinks I should sell my designs at Fields and Thomas. Maybe even start a boutique with Rachel."

It took almost two years for that to happen. In the interim, Jana honed her craft, learning everything she could about the properties of silver and gold, about how each could be worked. She also learned how to choose and set stones. By the end of the apprenticeship, Jana had developed her own unique style, a style that supported a growing reputation for being one of the most creative young designers in the country.

That's when Jonathan made Rachel and Jana an astounding offer.

"I want you to open a boutique in Fields and Thomas," he said one night over dinner. "It will just be for jewelry."

"Old or new?" Rachel asked.

"Both," Jonathan said. "That's the draw. The best of both worlds."

"We'll run it. Buy for it. And Jana will design for it. But will we own a piece of the business?"

"Well . . . I hadn't thought of that," Jonathan

said. "Trust you to come up with it," he added with a smile.

"Well?"

"It's negotiable," he said. "Certainly something to consider." Then he turned to Jana. "You've been awfully quiet. What do you think?"

"I'm stunned," she said. "I can't believe you've made such an offer."

"Well, I have," he said. "And why shouldn't I? Between the talents of you two women, Tiffany's and Cartier had better look out. They don't know it yet. But they are about to get blown away by the two most beautiful women in New York."

"I hope so," Jana said.

"You hope you're the most beautiful, or you'll blow away the competition?" Jonathan teased.

Jana laughed. "Both," she replied.

Chapter 14

Rachel sold the sapphire and emerald and all except one of her remaining diamonds to raise the money for their share of the partnership in the boutique. At her insistence, she was able to buy a fifty percent interest for herself and Jana. It would be their security, Rachel reasoned. Jana's security. This will give her a future, something to hang onto when I'm gone.

As for the last remaining diamond, Rachel returned it to the safety deposit box. Besides the brooch, the diamond had been Josef's prize, the rare, four carat pink stone he intended to turn into a necklace for Rachel. She couldn't bring herself to part with it. Nor could she bring herself to wear it. And so she put it away, thinking it would make a beautiful ring for Jana one day, a last sparkling legacy from a family who had lóved her well, but who had nothing to leave her except memories of that love and this one magnificent stone.

* * *

In formulating the policies for their boutique, Jana and Rachel decided to concentrate on only the best in antique and contemporary jewelry. They sought out pieces that were one of a kind, a necessity if they were to create the right appeal to the exclusive clientele that frequented the store. They attended estate sales. They scoured out-of-the-way places. They looked in every likely and unlikely location for unique brooches, rings, pins, and clasps. They bought Cartier hat pins and Tiffany rings. They bought a necklace worn by the Empress Josephine and a brooch given to a Russian Czarina. It took Rachel and Jana almost a year to gather the inventory for their venture. Their taste was discriminating and, considering the masses of jewelry they inspected, their purchases were few. Every spare moment was spent going to auctions, making phone calls, travelling, acquiring.

Because Rachel had begun to tire more easily, Jana did most of the travelling. She made three trips to Paris and two each to London and Rome.

On every one of these trips, Jana not only returned with new business acquaintances and some spectacular finds culled from the world of expensive jewels, she returned with the business cards of at least three men who wished to make her acquaintance. She accepted the cards, but not the invitations.

In spite of her growing maturity and her increasing experience, she was still frightened of men.

"I'm too busy," she would say. "I'm too involved in my business. My schedule doesn't permit it." All excuses to avoid the inevitable sexual advance. Just the thought of a strange man touching her was enough to send shivers down her spine.

On the other hand, several of the men Jana had met were attractive to her. They weren't dashingly handsome, nor were they particularly wealthy. But they did have a charming manner, a wit that appealed to her. As much as Jana wanted to get to know some of the men better, she was tormented by her inability to do anything about it. She didn't know where to begin. And, if she did find the courage to begin, she wouldn't know what to expect. For over twelve years, she had closed her mind to anything sexual. She had averted her glance, pretended sex didn't exist. She thought of it as make believe, like the lovers in *From Here to Eternity*. In reality, nothing really happened. In a way, she was still the young child she had left behind in Budapest when she had just turned seven years old. One afternoon, Margaret invited Jana for lunch at her new apartment. It was then that Jana decided to ask her friend the questions she had avoided for so long. She led up to the subject slowly. Yet when she finally asked her first question, it came as something of a shock.

"Does it hurt?" Jana asked shyly.

"I can't believe you're asking me this," Margaret said. "Of course it doesn't hurt. Oh, the first time can hurt, of course. But after that, it's wonderful!" Margaret paused and looked carefully at her friend. Her brow wrinkled in consternation. "Are you telling me you don't know anything about sex?" Margaret asked. "I've always known you were uncomfortable talking about it. So I tried to respect your privacy. You know how we English are," she teased. "I just assumed you were shy and didn't want to talk about it. But if it's more than that—if you want to talk, if you want to ask me some questions—please feel free. Ask anything."

Jana swallowed. Tears sprung to her eyes.

"What is it?" Margaret said. She leaned across the lunch table and touched Jana's arm.

"There's something I never told you about when Rachel and I escaped from Budapest."

Margaret remained silent, not wanting to scare Jana off.

"When we got off the boat, we were detained by a German soldier. He did more than cut my hair, Margaret. I told you about that." Margaret nodded silently. "He . . . raped my grandmother. He raped . . . Rachel and I was forced . . . to watch," Jana said. With that, Jana buried her face in her hands, covering her pain, trying to blot out the terrible vision she had carried in her head for so many years. "I can't stop seeing it," she cried. "Every time I meet a nice man, just the thought of his touching me like that makes me run away, makes me retreat. And I'm afraid . . . deeply afraid that I'll be alone the rest of my life."

Tears sprung to Margaret's eyes. No wonder, she thought. That's why she's been so indifferent to men all these years. She moved to Jana and put her arms around her. At first, she didn't know what to say. So she just let Jana cry. When the tears subsided, the two women moved to the couch where they could talk more comfortably.

"I'm sorry you didn't tell me this a long time ago," Margaret said finally. "I'm not sure I could have changed anything. But just telling me might have helped. I'm glad I know now, though. It explains so much."

Jana nodded, too exhausted to speak.

"The first thing that occurs to me is that in a strange way, you were traumatized more than Rachel. You were barely seven years old, for goodness sake! It seems to me that Rachel's all right. The most casual onlooker can tell she's a very sensual woman. Quite at ease with her sexuality. She and Jonathan obviously share a wonderful intimacy."

"Do you think so?" Jana asked naively. She had tried not to think of those things where her grandmother was concerned. It didn't seem right to her.

Margaret laughed. "Of course. They travel together. They spend weekends together. What do you expect? Separate bedrooms?"

"I guess not."

"About you . . ." Margaret said, trying to move Jana back to talking about herself. "How do you feel about men now?"

"About men," Jana repeated. There was a vaguely bitter tone to her voice. "I'm terrified. I'm terrified to kiss a man, much less to make love to him. Every time I think about it, I think of that Nazi raping my grandmother. And I think of blood."

"Blood?" Margaret asked.

Jana shook her head. "Yes," she whispered.

"When it was over—when the man was still on top of her—Marek threw a knife at him. It cut his face badly. It was hideous. Blood everywhere. Gushing. Dripping all over Rachel who was still beneath him. The man screamed. An awful, animal scream. And Marek grabbed Rachel and made her get up. He took us both by the hand and we started to run. That's when we lost the brooch."

The two women were silent then. Jana was exhausted from the effort of telling Margaret her worst secret. And Margaret simply didn't know what to say. She knew she had to offer something. Jana needed her words, her comfort. I'm flat out of wisdom, she thought to herself. What can I possibly say that would help her in any way?

"I don't know where to begin," Margaret said. "Except to tell you that you don't have to live like this for the rest of your life. Psychotherapy can help."

Jana looked startled.

"No, no," Margaret said, reading her mind. "Not with Joe. Of course not. It wouldn't be ethical or wise for him to treat a friend. But he can recommend someone."

"Do you think he can make the memory go away?"

"No . . ." Margaret answered carefully. "But he can help you put it in perspective. He can help you take control so that it no longer controls you."

"It does control me," Jana said. "I'm almost twenty-one years old and I've never been kissed."

"I want to tell you right now that you're missing

out on something great," Margaret said gently. "When it's with the right man, making love can be . . . transporting . . . beautiful. If you trust him, Jana, it will be good. You're going to have to learn to trust. That takes time. I think you'll have to tell him about it," Margaret added, "If he's the kind of man who deserves you, he'll understand. And he'll help you. Just remember: Take it one step at a time. Don't look ahead. That can be scary. Just accept the moment for what it has to give."

"I'll try," Jana said, promising herself she would not walk away from the next nice man she met.

Jana started talking to him on the flight home from Paris. He was in the seat next to her. Since it was such a long flight, they had plenty of time to get to know each other. His name was Pierre Jonas, and he was a lawyer with an international law firm headquartered in Paris.

Jana liked his looks from the moment he sat down. He wasn't too tall. Five-ten, perhaps. He was slim, muscular. He had dark, flashing eyes and brown curly hair that was worn longer than was currently fashionable in America.

They talked all the way across the Atlantic. And when they arrived at Idlewild Airport, he offered her a ride to her apartment.

Jana held her breath. One step at a time, she reminded herself. Just like Margaret said: accept the moment. "Thank you," she said. "That's very kind."

Pierre Jonas was delighted. He liked this lovely

young woman. There was something elusive about her, something mysterious. And yet she contained an attractive warmth that was subtly expressed in her shy and unassuming manner. She was an enigma, he thought. He had no idea that he had made more progress with this stunning beauty than the combined efforts of dozens of men before him.

As they walked through the airport, Jana found herself chatting easily with him.

It's not so hard, she thought, this taking one step at a time. He's nice. She looked up at him and smiled.

It was that smile, that warmth and delight, that Christopher Horvath saw as he walked toward Jana in the airport. But all that beauty shone on another man.

Earlier that day, Chris had called for Jana, and Rachel had told him she was arriving that afternoon on the Air France flight from Paris.

Deciding to surprise her, Chris had rented a limousine and went to the airport to pick up his cousin. A limousine, champagne and flowers, he thought. How can she turn it down? As it happened, Jana walked right past Christopher. She never even saw him standing there.

She never smiled at me that way, Christopher thought bitterly as he watched Jana collect her luggage and then get into a taxi with the man. She never went anyplace with me, either.

It was only a coincidence that Christopher overheard Rachel mention that she would be attending opening night at the Metropolitan Opera season. That was how he knew Jana would be alone.

When the doorman rang the intercom to announce Christopher's presence, Jana was surprised. Of course she invited him up. After all, he was her cousin.

"I was in the neighborhood and thought I'd drop by to see you," Chris announced. Jana was too inexperienced to detect the fact that he was a little tipsy.

"How nice," Jana said, not having the slightest idea of what she should say. "Why don't you come in and have a glass of wine."

Christopher smiled. "Terrific," he said.

As annoyed as she was by her cousin's visit, Jana tried to be pleasant. He *is* my father's last living relative, she reminded herself as she sat on the sofa and made polite, awkward conversation. I wish I didn't dislike him so much. I can't figure out why he makes me so uncomfortable.

"I thought maybe you'd like to go out and have a cappucino," Christopher suggested casually after he had been with Jana for about an hour. It had required two glasses of wine for him to find the courage to ask this offhand question.

"Thanks, but I really have too much work to do," Jana answered. "The opening of the boutique's less than a month away. And we still have lots of preparation."

"Ah come on," Christopher coaxed. "Just one cup of coffee won't hurt you. All work and no play

275

makes Jana a dull girl."

Jana smiled. "Then I guess I'll just have to settle for being dull," she said. Surely he'll take the hint, she thought.

"Come on," Jana," Christopher cajoled. "Loosen up."

"I really can't," she answered, standing up. "I really have work I must do."

Christopher stood up. With no warning, he lunged for her. Surprised, Jana stepped back. But Christopher caught hold of her blouse.

"Just this once," he said. His tone of voice was harsh, demanding. It matched the grasp he had on her sleeve.

Jana was angry. It never occurred to her to be frightened. "I have to work now. It's time for you to go, Christopher. Please let go of my sleeve."

"Not till you say you'll come out with me." He took hold of her arms. His grip was powerful, insistent.

"Stop it!" Jana said, choking out her words. "Let go of me." Panic rose in her throat. "Let go of me right now!"

Suddenly Christopher pushed her backwards onto the sofa. She started to scream. But he clamped his mouth over hers in a terrible, painful parody of a kiss.

Horror at the deepest level invaded every cell of Jana's body. She was no longer in the present. Without warning, without preparation, she was swept back to the most traumatic time of her life, a time of raw terror, of explosive hatred. A time when violence was stark and life was cheap.

Putting his hand over her mouth, Christopher shoved Jana into a prone position, pulling her legs up onto the sofa.

"This is what you've always wanted, you cold bitch," Christopher snarled. "All you women are the same. You tease us. Then you withhold the promise. Well, I'm not going to let you get away with that. I'm going to take what you've been offering. And I'm going to take it now."

Jana couldn't utter a sound. He was much stronger than she. More powerful. But somehow in her struggle she managed to free one hand. Blindly, she grasped desperately behind her head. Her hand brushed the lamp on the side table at the end of the sofa. Without thinking, she closed her fingers around the base. Then, with a strength born of twelve years of suffering, she lifted the lamp and swung it hard onto the top of her cousin's head.

When Rachel and Jonathan returned from the opera, Rachel was still bathing in the powerful glow of *The Magic Flute*. Mozart's music had soared that night, filling the Metropolitan Opera House to the rafters with exultation and beauty.

As they got to the apartment, Rachel looked up at Jonathan and smiled. After all this time, she thought, I still love him without reservation. How lucky I am to have met this extraordinary man.

Jonathan leaned over and nuzzled her cheek. "I love you," he whispered softly.

Rachel fumbled with the key. Laughing softly, she said, "See how you make me tremble."

"Don't ever stop," Jonathan said as they walked into the apartment.

When they entered the living room, Rachel and Jonathan were confronted with a terrible sight: Jana lay inert, dazed on the sofa. Her blouse was torn and bloody. Her face was bruised and her lower lip was red and puffy. Her right eye was swollen shut.

Beside her on the floor, Christopher Horvath lay unconscious. His head was bloody and a deep gash that looked like a ragged black-red line streaked across his forehead.

"Oh my God!" cried Rachel as she ran to Jana. "What happened!"

Jana looked at Rachel through wounded eyes that were glazed with fear and terror. "He tried to . . . rape me," Jana gasped. Then she closed her eyes against the pain she saw in her grandmother's face.

"I'll call an ambulance," Jonathan said, putting his hands on Rachel's shoulders. She nodded.

When the ambulance came, Jana refused to go to the hospital. The doctor examined her and said she didn't appear to be injured. So Christopher was taken alone.

After Rachel called the Horvath's to tell them about their son, she made one other phone call. She knew without even discussing what happened that the services of a psychiatrist were going to be needed. In ten minutes, Joe Dakin was at Jana's side.

"I'm afraid," Jana confessed. She had visited the psychiatrist every day for two weeks. She told the doctor about her childhood, about Christopher. Yet, she felt like she had just scratched the surface.

Dr. McGowain smiled. "That just confirms you're sane. Only a crazy person would be fearless at a time like this." He paused a minute. "Look," he said. "I differ from most of my colleagues in several ways. The most significant is that I don't adhere to one doctrine. This is 1957. A new era. I believe in doing what works. We don't need to spend months or even years trying to uncover the cause of your pain. The story you've told makes that quite apparent. It's no wonder you feel helpless. You'd be abnormal if you didn't. So our task isn't to uncover the trauma. It's to help you learn how to deal with it so that you can cope effectively with the present. It can be done. It will require a great effort from you. Because these changes aren't accomplished without pain and risk. And they're certainly not accomplished overnight. But if you'll make a commitment to try your hardest, Miss Horvath, I will, too. You're too strong, too intelligent to live half a life."

Jana thought about what he said. "I want to live a whole life," she said softly. "I don't want to live half a life anymore.

"Then, let's get started," said Dr. McGowain.

Chapter 15

"It's a long way from the mountains," Jana whispered to Rachel as they surveyed the bustling scene before them.

"Indeed," murmured Rachel, her voice subdued with quiet pride and the natural anxiety that precedes an important event.

In front of the two elegantly dressed women, an archway made entirely of plexiglass formed an entrance to a separate section of Fields and Thomas. Above the archway, suspended by invisible nylon thread, brass letters spelling THE DANUBE hung in shining announcement of the store's new and very expensive jewelry boutique.

In the corner of the store, a five-place stringed ensemble warmed up for an evening of Hungarian music. The musicians would be playing for five hundred selected guests. Everything was ready, everything was in place. But nothing shone brighter among the jewels and the glitter than Rachel von Weitzman and Jana Horvath. In their individual ways, both were extraordinarily beautiful women.

Down the center aisle of the store, a long table covered with pale pink linen was laden with a sumptuous feast of Hungarian food. A huge pot of *tokany*—a rich stew made of beef and veal spiced with sweet paprika and onions—comprised the main dish of the elaborate buffet supper. *Lesco,* a mixture of green peppers, tomatoes, onions, bacon and paprika, added a bright dash of color to the table, contrasting pleasingly with the more subtle dish of cold fish called *fogas.*

The far end of the buffet table featured a large selection of cheeses and pastries, the latter an elaborate variety for which the Hungarians have always been famous. And as an accompaniment to the desserts, an antique brass espresso machine had been installed on a separate table, a gesture to the Hungarian fondness for coffee houses.

Vintage champagne and Tokay—an elegant sweet wine for which the country is justifiably famous—flowed freely, leaving no doubt about how important and extravagant this opening was.

"Sometimes," said Jana during the quiet lull just before the guests arrived. "When I see all this luxury I feel guilty. I can't help remembering the times we were hungry, the times we were grateful for a thin, watery stew made of a scrawny rabbit and a few wild onions and nettles. I wonder why we should have all this, why—"

"Stop that nonsense," Rachel said in her characteristically firm manner. "The reason we have all this is because we worked ourselves to the bone for it. This boutique was not handed to us. It did not fall into our laps uninvited. We worked for it. Don't you forget it. We have paid, in one way or another, for every morsel of food on that table and every piece of jewelry in that case."

The case Rachel referred to was a U-shaped plexiglass counter that was lined in thick, rich midnight blue velvet just beneath the glass top. From a distance, the counter looked as if it were suspended in space. On one side, the case was filled with antique jewelry culled from the most prestigious estate sales that had taken place in America and Europe over the past year. The other side—glittering with gold, silver, precious and semi-precious stones—was made up entirely of new jewelry. A few of these pieces had been designed by Jana, others by some of the brightest and most creative designers of contemporary jewelry in the country. In all, it was a stunning collection, one calculated to appeal to the wide range of wealthy people who were already devoted patrons of Fields and Thomas.

"Don't ever forget that we've paid," Rachel continued, putting her arm on Jana's shoulder and giving her a hug. "I know what you've gone through. I wasn't a child forced to endure what you did. But I saw, Jana . . . I saw what was happening and I have a pretty good idea of what was going on inside you. It was more than any one human being—much less a child—should have to endure. We've both paid our dues, my love. So I don't want to hear any more talk about not deserving this. We deserve every last bit of it . . . and more, for that matter," she added with a gentle smile. "Lots more."

Jana nodded, knowing her grandmother's words were true. But it was intellectual knowledge. Not emotional conviction. Because there were still places inside . . . dark places only touched in the blackest part of the night, empty places that sometimes left her bereft of her rightful sense of self . . . that still clung to her, clawing at the shreds of confidence and vitality she had managed to salvage from her tragic and chaotic childhood. She was working hard with Dr. McGowain to change this. And she had accomplished a lot in the short time she had been seeing him. When she began, she did not think she would have the emotional strength to attend the opening.

Yet, here she was, elegantly turned out for the glittering show, making decisions, coping with stress. In many ways, she was still frightened, still a child scared of the dark. Sometimes she felt as if she were floating above her own self, a suspended, ethereal creature in a Chagall painting. But through it all, she did what she had to do, a lesson she had learned originally when she was only seven years old.

"Are you Miss Horvath?" a distinguished-looking woman inquired.

Jana hadn't noticed the arriving guests. "Yes," she said with a smile.

"Your designs are stunning," the woman exclaimed effusively. "Simply stunning."

Jana took a deep breath, made the appropriate response, then plunged into the evening. She chatted amusingly with the French Ambassador's wife and

Jasmine Conte, a used-looking young woman who had just opened in the Broadway season's newest musical hit.

She flirted discretely with one of the mayor's aides and smiled prettily at an upper-echolon manager of Fields and Thomas. She laughed, she accepted compliments graciously and offered them generously with a talent that had been honed to a fine art over the years.

She played the parts demanded of her with the consumate ease of a seasoned actress. And the role was enhanced by her stunning beauty. On that evening, she was dressed in a simple black matte jersey gown. Elegant and striking, everything about her was perfect: her long, golden blonde hair was piled high on her head, accentuating her graceful neck and bare shoulders. The only piece of jewelry she wore was a simple pendant, a glittering bar of her own design, made of emeralds and diamonds. Only Rachel recognized that this was a jeweled replica of an Italian medal that had once been given to her by a dying Yugoslavian hero.

Once during the evening when Jana found herself playing nervously with the necklace, a wisp of a thought passed vaguely through her mind: if it were only the Tiffany brooch. She was old enough now to understand the childish foolishness of such a wish; and she was honest enough with herself to understand that this incessant dream persisted because of her own lack of inner sustainment. No matter how hard she tried, no matter what substitutes she created, she could not seem to fill that vague but important void inside her self. She had been working harder at it over the past month since the incident with Christopher.

"There is no instant cure," Dr. McGowain had said. "It takes time. You must learn how to take care of that frightened child we all carry around inside ourselves, and that's not easy. But with time and effort you'll do it. That's when you'll discover yourself. And when you do, you'll find out you're stronger than you think."

Jana smiled and chatted amiably with dozens of important people. She moved where events took her, drifting from one beautiful person to another. Detached and serene, she was an ethereal young woman floating calmly in the eye of her own personal storm.

Jana looked at Rachel, still elegant and beautiful at the age of sixty-two. There was a regal bearing about her, a boldness that demanded attention with its powerful grace. Somehow, the harsh experiences that had clipped Jana's delicate wings were the same ones that had strengthened Rachel and had given her flight. Jana recognized this, envied it.

Jana walked over to her grandmother just as Jonathan approached.

"Rachel . . . Jana," he said with an easy smile. "You women are sensational! You've created something unique, just as we had hoped. Everyone loves it!" He tipped his glass of champagne to them, then his eyes drifted towards Rachel, resting a moment as they met hers. A secret smile played delicately between them. For a fleeting moment, they could have been mistaken for young lovers.

Rachel glowed with Jonathan's compliment. Almost shyly, she glanced away, as if she could not afford to continue her gaze for fear of revealing herself too intimately. Then, without warning, a stricken expression marred her face. She tried to hide it, to control her shock. But she failed.

"Excuse me, please," she mumbled clumsily to Jana and Jonathan. Then she walked through the crowd to the far side of the room as if she were being drawn by an invisible cord.

"It's happened again," Jana whispered to Jonathan.

They stood transfixed and watched as Rachel approached a strange man who was at least twenty years younger than she. She touched the man's shoulder tentatively and said in a trembling voice, "Josef?"

The man turned and looked blankly at Rachel. "Pardon me?" he asked, his brow furrowed in confusion.

Involuntarily, Rachel's hand flew to her mouth. Her face sagged and she suddenly looked every moment of her age. "Oh," she mumbled awkwardly. "I thought you were someone . . . I knew . . . a long . . . time ago," she offered in lame apology.

The man smiled awkwardly, clearly uncomfortable with the intensity of Rachel's reaction.

Helpless, Jana and Jonathan watched, both wanting to weep for Rachel, to put an end to her endless quest. And yet, they knew there was nothing they could do.

Since the moment Jana and Rachel arrived in Bari, Italy twelve years earlier, it had been like this. Jana wondered if the search would ever end. The thought flashed through her consciousness that Rachel's quest was the same as her own quest for the brooch: futile.

The first thing Rachel had done when she arrived in Bari was to go immediately to the Red Cross in search of her family. She had talked and corresponded with every Jewish aid society she could locate, with every agency that might be the slightest help in discovering the fate of her family. Over the years, the search had become an integral part of Rachel's life, never-ending, always elusive.

Several times a year, Rachel would see someone, a man or woman, who resembled Josef or Olga or Stefan. Each time she would approach the person with anticipation and part from him with sorrow. All that carried Rachel was hope, hope that somewhere, somehow, her family was still alive. But never once did she receive one concrete word about them. Never once did she hear their names uttered by a helpful stranger. Had their deaths been confirmed, had they been one of the millions whose names filled the death rolls of Auchwitz or Buchenwald, it would have been a merciful ending for Rachel. As it was, she simply continued the search for something she did not know existed. The idea that three people she had loved deeply and well had simply disappeared from the face of the earth was unthinkable to her. In order to validate their existence, to prove they hadn't lived in vain, she continued the search. Somehow, she felt that if she gave up she would negate their very existence. The abhorrence of this alternative condemned her to live forever haunted.

Jana walked over to her grandmother. The party swirled on around them, oblivious to the private drama taking place. Rachel looked at her grand-daughter with dark and haunted eyes. "I thought. . ." she began in lame explanation.

"I know, Buba," whispered Jana. "I know."

It was at that moment that Jana understood. For the first time, she saw clearly that—no matter how fast we run or how cleverly we hide—the past will always be with us.

Chapter 16

" 'The opening of The Danube marks a new era for Fields and Thomas. In recent years, the venerable institution had begun to rely more on its reputation than its marketing skill. But if last night's gala is any indication, Fields and Thomas has assured its place once again at the top of the department store ranks. Furthermore, the opening made it abundantly clear that if you want the best and the most unique in contemporary or antique jewelry, The Danube is the place to go.' So what do you think of that?" Jonathan asked Jana and Rachel as he read the *New York Times* review to them. His smile was filled with pride and delight.

"I think we couldn't ask for a newspaper review any better than that," Jana said. She felt giddy from the triumph of the night before and was thrilled that her sometimes controversial taste in contemporary jewelry design had been vindicated.

"It's wonderful," Rachel said.

"Wonderful is an understatement," Jonathan said. He leaned over to Rachel and kissed her cheek. "I love you," he whispered as his lips grazed her ear.

Filled with the triumph of the night before and the warmth of Jonathan's love, Rachel smiled. Under the table, she took his hand in hers and squeezed it in a silent response to his whispered words.

Jonathan looked at Rachel, his eyes assessing her expression. "What is it?" he asked.

Beneath her smile, Rachel's face appeared strained. Touched that Jonathan could read her so clearly, she protested, "I'm wonderful. Really I am. Please forgive me if I don't sound as enthusiastic as I should. Unfortunately, I think I am paying for my overindulgence in Hungarian pastries last night. If you don't mind, I think I'll go lie down."

"What's the matter?" Jonathan asked. He reached out and held her hand.

"Now don't worry," Rachel said. She touched his cheek tenderly. "You're always worrying about me." She skipped a beat. "Not that I don't appreciate your concern. It's just that this time, I have nothing but a little indigestion and there's not a thing to be worried about."

Rachel stood up and turned to them. "You two really are loves," she said. Suddenly, a stricken expression came over her face.

"What is it?" Jana cried.

Rachel's hand moved to her chest as her legs

folded beneath her.

"Call an ambulance!" Jonathan shouted as he lunged toward Rachel, catching her before she collapsed.

This can't be happening, Jana thought as she turned to the phone. It can't be happening.

At the hospital, Jana and Jonathan sat anxiously in the waiting room of the cardiac intensive care unit. Wordless, they held hands, each seeking silent comfort from the other.

The hours stretched before them as they waited for the doctor. When he finally appeared, they stood too greet him.

"She's suffered a massive coronary," Dr. Lamb said.

"Will . . . will she make it?" Jana asked. Her voice trembled in her effort to speak.

Dr. Lamb swallowed. "To be honest, Miss Horvath, I don't think her chances are very good."

Jana gasped as tears sprung to her eyes. She felt Jonathan's body stiffen beside her.

"May we see her?" Jonathan asked.

"One at a time," the doctor said. "And please make it a very short visit."

Jana stood by the door as Jonathan entered the room. She watched as he leaned over and kissed Rachel. There was something ineffably sweet and deep in the glance that passed between them.

Silently, Rachel's lips formed the words "I love you."

Jonathan nodded, clutching her hand in his.

"I love you, too," he whispered, as he brought her hand to his lips.

As she closed her eyes, a faint smile settled on Rachel's face.

Jonathan placed her hand gently on the bed and turned to Jana.

She entered the room on tiptoe. Although she was not asleep, Rachel's eyes were closed. The effort required to keep them open simply seemed to great.

Jana leaned over the bed and whispered to her grandmother. "Buba?" she said. "Buba? I love you."

Rachel opened her eyes. "I love you," Rachel choked.

"Please get well, Buba. Please."

"Be strong, Jana." Her words were barely audible. As if she were gathering strength, Rachel took a deep breath. "You have more power than you think."

Jana nodded, choking back her tears.

Rachel smiled. Her eyes spoke of the depth of her love. With all her strength, she squeezed Jana's hand.

Then, as if life were being turned off at a slow

but steady pace, the light dimmed in Rachel's eyes.

She died peacefully in the arms of the two people who loved her most.

Jana drifted through the funeral and its aftermath as if she had been turned on automatic pilot. She did not weep. There were no tears. She had nothing left with which to mourn the dead. Feeling had been cut from her just as surely as if a surgeon had excised all emotion from her with a sharp, gleaming scapel, then stitched her up to resemble a human being once more.

She continued to eat, to sleep, to work. She had an extensive repetoire of actions and reactions she could call upon at any given moment, and she used them all. She had trained herself well.

"Don't retreat now," Dr. McGowain cautioned her. "I know this is a terrible blow to you, Jana. But don't retreat from the pain. It's real. Feel it. Don't run from it. You can handle it, Jana. It will hurt. But it won't kill you."

"I wish I could believe that," Jana said, "Sometimes, I'm afraid that if I start crying I'll never stop. It's a prospect so terrifying to me . . . that I'd do anything to avoid it . . . including not feeling at all."

"I don't usually make promises to patients," Dr. McGowain said, "But this is one that I can make.

293

I promise that won't happen to you, Jana. You'll cry. Then you'll stop. And you'll cry some more. You may do that for weeks. But then it will be over. There will be an end to it. I promise."

"It's a lie," Jana said numbly. She had no feeling left.

At her lawyer's office a week after the funeral, Jana sat passively as Noah Benjamin read the provisions of the will.

"Rachel was a very wise woman," he said when he had finished.

"I know."

"Both your apartment and your business were set up as joint ventures. You avoid inheritance taxes that way. You are by no means an independently wealthy woman, Jana. But if you're careful. If you run your business wisely, you can continue to live the way you have been."

Jana nodded in acknowledgement. Numbness was the only feeling she had left.

"Are you all right?" Noah Benjamin asked.

"Yes," Jana said.

But the astute lawyer didn't believe her. He looked at this extraordinarily beautiful woman who sat before him. Her jaw was clenched, her face was impassive. He had the startling and peculiar notion that if he were to knock on Jana, there would be nobody home.

Six weeks after Rachel died, Jana's phone rang one evening. In a purely automatic response, Jana reached for the receiver.

"Hello? . . . this is Jana Horvath?" the male voice inquired in a charming French accent.

"Yes."

"This is Pierre Jonas."

For a fleeting instant Jana's heart fluttered. Then the feeling disappeared.

"Yes?" she said.

"I said I would call the next time I was in New York. This time I am here for a week. I wondered if we might have dinner together tomorrow night."

Jana hesitated. She would only lose him if she learned to love him. "I'm afraid that's not possible," she said.

Pierre hesitated. He heard the rejection in her voice, but he could not tell if it was temporary or final.

"Some other night then?" he asked.

"I'm afraid not."

"I see . . ." he said. There was no doubt that he did, indeed, see. "I am sorry," he offered lamely.

"I am, too," Jana said.

"Then it's *a dieu*," Pierre said.

"Yes."

Jana hung up the phone. She was overcome with the urge to scream. Then the feeling disappeared. There was nothing except blankness in it wake.

"Why are you doing this to yourself?" Margaret asked.

"Doing what?"

"Running away from life."

"Is that what I'm doing?" Jana asked. Her voice was a listless monotone, devoid of animation, of life.

"Yes. That's what you're doing. You're avoiding any situation that might make you feel, that might make you enter into the fray of life. If you're not careful, you're going to end up like a mechanical doll. You'll walk carefully through life sidestepping any pain, pretending you don't see any unpleasantness. I've got news for you, my friend. If you're going to live, you're going to hurt. But you're also going to laugh and love and feel. Pain comes with the territory, Jana. Granted . . . you've had more than your share. I wish I could wave a magic wand and change that. But I can't. All I can do is offer you my hand and ask you to walk alongside me till you feel strong enough to walk on your own."

Jana knew she was guilty of doing everything

Margaret accused her of. She *was* sidestepping life. During the two months following Rachel's death, she had spent her days like a robot. She stopped seeing Dr. McGowain. She was afraid he would force her into actually feeling her pain. And that possibility held more terror than Jana could cope with.

Her strange, detached behavior did not go unnoticed. The people she worked with in Fields and Thomas began to avoid her. They could not cope with her stony face and impassive eyes.

"It's not that I don't like her," a saleswoman told Dolly Mack, the woman Rachel had chosen to be her assistant and who now helped Jana in the daily running of the boutique. "It's just that she gives me the willies. I don't know how you can stand to work for her."

Dolly smiled. Sometimes she didn't know, either. She had been very fond of Rachel and held her in the highest esteem. She also had an enormous respect for Jana. She kept telling herself things would get better. But she was beginning to have her doubts.

Even Jonathan, who thought of Jana as the daughter he never had, tried to get through to her. At least once a week, Jana had lunch with him. Occasionally, they would have dinner and go to the theatre or the opera. But nothing Jonathan said, nothing he did, seemed to get through to her.

"I think," Jana said to Margaret, "That I've lost faith in the future. I'm afraid to love because I'm afraid I'll lose the person I love. It's happened to me every time."

"But it won't always be that way," Margaret said.

"I wish I could believe you. I'm so frightened," Jana said. She felt all the pain and fear of an abandoned child. "I'm terrified of losing control of my life, of starting into a spin that I can't stop."

Margaret put her arms around her friend and held her tight. "Hang on, Jana. Good things will happen if you let them. Just remember to take one step at a time."

In her desperate need to keep a grip on her sanity, Jana began to develop little rituals to insure the fact that she would retain control of her life. She started to make seemingly insignificant deals with chance. At first, it was innocent enough. Then, gradually over a period of months, it became a compulsion. In the mornings, if her routine was interrupted in any way, she would be convinced her day would go wrong. If she didn't catch a cab within a prescribed period of time, she would have bad luck. If, when she returned home at night, the doorman tipped his hat to her in greeting, she would make it through another night. If he didn't, disaster would strike in the night.

The problem with this sort of magical thinking, of course, comes when things don't happen the way you wish them to. Then, counter-rituals must be devised. Jana refused to think of these peculiar rituals in terms of anything except self-protection. She didn't tell Margaret. Even after she finally found the courage to start seeing Dr. McGowain again, she didn't tell him about her daily ceremonies. Somewhere, lurking in the dim recesses of her consciousness, she understood her behavior was becoming more and more bizarre. But she could not help herself. She had become an addict of sorts, a control junkie always in need of a ritual fix in order to maintain her grip on an increasingly precarious world.

One evening, almost a year after Rachel's death, Jana came home from work on a hot, steamy August evening. She was exhausted from the debilitating effects of the heat, weary from the noise of the traffic, the stink of exhaust fumes, and the short tempers of virtually everyone she encountered. She walked past the doorman, but he simply nodded, too hot and tired to tip his hat.

Jana was stunned. She had always been able to count on him. And now he had let her down. She didn't know what to expect, what terrible disaster might strike.

Instead of going upstairs to her apartment, she walked back outside again and went down to the deli on the corner. She bought some tuna salad for dinner and then returned to her apartment. As she walked past the doorman again, he managed a wan smile as he put his hand to the bill of his cap.

It was almost like tipping his hat, Jana thought with relief. Almost.

Upstairs in her apartment, she poured herself a glass of white wine. She took a sip and closed her eyes, trying to think of nothing, to clear her mind of all doubts and anxieties and fears.

The ringing of the telephone startled her out of her stupor.

Should I answer it? she asked herself. Maybe I shouldn't touch it. Maybe it's bad news.

Against her better judgement, Jana picked up the receiver.

"Hello?" she said.

The voice of the caller was strange. But somewhere, from the vague recesses of her memory, there was a familiarity to its deep, male resonance. She felt as if she were listening to a haunting melody that she had heard long ago. She had forgotten where or when she learned it, or what the lyrics meant. But she hadn't forgotten the tune.

"Is that Jana Horvath?" the caller asked.

"Yes."

"The Jana Horvath that was born in Budapest and lived with the Partisans in Yugoslavia?"

Jana's heart skipped a beat. "Yes!" she cried.

"My name is Marek Cetkovic."

Jana gasped. She couldn't believe what she had just heard. She didn't think it was happening.

"Marek?" she said breathlessly. "My Marek from the mountains?"

"It's you, Jana!" Marek exclaimed. "It really is you! I was afraid to believe it when I saw your name in the phone book."

"But how . . . where?"

"I've been in America for almost two years. But on the west coast. In San Pedro. I have also been travelling a great deal." Marek spoke English quite well. His accent was still heavy, but Jana had no trouble understanding him. "To tell you the truth, I think I have been afraid to call. I did not know if you would want to see me. Those were difficult times, after all. I didn't know . . ." His voice drifted away inconclusively.

"They were good times, too," Jana whispered in a choked voice. She was so filled with emotion, so overcome with a whirling mixture of feeling and memory, that she could barely contain herself.

"I had hoped you would be in New York. I remembered you had relatives there."

"Yes. I have relatives. But I don't see them

301

anymore."

"Jana . . ." Marek said. "How is Rachel?"

Jana took a deep breath. "She died a year ago."

Marek was silent. Finally he said, "I'm . . . I'm so sorry, Jana. So deeply sorry."

"I know you are," she said simply. "I know you loved her, too."

"I did."

"But you, Jana. How are you?"

"All right," she lied. "I'm all right."

"I don't hear that in your voice."

His comment didn't ask for an answer.

"Tell me, Jana. I am at the airport now. I must catch a plane to Los Angeles. But I'll be back in New York in six weeks. I'd like to see you then. Will you be in New York?"

No! she thought. Don't see him! a voice screamed inside her. It will break you if you lose him, too! And you'll never recover. Don't see him!

Jana teetered back and forth on the edge of the abyss. She took a deep breath. One moment at a time, she reminded herself. One moment at a time. The future will take care of itself. "Yes," she said finally. "Please call me when you get back. I want to see you."

"I'm glad," Marek said simply. There was relief in his voice. "I'll return on the first of September. I'll call you before I come."

"Wonderful," Jana said.

302

After they said good-bye, Jana hung up the receiver as if she were in a dream. She did not move for a long time.

It took a full thirty seconds before she realized she was holding her breath. She felt like she was choking. She opened her mouth and inhaled, her lungs begging for air. She didn't feel like she could get enough. Finally she relaxed.

Marek's here, she thought. Marek's here. Without warning, tears flooded her eyes. And she began to cry. Really cry.

Former Oberleutnant Fritz Walther walked unsteadily home. He was drunk again, too far gone to be interested in any of the women who advertised their wares from the windows overlooking the Reeperbaun. This precarious journey had become his nightly ritual. After dinner, he would walk around the corner to the bar and drink until he stopped feeling. Then, with a backward glance at Ingrid, he would stagger home.

As he turned the corner to his building, he wasn't alert enough to sense anything wrong. Even if he had been, it's doubtful whether he could have escaped the efficient professionalism of the three men who accosted him.

The first one grabbed him around the neck and dragged him into the shadow of the building.

Bam! Walther received a full blow to the stomach.

"That's a message from Gunther," said the man who hit him. "He doesn't like you messing in his deals. He says it's not good for you to do that."

"Don't try to muscle in on our territory," said the man who held him. "It's not healthy."

Bam! Bam! More blows to the belly.

"Do you understand the message?"

"Yes," Walther groaned. "I understand."

Several weeks earlier, the Rome treaty had been signed marking the beginning of the European Common Market. The German economy had begun to prosper. The Common Market would help it even more. That did not bode well for someone who dealt in contraband.

As the economy grew, there was less and less need for people to turn to the black market for their wares. They could be purchased in a store. This turn of events left Walther out in the cold. Until that point, he had depended on his illegal trading to earn a living. Business had already turned bad, and he was living on a pittance compared to what he used to make. He had enough money to pay the rent and buy his liquor. There was little left over for anything else. That's when he decided to grab a piece of the drug trade. It was only a small piece. Just a tiny corner of the market, he reasoned. Nobody would even miss it.

But his competitors didn't see it that way. They considered any piece to be too big. And this midnight boxing practice was their way of letting him know it.

"So you'll stay out of our business?"

"Yes, yes!" Walther moaned. "I'll stay away."

Without another word, the man let go of him. Walther crumbled into a dirty heap on the ground. It was almost morning before he found the strength to climb the three flights of stairs to his shabby room.

Chapter 17

"I can't see him, Jonathan," Jana said firmly. "I won't do it. Meeting Marek would just be too painful. Too difficult. You don't understand. I lost him once. That was enough. I can't go through that again."

"Now, see here, young lady. I am too fond of you to allow this nonsense to go any further." Jonathan's voice was stern and allowed no room for excuses. Jana had invited him to dinner as a way of thanking him for all that he had done for her. And now she was beginning to regret it. She certainly regretted telling him that she was going to cancel her plans with Marek. She had never liked listening to unsolicited advice, and Jana could tell that Jonathan was on a collision course with a major lecture. "Since when was it written that encounters should be easy?" Jonathan continued. "Since when was it ordained that loving doesn't require risk? My God! Look at me, Jana. I'm sixty-five years old. And I fell in love for the first time just a few years ago. Your grandmother was the best thing that ever happened to me. For years I just existed, a passive participant in a mediocre marriage. I did nothing about it. Oh, I played the game. I was a good enough father. I was a success in my work. I said and did all the right things. But I wasted most of my life living in mediocrity. It never occurred to me to ask for anything more, because I was raised to do what was expected of me, to do my duty, no matter what. Then, out of the blue, my wife left me. I was devastated. I figured at my age, my life was essentially over. And five years later I met Rachel. It wasn't ideal, of course. Nothing is. We had religious differences, ones that gave Rachel many more misgivings than they gave me. I wanted to marry Rachel and she refused." Jonathan shook his head, a hint of a smile on his lips. "I must have asked her to marry me at least once a month."

"I didn't know that," Jana said.

"There's probably lots you don't know about us. But there's one thing you should know: I was frightened when I met Rachel. She wasn't like the woman I had always known. Rachel was so . . . powerful. So enticing." His eyes filled with light as he spoke. "I was afraid of committing myself to another woman. Especially to one as strong as she. But I took the risk, Jana. And I mean it with all my heart when I tell you that I learned about

307

love from Rachel. She enhanced my life in every way. Communications with my two sons improved enormously after I met her. And I even learned how to forge a decent relationship with my ex-wife. I wouldn't trade my years with Rachel for anything. I don't regret one moment of it, even though there are some times when missing her becomes so acute that I think I might die of it. I, too, have had my share of sleepless, tear-filled nights. That's the price I've paid for loving such an extraordinary woman. She taught me how to live, Jana. And she taught me how to love. And I want more than anything in this world to pass that gift on to you." His voice softened. "After all, it's your heritage."

"I'm trying, Jonathan," Jana said in a subdued voice. "I really am. But I just can't seem to make it happen."

"Then try harder." His voice left no room for compromise.

Jana winced from Jonathan's obvious lack of sympathy. "But—"

"No more 'buts.' You're turning into what I call a 'Yes-But' person. Every constructive suggestion offered is met with a 'yes-but, I can't because.' " Jonathan reached across the table and took Jana's hand. "No more excuses, Jana. I've treated you with kid gloves since Rachel died. Because you deserved it. You're right: almost everyone you've

308

loved *has* died. But I love you. And I'm still here. Margaret and Dolly Mack are still here. You have a second chance now. Not many people get that opportunity. And you're a damn fool if you don't take advantage of it."

"How?" Jana asked.

"By taking the risk, Jana. By not backing out on seeing Marek. I know your background. I know how much he meant to you as a child. I know how much you loved him. And now you tell me that you don't want to see him because you would just lose him, anyway." Jonathan let go of her hand and pounded on the table. "Nonsense!" he bellowed. "Did it ever occur to you that you might get something back instead of losing something? Well . . . did it?"

Jana looked down at the table. "No," she whispered. She looked up at Jonathan. "I'm so frightened."

Jonathan smiled. "Welcome to the world."

Jana was drinking a cup of tea when the call came. It was late afternoon, and a gentle light shone through the livingroom windows, casting golden shadows across the blue and rose oriental carpet.

"I'm at the airport, Jana. Where shall we meet?" Marek's voice sounded excited.

"Here. Why don't you come here?" Jana said. "You know the address."

"I'll be there as quickly as I can," Marek said.

Jana smiled. She thought back over the past month. Since her conversation with Jonathan, she had visited Dr. McGowain three times a week. She decided that if she was going to take the risk of meeting Marek, she didn't want to do it as an emotional cripple. Of course, she did not effect an instant cure. But she did struggle. And out of that struggle, progress was made. She began to understand that all her bizarre behavior had been directed towards one end: to deny the human condition, to deny that death is our final companion and the grave waits for us all.

She learned that there was no magic to protect her from this end, nor was there a ritual that could control her destiny. And with this lesson came the knowledge that she would not be offered an endless series of second chances, that the time would come—if she did not change—that she would become so mired in fear, so entangled in a web of her own making, that she would no longer be able to find her way to the light . . . with or without the help of a psychiatrist. She knew that her insight was just the beginning of a long slow journey. Now, in order to reach her destination, she had to back up insight with action. By the time Marek called, she was ready to try.

Somewhere during the past month, she had made peace with the fact that if she only saw Marek this one time, she would always be grateful to him for calling her. Because it was his phone call that gave her the final impetus to begin to heal herself.

In just a few minutes, she would put some of what she had learned to the acid test. She was about to confront her past and did not have the slightest notion what it would bring.

Well . . . here goes, she said to herself. She turned from the phone and swung into action. She hurried to her room and changed into a crisply ironed pair of blue linen slacks and a simple white silk shirt. Then she applied a touch of mascara and put on fresh lipstick.

She was in the kitchen preparing a snack when the doorman buzzed on the intercom to inform Jana that Mr. Cetkovic was here to see her.

Her voice shook when she said, "Send him up, please."

Suddenly she was terrified. How had he changed? What if he had turned into some awful man? What would happen if she found herself liking him? How should she behave? What would she say? What if he didn't like her?

Waiting at the front door for the old-fashioned elevator to make its slow assent, Jana felt her heart create strange staccato rhythms in her chest.

She wiped her sweaty palms on her slacks. Then, with an ancient clacking and grinding noise, the elevator door slid open. Jana watched as Marek stepped out into the hall, looking to the right and left for her apartment number.

"Marek?" she called.

He looked at her one brief moment. Then he hurried to her. "Jana?" he said with awed delight. "My little Jana?" He dropped his suitcase and folded her in his arms.

She could not believe she was being hugged by this strange man who was not a stranger at all. The feel of his arms was familiar, as if they had made a permanent imprint fifteen years earlier. Even the scent of him touched some long-dormant memory, a memory of warmth and love and protection.

"Here," he said. "Let me see you."

There were tears in his eyes as he stepped back and held her at arm's length. He looked at her and laughed.

"I thought you would be beautiful," he said, his voice filled with amazement. "But not *this* beautiful!"

Jana laughed. "Come . . . come inside," she said.

He stepped in the door.

"You have a marvelous home," Marek said as he walked into the living room. The sky outside her windows had turned pink and lavender, as if nature were putting on a special show for Marek's arrival. "Your view is terrific." There was an awkwardness in his voice, as if he, too, was unsure how to proceed.

"Thank you." Jana suddenly felt shy, like a little girl once again. All her repetoire of canned responses didn't prepare her for a moment like this. A vague awkwardness hung in the air. Neither seemed to know what to say to the other, how to continue their meeting without snapping the gossamer tie that was suspended so tenuously between them.

"Would you like a drink?" Jana asked by way of bridging the gap. At least it would give her something to do, she thought.

"Yes. Please." His response was formal, noticeably strained, as if he realized for the first time that he was visiting a stunning woman, not a beautiful child.

"Wine? Whiskey?"

"Wine. Red, if you have it."

Jana walked over to the bar and chose a bottle of Chateau Margeaux from the rack.

"Here . . . let me," Marek said, taking the corkscrew from her hand.

Jana placed two Baccarat wine goblets on the counter as Marek pulled the cork and filled the glasses in silence. Then they picked up the goblets.

313

"To life," Marek said, touching her glass gently with his. The thin crystal rang with a happy clarity.

"Yes . . ." said Jana, remembering another time with Rachel when she had made the same toast. "L'chaim."

Jana looked at Marek and smiled. She remembered the first time she saw him. Then he was a frightened, couragous boy who still had traces of baby fat clinging to his lean frame. Now he was a man. There was no pot belly, no balding spot as she had imagined. Instead, his black hair was thick and slightly curly, and his body was hard and lean. She liked the way he moved, as if there were a panther lurking inside his frame, a wild animal held in check with perfect grace.

His eyes, dark and flashing with dangerous yet amused electricity, held hers as they toasted. Jana noticed that, somewhere along the way since she had seen him, he had broken his nose. It was sharper, slightly crooked, with a bump on the bridge. She had to supress an urge to reach out and touch his cheek. Somehow, she felt as if she had come home.

They stayed up until almost four in the morning. Marek told Jana how he had remained in Yugoslavia after the war, attending the university in Dubrovnik. Jana listened intently, relieved that his English was so accomplished. Until he arrived, Jana was afraid she would have to communicate in German, a language she had not spoken in years.

At first, everything was fine, Marek told her. But then, in 1948, the news of the Berlin Blockade had sent faint ripples of foreboding through Marek's head. Nevertheless, Tito had managed to avoid the worst of communist control. When a new constitution was proclaimed in 1953 and Marshall Tito was elected president, Marek hoped things would be all right. But the iron fist of communism infiltrated further into the lives of the people. And even though Tito's brand of communism was of a more enlightened variety, Marek chaffed under the chains of state control over his life. He was, after all, Montenegrin, a man to whom living free was just as natural as breathing.

He might have remained in Yugoslavia had it not been for the Hungarian Revolution in 1956. The brutality of the Soviet invasion shocked Marek. He wondered how long it would be before the Russians tried to do the same thing in his country. He decided he did not want to stay and find out.

He left Yugoslavia and fled to Italy where he applied for a visa at the American Embassy. His mother's second cousin lived in Southern California, he explained, just outside San Pedro. It was this man who had sponsored Marek in America.

"You've been here for almost two years?"

"Yes . . . in and out of the country."

"But why didn't you call sooner?"

Marek looked at her. His dark eyes softened. "I was afraid, Little One," he answered softly.

Jana nodded. "I understand," she said. She smiled at him and then asked, "What do you mean you've been in and out of the country?"

"Actually, it is more out than in," he said. "I joined my uncle's import-export business. Although I have applied for American citizenship, I am living in Germany at the moment, in Munich, where I opened the Europeon office of the company."

"I see." Jana already felt lonely for him. Munich was a world away, she thought.

Marek reached over and touched Jana on her cheek. "And you, Little One. Has it been hard for you?"

"Yes," she said simply. She felt no need to color the truth.

"Tell me about it."

So she did. She told him about coming to America, about her first days at school. She talked about about her friendship with Margaret, her terrible encounter with Christopher, the shock of Rachel's death and the fact that she was seeing a psychiatrist. She felt totally comfortable with

Marek, as if no subject was taboo. He listened carefully and lovingly. Best of all, he did not judge.

When she finished talking, he said, "In all this, you have never mentioned a man in your life. Have there been boyfriends?"

Jana looked down at her hands. "No," she said. "Never."

"Never!" Marek said, clearly shocked. "A woman as beautiful as you?"

"Men . . . scare me," Jana said. Her voice was barely audible. "Every time I think of being with a man, I think of that day in the woods. And now there's Christopher. I can't seem to get over it."

Marek reached over and touched her shoulder. "Someday it will be different for you, Jana. Someday you'll meet a man you trust."

"I hope so," she said. Then she asked Marek what she had wanted to know since the moment she set eyes on him earlier that evening. "Are you involved with a woman, Marek?"

"I have been. But I'm not now."

They looked at each other then. They were silent, lost in their own thoughts.

Marek stayed in New York for a week. He slept in Rachel's room, and for the first time since she was seven years old, Jana felt safe. She knew that, no matter what, Marek would protect her.

He was busy during the day with his business.

317

But they spent every evening together. They went out to dinner several times. They went to the movies one evening and saw *Dr. Zhivago*. But Jana's favorite times were when they stayed home together. It seemed they never ran out of things to talk about.

Jana tried not to think about Marek returning to Germany. Sometimes she would look at him and wonder if she would ever see him again. Please don't let anything happen to him, she thought. Please.

For his last night in New York, Jana spent the day cooking. She made salmon mousse for an hors d'oeuvre. And for an entree, she prepared veal with morelles.

It was a poignantly festive evening. Their animation and obvious affection for each other had an underpinning of sadness about it. Marek would be leaving early the next morning and Jana was unsure when she would see him again. For one entire week they had lived happily under the same roof like brother and sister. Marek was affectionate with Jana. He hugged her and kissed her on the cheek or on her forehead. But that was as far as it went.

On their last evening together, after dinner they settled in the living room with their espresso. It was then that Jana finally found the courage to ask, "Will you be coming back to New York soon?"

"I am not sure. My schedule is erratic," he said. "But you can count on the fact that I will take advantage of any opportunity to travel here from now on." Marek smiled broadly.

"Is there a way I can reach you when you're away?"

Marek wrote down the phone number of his home in Munich.

"Now you won't be lost to me," she said with a shy smile.

"I never was," Marek answered softly.

When they said good-night, Marek put his arms around her pulled her close.

"I love you, Little One," he said, whispering in her ear.

"I love you, too," said Jana. She wasn't certain whether they were speaking as brother and sister or as lovers. When Marek kissed her, his lips grazed hers as softly as the kiss of a butterfly wing.

Was it my imagination? she asked herself later when she was alone in bed. Did he kiss me in a different way? She lay awake late into the night. She wondered if she were fooling herself, if she was clinging to Marek as an object of love because there was nobody else in her life and he represented a safe harbor.

She smiled sleepily as she remembered the way his short upper lip curled slightly, giving him the look of an innocent child when he was caught off guard. She imagined how he would look when he slept, his mouth parted slightly, his dark, curled lashes resting quietly on his high cheekbones. She thought of what it would be like if she were to kiss his eyes as he slept, kiss him awake so that he would look at her lazily, his mouth curved in a hint of a smile. She imagined lying in his arms, kissing him, loving him. She imagined his warmth, his affection, his generosity. But she could not yet imagine making love to him.

Exhaustion finally overtook her thoughts and Jana drifted into a restless, dreamless sleep. When she awakened, Marek was gone.

Chapter 18

"Jana?"

"Marek!" Jana exclaimed into the telephone receiver. "Where are you?"

"In Munich. But I'll be in New York day after tomorrow."

Jana's heart skipped a beat. It had been almost five weeks since she had seen him. And every week had seemed like a month. After Marek left, she felt as if she were missing a vital part of her body. She tried not to depend on him, to depend on the thought of him. But still she missed him desperately.

"How long can you stay?" she asked.

"It looks like I'll be there at least a week. We are having trouble in the New York office. I may have to go to Washington for a few days. But I won't know until I get there."

"I can't wait to see you."

"I can't wait to see you," he said.

During the month since he had been gone, Marek had written Jana several letters. They were very warm and friendly, filled with news about himself and personal observations about his life. Much to her surprise, Jana found herself longing for him to say that he wanted to hold her in his arms, that he wanted to kiss her. These were new feelings for her and she wasn't quite certain what to do with them, except to try to convince herself that the feelings were foolish. Because in all his letters, there was never even one hint that he loved her in any way except as a sister. In spite of this, she thought about him constantly, about his touching her, holding her. Finally, in self-preservation, she drew back, chastizing herself for her fantasies. Stop these silly delusions! she told herself. Lower your expectations! Marek's given you no reason to feel this way. None at all.

After Marek's phone call, the next thirty-six hours crept by at a snail's pace. She spent as much time as possible at work. Being with other people helped pass the hours. Besides, she was enjoying her work again. As Jana recovered, she and Dolly Mack had begun to forge a strong friendship. And out of that new relationship emerged the ability to run the boutique as if they had been partners forever. Dolly naturally gravitated to the business end, while Jana took total charge of the acquisitions and aesthetic decisions concerning the boutique. They were a perfectly coordinated team.

Furthermore, Jana's slow recovery had begun to have a positive effect on the people she worked with. They no longer avoided her. No longer was her strange behavior a subject of lunchtime gossip. Even Jonathan stopped by more often, frequently inviting her to lunch or dinner.

"It's nice to have you back to your old self again," he said.

"But I'm not my old self," Jana said with a new confidence.

Jonathan smiled at her. "You're right. You *have* changed. And it's a pleasure to see. It looks to me like you took on your monsters and you've dealt them some serious blows lately."

"You're right," Jana said. "At least, I hope so."

As soon as Marek walked through the door, he gathered Jana into his arms.

"I've missed you," he whispered, his face touching her hair. "Missed you so much." He stepped back and looked at her. And a cloud passed over his face.

"What is it?" Jana asked.

Marek just shook his head. Then he let go of her and walked into the living room.

That evening, they went to The Coach House for dinner. Just around the corner on Waverly Place, it was one of Jana's favorite restaurants.

They spent a perfect evening and arrived home laughing.

"Please excuse me, Jana," Marek said as soon as they walked in the front door. "I must go to bed now. I'm afraid jet lag has caught up with me all at once."

"Of course," Jana said, trying to keep the disappointment from her voice. "Your room is ready."

Marek reached over to her and pulled her close.

"Sweet dreams," he whispered.

Jana looked at him. Once again the dark cloud passed over his face. This time she didn't ask him what was the matter. She knew he wouldn't tell her.

"Sweet dreams," she said.

Two night later, unable to stand the tension any longer, Jana went to him.

They had spent three evenings together. The days had been occupied with their work. But the nights were theirs. Marek had been affectionate with her as usual. He kissed her on the cheek. He patted her head. He hugged her . . . big brotherly hugs. But that was as far as it ever went. And Jana wanted so much more.

If I go to him, Jana thought, what he would do? Would he reject me? Would he back away, filled with apologies because he had misled me? I don't think I could stand that. Does he want me at all? she asked herself. Maybe I'm not attractive to him.

"Why don't you just ask him," Margaret suggested as they ate lunch at a neighborhood Italian restaurant on the third day of his visit. "Ask him if he wants to make love to you."

"Never!" Jana said. "I don't think I could ever ask that."

"Why? Is it a sin?" Margaret asked. "From what you've said, the two of you have been incredibly close in every other way. You've been totally honest with each other. You talk about everything. I don't see why you can't talk about this."

"Just the thought of it makes me cringe," Jana said, fiddling with her napkin. "I suppose if I had some experience, I might not feel this way. But I just can't imagine *talking* about it, actually *asking* him if he wants to make love to me."

"It's a risk, Jana. Everything's a risk."

"But what if I'm mistaken? What if he doesn't want me? What if he only thinks of me as his sister?"

"Like I said: everything's a risk." Margaret smiled at her. "But you're strong enough to take it."

"I don't know . . ." Jana's voice drifted off. "It's so scary," she said.

"Regret is scarier," Margaret commented wryly.

* * *

She didn't knock on his door. Jana was so nervous, she didn't have the strength to raise her arm. Regret is scarier, she reminded herself. Regret is scarier than just walking away, she said as she reached out and touched the doorknob. One, two, three, go! She opened the door quietly and stepped inside the room where Marek slept. The reflection from the streetlights below created a dim light in the room. She stopped for a moment so that her eyes could adjust. Then she tiptoed to his bed.

He's so beautiful, Jana thought as she looked down on him. So beautiful. I couldn't stand it if he didn't want me. With that thought, Jana was overcome with second thoughts. She turned to leave.

"Jana?" Marek said sleepily. "Are you all right?"

Jana stopped. "I just . . . I just wanted to . . . be with you."

"Sit down, then." Marek patted the edge of the bed. "Tell me. What is it? Did you have a bad dream?"

Jana sat down. The long skirt of her midnight blue nightgown cascaded to the floor. Without warning, tears filled her eyes. She lowered her head to hide them.

"What is the matter?" Marek asked. Even though he could not see her tears, he sensed them.

Jana swallowed. "I want you," Jana said, her

voice barely audible. "I want to . . . be with you."

Her words were met with silence. Then Marek reached over and took her hand.

"What do you mean, Jana?" His voice was hoarse.

Feeling vulnerable and raw, she looked at him. She felt shy beyond imagining. "I want . . . to make love," she whispered. "I want to make love with you."

The room filled with an explosive silence. Jana felt Marek take a deep breath.

"Are you certain?" Marek asked at last. He was wide awake now.

"Yes," she said, her eyes closed, her heart beating faster.

Marek gasped. "Ah, Jana," he said. There was a catch in his voice. "You cannot imagine how much I have wanted to make love to you. But I was afraid that if I did anything you would run away."

"I won't run away," Jana said breathlessly, her body flooded with relief. "I won't ever run away."

With those words, Marek folded her inside his arms.

There was no past. There was no future. There was only now, this continuous now of loving. And they were suspended in its magical embrace.

Marek leaned away slightly and took her face between his hands. He kissed her eyes, her nose, her cheeks, his lips tracing her features. Finally, when Jana thought she could stand it no longer, he kissed her lips. He was gentle and unhurried as they played games with their mouths, nibbling, kissing, longing.

"I love you, Jana," Marek said. His voice was husky with desire.

"Oh, Marek, I love you, too," she managed to utter between kisses. "I love you."

Then Marek's voice turned serious. "I do not want to do anything to frighten you, Jana. Anytime you want me to stop, I will. I will tell you before I do anything. There won't be any surprises. Do you understand what I am saying?"

"Yes," she whispered.

"May I take off your gown?"

Jana's heart skipped a beat. She nodded.

Slowly, he lifted the silken gown over her head, then dropped it to the floor beside the bed.

"My God, you're beautiful," he gasped. "So beautiful."

Then he pulled her down beside him, covering them both with the quilt. Marek's hand grazed over her face, her neck and shoulders. Then he cupped her breast gently in his hand.

"I want to kiss you," he said, leaning over to cover her breast with his mouth. His tongue teased her nipples until they were hard.

"Ah, Jana, I love you so," he moaned.

Jana's hands roamed over his body, eagerly massaging his muscular shoulders and back. She wrapped her fingers in his dark curls as he moved down to kiss her belly. Then he moved back up to her lips.

"Touch me, Jana," he whispered. "Please touch me."

"I don't know how."

"I'll show you."

He took her hand and gently moved it to him. She was amazed at his fullness, his hardness.

"I want to touch you, too," he whispered.

His hand moved slowly down to her. For a moment she was frightened. Then she felt the fire. Greedy for more, she moved her body closer to him, urging him instinctively with her pelvis to enter her.

"No, love. Not yet," Marek whispered between kisses. "We have all the time in the world."

Jana understood what he was saying, what he was telling her, asking of her. He wanted the first time to last, to be perfect. He wanted to make certain he had kissed, had loved, all of her fear away.

He cradled Jana in his arms, stroking her, loving her. With every kiss, every touch, their passion increased. Her arms held him tight as her hands warmed him, told him of her love. They spoke in the language that only true lovers know: the silence that is filled with words. They spoke with their hands, their arms, their eyes, their mouths, making small appreciative noises as they explored the depth of their love. They spoke with every part of their bodies, telling each other of their commitment, their passion.

Once again, Marek's hand moved to her. She was wet, ready. Jana's desire was so great she thought she might die of it. Yet, she was so startled by the intensity of the sensation Marek created that she drew away from him.

"It's all right, Jana," he whispered. "It's all right. This belongs to you. This is yours. Just let go and let it happen, Jana. Let go, my love. And come to me."

And she did let go. She let go of all images, all feelings. She let go of everything except the passion she felt at that moment. Trusting Marek completely, loving him completely, she gathered in her strength. She could feel something wonderous beginning to happen. Her head arched back on the pillow, her eyes closed, she moved into a world all her own. Floating on the wings of passion, she climbed a spiral, a whirlwind, moving closer and closer to the peak.

She cried out his name then, cried out her joy to him, as the exquisite sensation spread through her body. Marek held her close to him, never leaving her, offering only pleasure. Even before it had ended, Jana pulled him over on top of her.

"Please. Now." she gasped. She felt his pulsating hardness ready for her.

He moved slowly, barely entering her. He felt her membrane preventing his entrance.

"This could hurt, my love," he said.

"Never!" Jana cried, as she thrust herself to him. The momentary flash of pain was totally obliterated by the joy she felt at his filling her. Wordlessly, she urged him to take his passion without reservation.

She watched his face, his beautiful face as he called out to her.

"Yes, Jana! Yes!" he cried joyfully.

She held him tight when he came, repeating his name like a litany of hope and salvation and indescribable, unbearable happiness.

Later, their arms and legs tangled together in their effort to stay close, Jana said with wonder. "I never knew. I just never knew."

"I didn't either," Marek said, his voice filled with awe.

Marek stayed with Jana for five more days. Then he had to go.

"I'll be in California for a week," he said, "Then I'll return to Munich. I don't know how long it will be before I get back to New York again."

Jana hesitated "I'll be in London at the end of

331

November."

Marek grinned, his eyes crinkling at the corners. "This is wonderful! Why didn't you tell me?"

Jana felt suddenly shy. "I waited till I was certain you wanted to be with me," she said. "I didn't want you to feel . . . obligated."

"Obligated?" Marek laughed. "Never! How could you ever have thought that?"

Marek's brow crinkled "After we made love," she said softly, "I was afraid you might feel it was the honorable thing to do to stay with me."

"Honor never entered into it," Marek whispered as he folded Jana in the strength and comfort of his arms. "Only love. Love was my consideration. From the moment I saw you three months ago, I loved you."

Jana laughed. "Think of all the time we wasted," she said.

Chapter 19

"Welcome you to Heathrow Airport, ladies and gentlemen." The stewardess spoke to the passengers in a clipped British accent. "On behalf of British Overseas Airways, we apologize for the delay in the flight and hope that your stay in London will be an enjoyable one."

It had been a grueling trip for Jana. Because of a flight delay in New York, there would be no time for her to do anything except drop her luggage at the Dorchester, where she would be staying, and then go on immediately to Wellington's.

Wellington's, Jana thought as the plane taxied to a stop. It was the most discriminating auction house in the Western world. This particular auction was by invitation only, limited to the most prestigious customers on the Wellington list. When Jana received her invitation, she knew she had finally arrived in the most exclusive circle of influential buyers in the world of fine arts.

She had expected the auction catalog to follow her invitation. But it never came. She was so excited about seeing Marek that she didn't become aware of the oversight until it was too late to have a catalog sent to her.

She had intended to arrive early so she could inspect the items being sold. But now, she thought, she wouldn't have time to view the jewelry or even read about it before the auction began. She could only hope that her perceptions were good enough to judge the quality of the pieces on first sight, enabling her to bid wisely with practiced and professional eyes.

Fortunately for Jana, she made it through customs with a minimum of confusion. The trouble began on the way to London from the airport. There was an accident on the road, and the traffic was a nightmare. Jana tried to remain calm, to avoid becoming agitated, as her taxi crept toward the city. By the time they reached the Dorchester, she was ready to scream with frustration.

"Please wait here while I check into the hotel," Jana instructed the driver. "I'll return as soon as I can."

"Of course," said the driver, pleased that his tab would be even larger.

In a jet-lagged blur, Jana checked into the elegant hotel, arranged for her luggage to be sent to her room, and then continued the ride to Wellington's.

In the cab, she tried to make herself look pre-

334

sentable, to apply fresh make-up and smooth some of the wrinkles out of her green jersey dress. The fact that she would be attending the most exclusive auction of her life in clothes she had already been wearing for fourteen hours disconcerted Jana. She had planned to wear a charcoal grey wool suit, appropriately businesslike for this important occasion. Instead, she felt rumpled and worn out.

A uniformed man opened the door of the taxi and waited patiently while Jana paid the driver. Then she stepped to the curb in front of the imposing facade of the Wellington building.

"Your invitation?" the doorman asked politely.

"Yes," Jana said, handing him the cream-colored envelope that held the engraved invitation.

The ritual complete, he opened the door to Wellington's.

Inside, Jana paused to admire her surroundings. The entry hall — larger than her living room on Washington Square — was floored in black and white marble squares. To the left of the entrance, a fire burned brightly underneath an ornately carved mantle, warding off the penetrating chill of the gray November day.

To the right, a handsome gray-haired woman sat behind a Louis XIV desk.

"May I help you?" she inquired politely.

"Yes," replied Jana as she handed the woman her invitation.

"Oh, Miss Horvath. I had begun to wonder if you would be coming. We had expected you sooner."

"My plane was delayed," Jana explained lamely, feeling the subtle censure in the woman's voice.

"The auction has begun, of course," the woman said, with a bare hint of annoyance. "Why don't you just take this catalog with you so you can read about the pieces before they come up."

"Thank you," Jana replied quietly, taking the full-color brochure the woman offered.

"Just come with me," the woman said bruskly. "I'll help you find a place inside."

Jana followed the woman through a reception hall furnished with priceless antiques, walking across a magnificent Aubousson carpet to the other side of the room. The woman opened two massive wooden doors.

At the far end of the room the auctioneer, a distinguished older man dressed in a impeccably tailored three-piece suit, spoke briefly to the audience of perhaps sixty people.

Jana sat down and opened her catalog. Thumbing through it quickly, she tried to familiarize herself with the items that would go up for sale.

"Oh!" Jana gasped in a moment of silence. The people nearest her turned to stare. Jana couldn't catch her breath. The image on the page swam before her stunned eyes. There, before her in full color, was Rachel's Tiffany brooch. And across the photograph one word had been written: WITH-DRAWN.

Jana lay on her bed in the hotel, still too shocked to move. She could not believe what had happened. It played through her imagination like a strip of film mounted on a continuous loop of anxiety and hope. And she felt totally depleted by the process.

Because the thought of finding the brooch had acquired such overwhelming significance in her fantasies, it had taken Jana a moment to realize that she was, indeed, looking at the object of all her hopes and dreams. There it was, pictured in color with a detailed description of the brooch that even included the engraving of "Always Rachel" in the back. As soon as Jana registered that this was, indeed, her brooch, she stood up.

Too stunned to think logically, tears of desperation rolling down her cheeks, she ran out of the room.

Jana burst upon the quiet, unsuspecting woman at the front desk with the force of a mack truck.

"Where is it" Jana asked frantically, pointing to the picture of the brooch. "Why was it withdrawn? Where is the brooch now?"

"Miss Horvath!" the woman said, shocked at the

noisy intrusion in this traditional bastion of quiet good taste.

"The Tiffany brooch! I must talk to the owner!" Jana said breathlessly.

"I'm afraid that's not possible, Miss Horvath," said the woman. "Please . . . calm yourself."

"I can't be calm. Please tell me who the owner is. Where he lives. I must talk to him. I must!"

"Miss Horvath . . . take hold of yourself," the woman said in the tone of voice reserved for servants who forget their place.

Jana leaned over the desk, her hands gripping the edge. She hovered over the woman as she spoke. Somewhere in that part of her brain that was still functioning rationally, Jana understood she would not get what she wanted if she continued to behave like a maniac. So she took a deep breath and wiped the tears from her face with the back of her hand. Then she willed herself to speak slowly, to enunciate her words clearly, while still conveying the urgency of the message.

"Please understand, Miss—"

"Smythe-Rainey," the woman replied.

"Please, Miss Smythe-Rainey," Jana said. "I must find the owner of the brooch. I must talk to him. It's urgent."

Miss Smythe-Rainey leaned toward Jana. "Wellington's has policies, has rules and regulations. And one of the most important ones is that we never divulge the identity of our customers. You must know that, Miss Horvath. Our reputation rests on confidentiality, on trust. Surely you understand."

"Yes, I do," Jana said. "But this case is different."

More than anything at that moment, Jana wanted to grab the contained, controlled neck of the woman in front of her and throttle her until she divulged her secrets. Instead, she continued to talk in the most reasonable voice she could muster.

"I understand what you are saying, Miss Smythe-Rainey," Jana said. "I understand the necessity of maintaining your reputation and your integrity. And I respect that. But I assure you that my need to see this man is important enough to supercede your rules."

"And why is that?" the woman asked archly.

"Because the brooch belongs to me," Jana said.

Miss Smythe-Rainey smiled indulgently. "I fear you're overwrought," she said. "Naturally, I understand how one can see something one really desires and think it belongs to one."

"That's not it!" cried Jana. "That's not it at all! Please. Please let me talk to Victor Wellington."

"I'm afraid that's not possible. This is a very important auction. And Mr. Wellington is a very busy man."

"Please!" Jana cried. Desperate now, Jana

reached across the desk and grabbed the woman's arm. Miss Smythe-Rainey jerked away with obvious distaste.

"Miss Horvath! If you don't cease this nonsense, I shall summon the guard!"

Chastized, Jana pulled away her hand. "Please," she implored softly. "Please just listen to me a minute. I beg of you."

"I have listened to enough, Miss Horvath. Do you understand? Rules are rules."

Stunned, Jana stared at the woman. Compassion had been wiped from her heart years before. And Jana suddenly knew that, no matter what she said, no matter how valid her argument or great her need, the woman sitting before her would not be moved. Because rules and regulations would always be more important to Miss Smythe-Rainey than truth.

"I understand," said Jana.

Conceeding the first round, Jana turned to go. And she found herself staring right into the eyes of Victor Wellington, III. She recognized his picture from numerous auctions and charity events.

"What is it, Miss?" the man asked. "Are you all right?"

This is my last chance, Jana thought.

"No, I'm not, Mr. Wellington. I'm not all right." Jana looked into his eyes and thought she saw the residue kindness resting there. "My name is Jana

Horvath."

"On, Miss Horvath. From The Danube in New York. Am I correct?"

"Yes," Jana managed to say politely, shaking his hand.

"What can I do for you, Miss Horvath?"

"I need help and you're the only person who can give it to me."

Victor Wellington smiled. "How can I resist a call of distress from such a lovely young woman?" he asked as he pulled his handkerchief from his pocket. "Perhaps this will help."

"Thank you," Jana said. She wiped the tears from her face.

"That's better," Mr. Wellington said. "Now. What can I do for you?

"You can help me get something back that was stolen from me."

Jana made every effort to control her tears, but still some escaped as she began her story.

"The Tiffany brooch in the catalog," Jana continued. "The one that was withdrawn. It belongs to me. Truly it does, Mr. Wellington. My grandfather bought that brooch from Louis Tiffany himself." All the time she talked, Jana had a vision of the man who owned the brooch moving farther and farther away from her.

"Do you have proof?"

"No."

"Then I'm afraid I can't help you," he said politely. "There's got to be some sort of proof before we can go to the police."

"Please. I beg of you. Please listen to me," Jana said. "The brooch was in the family until the war when . . . it was taken from us. I was there when it was stolen, Mr. Wellington. I was only seven years old. But I remember it well. Because . . ." Jana stumbled then. For a moment her embarrassment silenced her. Then her determination took over. She knew she had to tell the whole truth if she was to convince the man that the brooch truly did belong to her. "I remember it because," she continued, "It was hidden in my hair. The man who stole it — a German soldier — cut the brooch out of my hair, Mr. Wellington. Then . . . then he raped my grandmother . . . while I watched."

Jana lowered her head. Tears streamed freely down her face now. She didn't know how she could continue to speak.

"My grandmother's name was Rachel . . . the name inscribed on the back of the brooch. She died a year ago. I lost everything in the war. I have no family. They were taken away in 1944. Please help me recover that brooch, Mr. Wellington. It's all that's left of my family."

Jana took the train to Oxford the next morning.

342

She briefly considered waiting for Marek, who was due in London the following day. But she couldn't wait.

She imagined how wonderful it would be if she met Marek wearing the brooch. What a fantastic surprise, she thought, as she rushed to catch the train.

Having spent the greatest part of her life in America, where a building constructed before the turn of the century was considered old, Jana was enchanted with Oxford. There, an old building meant it was constructed in the thirteenth century.

She had been in Oxford for over four hours, and still had not visited the man who brought the brooch to Wellington's. Wandering aimlessly through the town, with no plan in mind except to avoid the inevitable, she could not bring herself to enter the jewelry shop of Mr. Lawrence Dennis.

All morning long she had felt a knot in her stomach that tightened as the minutes stretched on, a knot that held her imprisoned in its grip. She walked for miles, hoping the exercise would help. She took deep breaths, trying to make it disappear. Yet, she had the distinct impression that if it did go away, her arms and legs would lose their strength. She felt like one of the little puppet animals she had as a child: when she punched the bottom, the elastic strings that held the animal together were loosened and the animal flopped in every direction. She felt drained of all strength and was horrified she had lost it at the moment she needed it most.

Earlier that day, she had bought some cheese and bread and wine from a small shop and had lunched by the Thames, the river that ran tranquilly through the city where it met the Cherwell River at Christ Church meadow. Looking out on the water from behind a partial shelter of willow branches, Jana envied the students she saw walking briskly along banks. She had missed that part of life, she thought, the life of a university student whose biggest worry is to pass an exam. Despite the demanding rigors of academia, Jana knew that it carried with it a certain innocence that was beyond her now; an innocence she had lost long ago in darkness and in war.

After lunch, knowing that she could delay the inevitable no longer, Jana finally decided to pay a visit to the mysterious Mr. Dennis.

Through the window, she could see a man polishing the glass counter. He glanced up when Jana entered the shop.

"May I help you?" he inquired politely.

"I'm looking for Mr. Lawrence Dennis," Jana said.

"That would be my brother. I'll fetch him," the man said with a polite nod of his grey head. "Just one moment, please." Then he disappeared to the back of the shop.

In the two minutes it took for Lawrence Dennis to appear, Jana thought she might faint from anticipation. She tried to relax, but every muscle in her body refused to cooperate.

"How may I help you?" asked the older gentleman as he entered the shop through the door behind the counter. He spoke with an eastern Eurpeon accent.

"Mr. Dennis?" Jana said. "Mr. Lawrence Dennis?"

"Yes."

Jana smiled at him. She liked his looks immediately. In his late sixties, he was a man with taut features that set off soft eyes. A fringe of white hair lined the bottom of his scalp.

Jana took a deep breath. Here goes, she thought. "My name is Jana Horvath, Mr. Dennis. I believe Victor Wellington called about my seeing you?"

A dark cloud passed briefly over the man's eyes. "Yes, Miss Horvath," he said, extending his hand. "It's a pleasure to meet you."

"Would it be possible for us to talk privately for a few minutes?" Jana asked.

"Of course," Mr. Dennis said politely. He was clearly curious about the purpose of the visit by this attractive young woman. Victor Wellington had told him nothing about her, beyond the fact

345

that it was absolutely necessary that he see her. But behind the curiosity, Jana sensed a wariness she could not identify.

She walked with the man to the small office behind the shop.

"May I get you a cup of tea?" he asked politely.

"Yes. I'd like that very much," Jana said. She felt her throat constricting in panic and hoped the warm liquid would soothe it.

The familiarity of the tea-making ritual comforted Jana. She watched as Mr. Dennis warmed the pot before he poured the water over the loose tea leaves. Then he put the teapot on a tray and brought it to the desk.

"Cream and sugar?" he asked.

"Yes, please," said Jana. Her hands shook visably as she accepted the cup from Dennis.

"Are you all right?" Dennis inquired.

"Yes . . . no . . . I don't know," Jana fumbled. "I'm just nervous."

"Then perhaps you should get this over with," he said, his voice softening. "I have found it's usually the best way."

Jana thanked him with her eyes. Then she took a deep breath.

"I have come about the brooch," she said abruptly.

"The brooch?"

"The Tiffany brooch. The one you withdrew

346

from the Wellington's auction."

Lawrence Dennis nodded. "Ah, yes," Mr. Dennis said. "A magnificent piece. Haven't seen anything of that quality in years."

"Nor have I," Jana said, privately appreciating her irony.

There was an awkward silence that Dennis finally filled.

"Just what is it about the brooch, Miss Horvath?"

"I want to buy it from you."

"I'm afraid that's impossible," he said.

"But it belongs to me! At least, it used to belong to my grandmother!"

Lawrence Dennis gasped, making no effort to hide his shock. But Jana was too wrapped up in her quest to notice.

"Please, Mr. Dennis. Please let me buy it from you," she pleaded.

Lawrence Dennis' eyes opened wide. His cheeks were drained of color. "You . . ." he said at last. "You are Josef von Weitzman's granddaughter?"

Jana was too stunned to speak. Did he say what I think he said, she thought. Did he really ask me that? She barely managed to nod her head in response.

"In Budapest . . . before the war, Miss Horvath . . . my name . . . my name was Laslo Denes. I changed it when I immigrated from Hungary after

347

the war. I am the man who engraved the brooch for your grandfather."

"Then . . . why won't you sell it to me?" Jana gasped.

"Because I don't have it."

On the late afternoon train to London, Jana mulled over the story that Lawrence Dennis had told her.

"The brooch was brought to me by a friend of mine who lives in Amsterdam," Dennis had told her. "You can imagine my astonishment when I saw it, Miss Horvath. I was overcome. Overcome," he said, clearing his throat, "with memories and guilt."

"Guilt?" Jana asked.

"Guilt," he confirmed. There were tears in his eyes as he spoke in a soft, hesitant voice. "Your grandfather came to me and asked me for help, Miss Horvath. He asked me to help him escape. And I am ashamed to tell you that I turned him down."

Jana felt as if she might spin off the edge of the universe.

"I was afraid, Miss Horvath. I don't know whether you can understand that. In truth, it is no excuse. But those were terrible times. Terrible. And I knew that if I helped Josef, I would be risking

348

the lives of my family. I am ashamed to tell you I was too frightened to help. So ashamed. Especially when I heard what happened." Dennis paused to clear his throat and wipe his face with his linen handkerchief. "I had no idea that you and dear Rachel had escaped. For Joseph's sake. For the von Weitzman's sake, Miss Horvath. I am happy you are here. And I will help you in any way I can."

Unable to speak, Jana reached over and touched Dennis' arm. She was surprised that she bore the man no ill will. She could see that he had suffered, that his pain was real and had cut a deep and lasting swath through his life. He had paid, she thought.

"What I need now," Jana finally managed to say, "Is information. Who has the brooch?"

"I can't tell you that," Dennis said, shaking his head. "My friend brought it to me. He knew I had connections at Wellington's. But the brooch doesn't belong to him. I don't know who the owner is. I can only tell you that Hans was given the brooch to sell on a commision basis. Because it was a Tiffany piece, he knew the brooch would fetch the best price at auction. But then, after everything had been arranged, the owner changed his mind."

"Where does Hans live?"

"In Amsterdam," Dennis said as he turned to his

cluttered desk. He picked up a card. "Here is his business card. Would you like me to call him?"

"Yes. I'd appreciate that," Jana said.

Her heart beat in erratic flutters while Dennis placed the call.

"No answer," he said, hanging up the receiver. "He's probably closed up the shop for the day."

"I don't want to waste any time," Jana said, feeling more decisive, now that she had survived her first confrontation. "I am going to catch the next train back to London. I'll fly to Amsterdam first thing in the morning. I'd appreciate it very much if you could try to call him again in the morning, so my visit won't be a total surprise."

It was a poignant parting between Jana and Lawrence Dennis. She knew it was very unlikely she would ever see him again. And yet she had the distinct feeling she was departing from someone dear, from a last connection with her past.

That night, Jana tried to call Marek and tell him what had happened. She couldn't reach him. If I don't talk to him before I leave in the morning, she thought, the best I can do is leave him a note and let him know where I will be.

It was difficult being alone that evening. Without warning, the tension of her quest had become unbearable. Her disappointment at not finding the brooch in Oxford was taking its toll. The letdown had created some major cracks in her confidence.

She could feel them. Her entire inner being felt like the hard-baked earth in times of drought, the cracks lengthening and deepening as the land grew more parched. She almost expected to look in the mirror and see her face filled with tiny telltale lines that predicted calamity. Instead, she saw a beautiful young woman with worried eyes. Her skin was flawless, her face unchanged. Only her imagination had undergone the transformation.

She ate a late dinner at the hotel dining room that evening. She was alone, but she did not go unnoticed. There was not a man in the restaurant who did not take note of the beautiful woman sitting at the corner table. Several men considered approaching her. But there was something about her — a privacy, a distance — that deterred them. It was as if Jana's quest had suddenly become so consuming that there was no room left for anything else.

Before she went to bed that night, Jana left a note for Marek. She told him about Lawrence Dennis and said she was going to Amsterdam on the morning flight. "If I'm lucky," she wrote, "I'll be back in London by afternoon. And I'll be wearing the Tiffany brooch."

Chapter 20

"Mr. Dennis?" Marek said into the telephone receiver.

"Which Mr. Dennis? There are two of us," the man on the other end of the line said.

"Well, I am not certain," Marek said. "I am calling the Mr. Dennis who met with a young woman yesterday named Jana Horvath."

"I am the one who met with her," Lawrence Dennis said.

"Good. Let me explain why I'm calling," Marek said. "My name is Marek Cetkovic and I am a friend of Jana's. I was supposed to meet her in London today. But she left me a note saying she had gone on to Amsterdam to talk with the man who brought the brooch to you. I thought I might fly over to meet her there if I could find out where she would be."

"She's gone to see my friend Hans Van der Zee," Lawrence Dennis said. "I'm glad you want to be with her. I am worried about her. I forgot to tell her that the man who owned the brooch was a very unsavory character. I should have told her. But I was so shocked by her story, I forgot. When you see her, please warn Miss Horvath about him."

Marek's heart raced faster. "How can I reach her?" he asked.

"I'll give you Han's address."

Jana walked away from Hans Van der Zee's shop with a renewed determination. Van der Zee was probably exaggerating when he said the man was scary, Jana thought. He just wanted to make certain I would take someone along with me. If this Mr. Walther wanted to sell the brooch once, it probably means he needs the money. I'll offer him everything I've got, she decided. Surely he'll sell it, especially when I tell him my story.

Jana walked across Dam Square in search of a hotel where she could find a telephone and a travel agent. She wanted to call Marek and tell him about her change of plans. She also needed to buy a plane ticket to Hamburg.

When she finally reached the Dorchester by phone, Jana was informed that Marek had checked into the hotel that morning, but that he wasn't in his room at the moment.

"I wonder if I could leave a message for him?" she said.

"Of course, Madam," said the hotel clerk.

"My name is Jana Horvath. Tell Mr. Cetkovic, please, that I am flying to Hamburg this afternoon. I'll be staying at the Hotel Metropole. I want him to meet me there."

After the clerk confirmed the message, Jana hung up the receiver. She ate a quick lunch, then she went to the airport where she caught a one o'clock flight to Hamburg.

Marek walked briskly on Damrak, the street leading toward Dam Square in Amsterdam. He was headed toward the royal palace and the small street just off the square where he would find Hans Van der Zee.

Marek had never been to Amsterdam, and he wished he weren't in such a hurry. He liked the feel of the city, its charm and its warmth. The tall, narrow gabeled houses were comforting and cozy. The canals, dotted with houseboats and barges, spoke of days that still allowed time for leisure and contemplation. There was a tranquility about the city, an orderliness that indicated a reverence for the past and a belief in the future. Being there gave Marek a better understanding of the national character, of the Dutch tolerance for individual differences, while still maintaining values and standards that formed a solid central core of life.

The pleasant tinkling of a bell greeted Marek as he opened the door to the jewelry shop. To his right, a long, old-fashioned wood and glass counter ran the length of the narrow room. At the back, sitting behind a work table with a bright light suspended directly overhead, a man sat repairing a watch.

His hair was blonde mixed with gray, spread sparsely over the top of his head. He wore thick glasses, the result of years of laboring on the minute workings of watches. He glanced up and smiled when he heard the bell.

"Do you speak English?" Marek asked, knowing that almost everyone in Holland had studied English in school.

"Yes," answered Van der Zee.

"My name is Marek Cetkivoc, and it is my understanding that a young woman named Jana Horvath visited you today."

"About the brooch?" Van der Zee asked.

"Yes."

"She left several hours ago," Van der Zee said. "Are you a friend of hers?"

"Yes. I had hoped to find her here."

"I'm sorry you missed her. Are you the friend she said would go with her to Hamburg?"

"Hamburg?" Marek asked. "Why Hamburg?"

"That's where the man lives who has the

355

brooch."

Van der Zee then told Marek the story of Fritz Walther; of how Walther brought the brooch to Amsterdam because it was the diamond capitol of Europe. He assumed that was where he would get the best price for the stone. Van der Zee informed him that, because it was a Tiffany brooch, he could get more money for the brooch at auction, rather than selling the diamond separately and cutting it into smaller stones.

"I could see the man was in need of money," Van der Zee told Marek. "He asked me if I would handle the brooch at an auction. Even though he scared me slightly, I knew I could collect a sizeable commission, so I agreed to supervise the sale. That's how it happened that I took the brooch to Lawrence Dennis."

"You said the man scared you?" Marek asked.

Van der Zee paused, as if he were considering just how frightening Fritz Walther really was. "Yes," he said firmly. "He didn't do anything threatening. And yet, to be honest, I didn't trust him. When he asked me to withdraw the brooch from the auction at the last minute—something that is unheard of—I had no doubt that if I failed to get the brooch back, the man could become violent. It was for that reason that Lawrence was able to convince his friend Victor Wellington to withdraw the brooch from the auction. And it is also for that reason that I made Miss Horvath promise she would take someone along with her to visit this man."

"I see," said Marek. "Do you know Walther's address?"

"No. He never gave it to me," Van der Zee said. "He does not have a phone. But he gave me the address and phone number of a bar near his home where he could be contacted. From our conversation, I think he lived close to the Reeperbaun."

"What does he look like?"

"Ah, he will be easy to recognize," Van der Zee said. "He has a scar on the left side of his face from his eye to his jaw."

"A scar?" Marek asked, his inner alarm jolting him with an explosive force.

"Did you tell Miss Horvath what the man looked like?"

"She did not ask," Van der Zee said with a shrug. "I just gave her his name and the address of the bar."

"Was the scar severe?" Marek asked, hoping his fears were exaggerated.

"Quite. Whatever cut him must have severed the nerves," said Van der Zee. "Because that side of his face droops. He is grotesque. Especially when he smiles. Very grotesque."

Marek closed his eyes and pictured the knife flying through the air. He remembered how it laid open the cheek of the German Lieutenant, how the red line appeared on his face before the blood gushed forth. That kind of cut could easily sever the nerves, Marek thought.

Panicked, he asked, "Do you know if Jana was flying to Hamburg today?"

"That was my understanding," said Van der Zee.

Jana arrived at the Hotel Metropole in mid-afternoon. The first thing she did after she checked into the hotel and discovered there were no messages for her, was to call the Dorchester in London again and ask if Marek had picked up his message.

"No he hasn't, Madam," the clerk said.

"Are there any messages for Jana Horvath?"

"Just one moment and I'll check," said the woman.

Jana lay down on the bed.

"No. I'm sorry, Madam. There are no messages for you," said the clerk.

Maybe he got delayed, Jana speculated. He should pick up my message soon.

Deciding she would call the Dorchester again in an hour, Jana lay down and took what she intended to be a brief nap. Exhausted, she fell into a deep sleep and awakened two hours later. It was almost six o'clock when she put in another call to

London. When it was confirmed that Marek still had not picked up his message, she became concerned.

Something's happened, Jana thought. There's no sense in wasting anymore time waiting for Marek. I can do this alone. After all, I know the man's name and the bar where he can be contacted. If I don't have any luck this evening, I'll return to London on the next flight. And then I'll hire a detective. But if I *am* lucky, maybe I'll be back in London with the brooch by morning.

Marek's flight arrived in Hamburg at dusk. He didn't waste a moment.

"Please take me to this address," Marek told the taxi driver in impeccable German.

"Of course," the man said with a raised eyebrow. "Whatever you want, you're guaranteed to find it in the Reeperbaun."

The whore leaned out the window and glared malevolently at the beautiful young woman who approached the shabby brick building.

"Get out of here!" the whore hissed in low, gutteral German. "You'll spoil my business!"

Preoccupied with her own throughts, Jana never even noticed. She continued to walk down the sidewalk, glancing from time to time at a piece of paper she held in her hand. Toward the end of the block, she stopped and compared the address on the paper with the faded numbers painted over the doorway of a gray, frame building. It had once been a pleasant place to live, but the building had not known the kindness of a coat of paint in thirty years. Indifference and neglect had taken a heavy toll. Just looking at the seedy, dilapidated building made Jana feel grubby, and she wondered why anyone who owned the brooch would choose to live in such a squalid place. Suddenly, she was seized with doubt, certain she was in pursuit of the wrong man.

Determined to follow the lead to the end, however, Jana climbed up the rickety stoop as the steps creaked wearily beneath her feet. The front door was unlocked, obviously indicating there was nothing in the building worth stealing.

Inside, one naked light bulb hung from a cord at the top of the landing. It swung slowly back and forth in the breeze created by the opening of the door. Dark shadows undulated across Jana's face, casting a mysterious veil over her fresh, innocent beauty. At the same time, it illuminated her filthy surroundings.

To her right, a list of tenants was tacked on the wall. Jana scanned the names. There it was: Fritz Walther, 4-B

On the stairway, small heaps of debris had been shoved to the side of each step, as if people who climbed the steps simply pushed it aside with their feet as they trudged wearily up and down their dismal journey to nowhere. There was a foul stench about the place. The vague scent of urine mixed with stale cooking odors clung stubbornly to the walls.

As she climbed the stairs, the Jana started to hold onto the bannister, then thought better of it. Without even touching it, she was certain the rail was sticky with accumulated layers of filth.

At the landing on the fourth floor, she stopped. The light was dim and she could not see the numbers on the doors. She walked close to the first door. "4-E" it said in faded writing. Jana checked every door. Finally, at the end of the hall, was a brown wooden door with the letter "B" painted crudely in the center. She raised her hand, but stopped suddenly in mid-gesture.

Is this the end of my journey? she asked herself. Or is it the beginning?

Taking a deep breath, she knocked. For a moment, there was only silence. Then she heard noises on the other side of the door as lethargic, shuffling footsteps moved toward her. Rooted in place, Jana watched the knob turn. Then the door opened.

"Ya?" said a man, his voice raspy from drink. The sour smell of alcohol drifted from him.

When her eyes adjusted to the light, it was all

Jana could do to prevent herself from gasping at the sight of the man's hideous face. It was a used face, a hopeless one. The years have not been unkind to him . . . they have been brutally cruel, Jana thought. He looks like a living symbol of the classic theatrical masks representing comedy and tragedy.

Swallowing hard to contain her shock, Jana said, "Fritz Walther?"

"Ya."

"Sprechen sie englisch?"

"Nein."

"Sprechen sie Francais?"

"*Ya . . . oui.*"

"*Je . . . je m'appelle Jana Horvath,*" she said, gathering her courage. "*Je suis ici* . . . I am here in search of a brooch," she continued, just as she had rehearsed on the flight to Hamburg. "It is a diamond and pearl brooch that once belonged to my grandmother." Jana showed Walther the crumpled photograph from the Wellington's catalog.

"*Ya?*" Walther said, his eyes dancing crazily. *Entrez* . . . Come in."

Jana hesitated. "This brooch . . ." she said, pointing to the picture. "Do you have it?"

"*Ya,*" Walther said, smiling grotesquely as he patted his pocket. "I have it. Come in. I will show it to you."

Afraid to enter the apartment of this strange,

362

grotesque man, Jana hesitated. I've come too far to stop now, she thought. Then she stepped across the threshold. Behind her, Walther locked the door and pocketed the key.

"Votre grandmere?" Walther asked, walking to the center of the room before turning to face her. "You said the brooch belonged to your grandmother?"

"Yes."

"Were you . . . by chance . . . there when she . . . lost it?"

"Yes. It was hideous. I—"

Jana stopped. She remembered the knife flying through the air. She heard the soldier scream and saw his face, grotesque and bloody, as he shrieked like a wounded animal. Suddenly she knew: she was locked in the room with the monster who had raped her grandmother. Her brain exploded in the effort to process the nightmare of the past as it collided explosively with the living presence of this man. Her hands groped wildly behind her as she backed toward the door.

"Don't bother," the man laughed. "It is locked."

"You!" Jana gasped. "You!"

"You!" Walther mimicked. He took a step toward her. "You're a very beautiful woman. A real lady. Just like your grandmother."

"Get away from me!" Jana cried. She felt like her life was melting before her eyes.

"Get away! Get away!" Walther taunted, toying with her as a cat plays with a mouse before killing it.

Jana scanned the room looking for a weapon. There was nothing in reach that she could grab.

The man stepped closer, daring her to defy him.

"Don't touch me," Jana cried.

"Don't touch?" Walther asked. "I can touch anyone I want. Remember?"

"And you paid," Jana said recklessly, trying to stall for time.

"And so will you," Walther said. "Your friend cut me, gave me this face. And now I will do the same to you." With that, he reached into his pocket and pulled out a folded knife. With a flick of his thumb, a wicked blade sprung from the case.

Jana's eyes opened in horror.

Walther stepped closer.

"Nooooo! she choked. "Please . . . NOOOOOOO!"

In 1957, Hamburg was the largest seaport in the world. It was also a city that had the pragmatic good sense to look after the welfare of the sailors. Because of this realistic approach, the streets of the city were safe.

The focus of this common sense attitude was a

section of the city known as the Reeperbaun. There, a licensed prostitute could live and ply her trade without fear of interference or reprisal. And it was there that Merek began his search.

"Hey, mister," a woman called from a window. Dressed in leather panties and bra, she moved her body suggestively when Marek glanced at her. "Anything you want, mister. Anything," she added provocatively.

Everywhere he looked, prostitutes called to him, leaning out the windows and advertising their various specialties. Skinny or fat, tall or short, blonde, brunette, redhead. A man could satisfy any number of preferences and appetites. It was simply a matter of choosing.

Marek entered the bar his taxi driver had directed him to and made his way past crude wooden tables filled with listless drinkers. He walked directly to the bar and ordered a beer.

"I'm looking for a man named Fritz Walther. A man with a scar on his face," Marek said, drawing a line down his cheek with his finger.

"Ya," said the bartender. "I know a man who looks like that."

"Does he come in here often?"

"He used to be here every night. I think he liked Ingrid. But I haven't seen so much of him recently."

"Who is Ingrid?" Marek asked.

"There," said the man pointing to a red-haired barmaid.

Marek nodded, paid for the drink and the information, then approached the barmaid.

"Excuse me," Marek said. "The bartender tells me you know a man named Walther"

"My God!" Ingrid said. "You're the second person to ask me about him today. Is he in trouble or something?"

"No," Marek assured her. His heart raced faster. "No trouble. Who was the other person who asked you?"

"A woman. A pretty woman. She was here just fifteen minutes ago. I can't believe the coincidence."

"Listen," Marek said, reaching into his pocket and pulling out a wad of bills that he stuffed in her hand. "Do you know where Walther lives? This is important. Very important."

"Sure," Ingrid said. "He lives in the gray building just around the corner and down the block. It's the one with the broken glass in the front door. You can't miss it."

"Thanks!" Marek called as he started to run.

This building should have been condemned years ago, Marek thought when he saw the wretched five story tenement.

Without further speculation, Marek hurried up the stoop. The front door was unlocked. To the right, a list of tenants was tacked on the wall. Quickly, Marek scanned the names.

Fritz Walther 4-B.

That's it! Marek thought. Then he raced up the stairs. He did not notice the filth. He did not pay attention to the stench. His only goal was to locate Jana.

He was halfway up the second flight of stairs when he heard the scream.

"Noooo! Please, noooo!"

Jana! Marek thought. He took the remaining stairs two at a time.

It was dark in the hallway. Dark and silent. Which one is 4-B, Marek thought frantically. Where is she?

"Jana!" he yelled. "JANA!"

The doors of two apartments opened. A woman put her head out.

"Shhhh!" she said. "No yelling! I'm trying to sleep."

"MAREKKK!"

The scream came from the end of the hall. In an instant, Marek was at the door. A heavy object crashed into the door with a resounding thud as the sounds of Jana's struggle only a few feet away tore into Marek's heart.

"NOOOOO!" Jana screamed.

Marek tried the door. It was locked. He hesitated only long enough to take the knife from his pocket. Then he threw his full weight against the cheap, flimsy door and burst into the room with a crash.

Seeing the intruder, Walther grabbed Jana from behind, hooking his arm around her neck. He positioned his knife beside her face. The steel gleamed wickedly as it caught the light.

"Don't come any closer," Walther said, "or I'll slice her face to ribbons."

My God, thought Marek. What will I do?

"Let her go," Marek said. "Just let her go and we won't bother you anymore."

Walther laughed malevolently. "Are you scared I'll hurt her?" he asked with a grin. "Scared I'll cut her face?"

"Yes. I am scared of that," Marek said. "But it would be stupid of you to hurt her when you can actually do it to the man who cut you."

Walther was silent. He stared carefully at Marek. Then a terrible look of recognition spread hideously over his face, turning his twisted expression of rage into the embodiment of evil.

"You!" he spewed, shoving Jana aside as if she were a sack of grain. She fell helplessly to the floor. "You're the one who did this to me!"

"Yes," Marek said. He stood on the balls of his feet, ready for action, ready to spring. Without taking his eyes from Walther, Marek said, "Get out of here, Jana. Just get out of here now."

Her eyes wide with terror, Jana crawled to the side of the room.

"IIIEEEEEEE!" screamed Walther. His cry filled the room with a pure distillation of bitterness and hate as he lunged toward Marek, his knife at the ready.

Without thinking, Marek's old training took over. Deftly, he stepped aside, then reached out and plunged the knife deep into Walther's belly. He pulled the knife up, slicing through Walther's stomach and intestines. When the blade hit the rib cage, he tilted the point upwards, turning it as he did so. The full weight of Walther fell on his arm.

In a cold, businesslike manner, Marek pulled the knife out of Walther's dead body and shoved him aside. He fell in a bloody, crumpled heap to the floor.

"Oh, God!" Jana screamed as she saw Marek's blood-covered arm. "Oh God no!"

Two neighbors peeked inside the door.

"The police!" called one of them. "Get the police!"

Marek leaned over the fallen man. Instinctively, he felt his pockets. Before any onlookers knew what was happening, Marek reached in Walther's pocket and pulled out a worn, leather pouch that he recognized from years earlier. Without looking inside, Marek knew he was holding the brooch.

He turned to Jana. "It's all right, Jana," he

369

said, hurrying to her. "It's all right."

Marek bent over and picked her up. He handed her the brooch.

"Put it on," he whispered desperately. "Do it now."

Mute, Jana nodded and then took the brooch in her hand and pinned it to her dress while Marek shielded her from view. That done, her hands fell limply to her sides. She could not move. She could not utter a word. Cradling her in his arms, Marek rocked her gently, holding her tight and soothing her as he would a frightened child. "It's all right now, Jana," he whispered, his face flooded with relief. "It's all right."

"You're wrong," Jana choked. "It's starting all over again."

"No it's not," Marek said, rocking her gently. "I promise. This is the end," he whispered. He heard the wail of the police siren approaching the house. "It's all over now, Jana. The nightmare is over."

Silently, Jana began to cry. She looked up at Marek. All the love she ever wanted shone from his eyes.

"Come now," Marek said gently, lovingly. "It's time to go home."

Epilogue

One Year Later

Jana held Marek's hand as they stood in front of the carved oak door. There was an ethereal quality about her that day, a serenity born of anticipation and sadness. She wore a cream-colored wool dress and her blonde hair cascaded in soft waves over her shoulders. She was simple beauty and golden light.

Looking up at Marek, her blue eyes clouded to grey. "I don't think I can do it," she said.

"Of course you can," said Marek as he squeezed her hand. "We haven't come all this way just to look at a yellow house on Batthany Square. After all, it wasn't easy to get here."

Indeed, procuring their visas and receiving permission to visit an iron curtain country had taken Jana and Marek over six months. There were moments when Jana didn't think it would actually

371

happen. But she persisted, because she knew that going home for the last time would complete the long and painful journey she had begun when she was only seven years old.

Jana took a deep breath and then turned to Marek. For a moment, he saw the frightened child that Jana once was: The child that entered a secret hiding place fifteen years earlier and emerged into a life that was changed forever.

A wisp of a smile, played over her lips. "Well then, here goes," she whispered. Then she reached up and pushed the doorbell.

A pleasant-looking, middle-aged woman opened the door.

"Yes?" she asked her eyes narrowing with a hint of suspicion.

"Good afternoon," Jana said in halting Hungarian as she gripped Marek's hand for strength. "My name is Jana Horvath. This is my husband, Marek Cetkovic. I once lived in this house."

"Oh?" the woman said non-committally.

"I lived here till 1944," Jana said.

"I see," the woman said. "What may I do for you?"

"I know this sounds preposterous, but when I lived here, there was a secret hiding place in the attic," Jana said. "I would appreciate it very much if you would let me see if it is still there."

"A secret hiding place?" the woman said with

disbelief. "Surely we would have known about it. We've lived here for ten years. My children played in the attic frequently. But none of us ever found anything like that. I'm sorry, but you must have the wrong house," she said firmly. She started to close the door.

"No! Please," Jana said. The woman hesitated. The desperation in Jana's voice stopped her. "Please don't close the door. I know this is the right house. I lived here for the first seven years of my life. The reason you haven't seen the hiding place is because I am the only person alive who knows about it. The others . . . all my family except my grandmother and me . . . were taken away."

An expression of understanding spread slowly over the woman's face, an expression soon replaced by unguarded compassion. "I'm sorry," the woman offered lamely. "of course, you must see this place. My name is Olga Komczek." She offered her hand to Jana. "Please. Come in," she said to Marek.

As Jana entered the house, a silent chill of recognition fell over her. At that moment, she was the victim of so many simultaneous conflicting emotions that she didn't know whether to weep or to celebrate.

Everything seemed smaller than she remembered; yet, it was all very familiar. The furniture was different, of course. But Jana immediately recognized the rose-colored carved marble mantle in the parlor that arched over an inviting, crackling fire. She warmed herself before it as she talked. Briefly, she told Olga Komczek about how her grandfather had built the hiding place and how it had saved her and her grandmother's lives.

"I am hoping I will find my family momentos there," Jana said. "There were things we had to leave behind because they were too heavy."

"You must be anxious," Mrs. Komczek said. "I'll take you upstairs right away."

The three of them walked single file up the stairs. "All these years," the woman muttered as she moved her head back and forth in disbelief. "All these years, and we never knew there was a secret room in our very own attic."

Jana followed Mrs. Komczek, griping the bannister tightly with her hand. Marek walked behind her, quiet, resolute.

On the second floor, they walked to the end of a long hallway. "I'll leave you here," said Mrs. Komczek. "You'll probably want privacy. The light switch is to the right of the door."

The attic door was painted white, just as it had been when Jana lived there. It, too, was smaller than she remembered, diminished by the passage of time.

Jana turned to Marek with a silent plea in her

374

eyes, a plea for him to lend her strength and courage.

"You can do it," he said. He reached up and touched the side of her face. "You've got all the strength you need."

"I hope so," Jana whispered. "I hope so." Then she reached out, opened the door and climbed up the narrow stairway.

There was little light filtering through the dormer windows. Dusk had fallen, and the bare lightbulb hanging from the center of the room cast shadows in the far reaches of the attic. It was exactly as Jana had remembered it. Only the family possessions had changed.

Jana willed herself forward, willed herself to walk, shaking and frightened, across the planked wooden floor to the brick chimney on the far side of the attic. There's no turning back now, she thought. The only way to get to the other side is to move through the experience.

Reaching out tentatively, she touched the old chimney bricks, her fingers searching for the crevice where the latch was hidden. She had never opened the door herself. But the image of Rachel unlocking the door was frozen in her memory.

Although she did not see it, her fingers felt a metal rod barely protruding from the mortar. She pushed it and heard a distinct click. She tugged on the door, but it did not budge.

"Let me help," Marek said.

Pulling together, the door moved, creaking with the weight of years as it inched slowly from the wall.

Transfixed, Jana stood perfectly still and stared into the hiding place. Without warning, the darkness reached out to her, its ageless arms clutching, engulfing her in its claustrophobic embrace. All the fears of her lifetime lurked in the shadows of this dark place. Terrified that she was opening Pandora's box instead of closing the final chapter on her fear, Jana supressed the urge to scream.

Silently, Marek offered her a flashlight. She nodded but did not take it. She took a slow, deep breath. And then she stepped inside.

The air was dank and musty as she breathed in its essence. She stood motionless, allowing herself to feel, to experience the dark.

She felt a scream boiling up inside her. Then something happened that was totally unexpected: The scream rose to the top of her consciousness and slipped into a kind of strange peace that settled gently over her like a silken cape. She had met the enemy and she had not run away. Only then did she allow herself to switch on the flashlight.

The soft light filtered into the tiny, cramped room. When her eyes adjusted to the dimness, Jana gasped. On the floor was the quilt that had

376

been left behind, its dusty, frayed design faded into dim shadows. In the corner of the room, were two satchels. Kneeling carefully on the quilt, Jana hesitated for a moment, imagining the other loving hands that might have carried the satchels to safety.

Taking the flashlight from her hand, Marek directed the light while Jana opened the satchels. One by one, she pulled out the last remnants of her family: items of clothing that had been meant to warm her parents and her grandfather; extra soap and a chocolate bar that had crumbled into dust; five silver spoons and forks, tarnished into a black sheen; a delicate pair of brass scissors and a small sewing kit.

Laying the precious objects carefully beside her, Jana caressed each piece as if it were alive, remembering now the feel of her father's rough wool sweater against her cheek, the touch of her mother's hand upon her brow. Gone. Gone forever.

There was only one item left, something heavy. Puzzled, Jana reached inside the larger of the two satchels and pulled it out. It was the family Bible that Rachel had said sadly was too heavy for them to carry; the Bible that had been replaced so long ago with sausages and cheese and extra clothing for a woman and child.

Laying the book reverently in her lap, Jana opened it. Inside, written in faded ink in a variety of spidery handwriting, was the record of five generations of von Weitzmans; generations whose blood had finally come to rest in the life of Jana and the delicate life that she now carried so preciously within her.

Reading each name, Jana stared at the pages. Fragments of family stories her grandfather told her drifted past her consciousness. It was as if for one moment they had come alive, laughing and dancing and singing beside her in the dim light.

Overcome with the power of the moment, Jana closed the Bible and held it to her breast. As she did, a folded piece of paper slipped from between its pages. The paper was brittle with age, and Jana opened it with great care.

She could not believe what she saw: it was a letter written to her. Through eyes blurred with tears of sadness and joy, Jana read the faded words.

"My dear little Jana," it began. "I feel somewhat strange writing a letter to you when I only tucked you into bed an hour ago. I tucked you in and kissed you as I always do.

Soon it will be your birthday. You will be seven years old, and I want to write you while there is still time.

I wish I could rejoice in your coming birthday. But it is difficult. Because, in the days ahead, I cannot envision you living with the kindness and beauty and grace I have always wished for you. There is a dark cloud hanging over our lives now. It is born of hatred and fear. I am so afraid it will rob you of the wonder and joy with which you have lived your life until now.

There are nights, such as now, when I cry out to our God in dispair; nights when I see nothing except darkness and sorrow before me. I struggle to find my way past my torment. It is difficult, but I have faith.

Soon you will set out on a long journey. I wish I had the gift of prescience so I could be assured that you reach the end. I cannot know if I have made the correct decision in taking our family from Budapest. But I want you to understand that I have done my best. I have tried with all my wisdom and strength to make the right decision for all of us, even though your mother and father are resisting. Perhaps our leaving is too hasty. Perhaps I have waited too long.

I am an old man now. I do not know if I have the strength to survive this last journey. But you are young and strong. It is my constant prayer that you, Jana will survive. No, not just survive. It is my hope that you will persevere, that you will endure. Because you have been the joy of our family, it follows that you are also our hope.

It breaks my heart to tell you that I know now, without question, that evil exists. It is not just an abstract concept tucked into the stories of the Bible. I have seen it. It is a real and living presence stalking the earth, defiling everything it touches.

I can also tell you that, because of this knowledge, evil's opposite must also exist. Simple goodness is a quality that is overlooked in our search for more tangible glories. But I have seen it, Jana. I have seen goodness in the faces of those I love. And I have seen it in the eyes of strangers. I believe in this goodness, Jana, just as I believe in you.

If there is one gift I can give you, along with this history of your family, I hope it is this: that you be blessed with faith in yourself and faith in the ability of mankind not only to endure, but to triumph. You must not bow under the challenge that the future is likely to give you. You must persist and overcome.

From the moment of your birth, you have been loved deeply and well by your family. I would ask you to remember this and take comfort from it during the trials I fear you must face in the future. You are so young, so fragile, and I feel it is an affront to your innocence and youth to ask this of you. And yet I must.

But I also ask this of you, dear Jana: that you remember the beauty and the singing and the light; that you remember the grace and the goodness; that you remember the love. Even on the darkest nights, these things cannot be taken from you. They are yours forever, if only you will endure.

With deepest love and unending affection from your Grandpa Josef. 8 April 1944.

It was a long time before Jana left the hiding place. Perhaps, in some ways, she never would leave. It was part of her now, but she had made peace with it. The demons had been banished.

With tears in her eyes, she looked at Marek and smiled.

"It's time to go home," she whispered.

ZEBRA ROMANCES FOR ALL SEASONS
From Bobbi Smith

ARIZONA TEMPTRESS   (1785, $3.95)

Rick Peralta found the freedom he craved only in his disguise as El Cazador. Then he saw the exquisitely alluring Jennie among his compadres and the hotblooded male swore she'd belong just to him.

CAPTIVE PRIDE   (2160, $3.95)

Committed to the Colonial cause, the gorgeous and independent Cecelia Demorest swore she'd divert Captain Noah Kincade's weapons to help out the American rebels. But the moment that the womanizing British privateer first touched her, her scheming thoughts gave way to burning need.

DESERT HEART   (2010, $3.95)

Rancher Rand McAllister was furious when he became the guardian of a scrawny girl from Arizona's mining country. But when he finds that the pig-tailed brat is really a voluptuous beauty, his resentment turns to intense interest; Laura Lee knew it would be the biggest mistake in her life to succumb to the cowboy—but she can't fight against giving him her wild DESERT HEART.

Available wherever paperbacks are sold, or order direct from the Publisher. Send cover price plus 50¢ per copy for mailing and handling to Zebra Books, Dept. 2377, 475 Park Avenue South, New York, N.Y. 10016. Residents of New York, New Jersey and Pennsylvania must include sales tax. DO NOT SEND CASH.